CW01272339

The Furniture Being

Simon Ingsworth

Grosvenor House
Publishing Limited

This book is published by
Grosvenor House Publishing Ltd
Link House
140 The Broadway, Tolworth, Surrey, KT6 7HT.
www.grosvenorhousepublishing.co.uk

A CIP record for this book
is available from the British Library

ISBN 978-1-83615-118-0
eBook ISBN 978-1-83615-119-7

Acknowledgements

I would like to attribute this book to my supportive friends and family as it is thanks to their help and support that I am able to write this novel. I would like to give a very special acknowledgement to my mother who unfortunately died of cancer in 2017 as she was the inspiration for much of the book and she would always encourage me to read books. I wanted to dedicate this book to neurodiversity, since it is a challenge which many people must live with, and I hope that people are able to see the positive side of neurodivergent people through reading this story. Another central aspect of this book is symbolism and spirituality, the belief that incredible things do actually exist and the power of emotionality-what people can experience through memories and self-reflection.

Prologue

Opening scene, 1890, in the afterlife

A day many ago, a sight to behold. A masterpiece never to be forgotten.

A family of Victorian carpenters are polishing their creation. Staring in awe at what they have invented. In this dusty old workshop stands a marvel, something that has never been witnessed before. The joy on their faces is one of relief and excitement. They are constantly wiping their fingers and hands on different rags to avoid fingerprints appearing. All four of them are daring each other to touch this mind-blowing creation. Fingers skating up and down on the varnished oak, palms glued to the face of this extraterrestrial being – a being of their own creation.

The father carpenter counts the numerals on both clock eyes, his left and right middle fingers orbiting around the clocks in a clockwise direction, he completes three laps with the fingers, synchronising in perfect harmony. The mother carpenter dusts the cupboard and wardrobe. The son and daughter carpenters stand at each side, preparing to ring the bell pull. One, two, three – they ring the bell pull, the chimes of heaven, ringing for all to hear. In comes a small army of servants, rushing to deliver service. A servant ignites the candles with different matchsticks. A maid makes the bed. A lamplighter rushes in with a stepladder; he carefully lights up the streetlight, then the oil lamp. The desk lamp lights up. To finish off, the lamplighter lights up the chandelier. Each of the five lights are carefully lit, creating a crown of enlightenment.

The clock eyes: two mysterious clocks that stare into your soul, tick to your heartbeat and hypnotise your conscience. These eyes have a swirling vortex in the centre that sends subliminal messages. Above these clock eyes rest the eyebrows; two grey dusty lines, a hundred years of collected dust forming the wise eyebrows of a god. Beneath the clock eyes sit the two wooden fans. These wooden fans are joined together to create a propeller that blows an ethereal breeze.

The Victorian light crown: five individual lights all working together to form a light crown. The light that reads everything, the light that shines visions, the light that reveals hidden messages, the light that never forgets and the lights that foreshadow the world. The Victorian streetlight is placed on the forehead creating a striking presence. The oil lamp on the left side of the wooden head shines visions of the future. The lantern projects warnings of the near future. The white desk lamp casts fond memories into your soul. The chandelier casts shadows that will symbolise your future. All placed to signify the brainpower of history, five brains working as one. Over the clock eyes rests two grey dusty lines that resemble eyebrows – the eyebrows of a wise god.

The bottom half of the wooden head is the wooden chest mouth. This contains the bottom and top row of the candle teeth. The candle teeth are like shining white arrows that point upwards or downwards. The top row points downwards, and the bottom row point upwards.

This represents the world that faces downwards and crushes everything and the world that faces upwards and hopes that everything will be all right. In the middle of these two rows are two protruding candle teeth that resemble fangs. These candles have flames that may expand into raging infernos. These infernos may symbolise frustration, desire or hope. These shining teeth give this being a dragon-like appearance.

The carpenters attached a collection of bells to their creation, these bells were designed to attract the attention of the chosen one, the mellifluous sound will reach the chosen one before they come face to face with this furniture being. There are three different types of bells: the six desk bells, two servants' bells and one house bell. The six desk bells are dotted around the edge of the wooden face to form a circle. These bells make a persistent pinging sound. The two servants' bells are located on the wooden shoulders. The wooden shoulders are two flat wooden pillars that are on the left and right side of the wooden head. These flat wooden pillars stretch from the top of the wooden table leg to the bottom of the overhanging bed. The shoulders are painted in black and white stripes symbolising the Victorian era. These two bells are connected via a wire that is activated by pulling the bell pull located on both sides of the shoulders. These bells ring at a colossal speed, creating a drilling sound like you would hear from an alarm clock or a machine gun. Once these bells have been rung, the spirit of a servant will instantly be there to help you. The house bell is hanging down from the chin of the wooden head. This bell rings when the wooden head shakes with persistence, creating a harmonious sound that can only be described as a sea of church bell chimes.

When Pvormlu wants to summon your attention, it will sound church bell chimes followed by the drilling of the servant bells, followed by the persistent pinging of the desk bells creating a euphony that is terrifying and beautiful at the same time.

In between the wooden head and wooden body is the coffee table chest. This is a coffee table that is placed sideways to resemble a wooden cloak. It spins to greet the chosen one.

This creation contains four wooden table legs, each leg is half sculpture and half mechanical. The joints are mechanical discs, and the upper and lower legs are sculpted out of wood. These are three metal discs: the top disc is the hip joint, the middle disc is the knee joint, and the bottom is the ankle joint. Attached to each wooden table leg is a small metallic Victorian wagon wheel which Pvormlu uses to move around.

On the sides of the body hang two ghostly white curtains. These curtains conceal the furniture torso like a fog that will only clear when Pvormlu wants to show you a display.

Above the furniture torso sits the large Victorian bed. This bed resembles a throne that is carried by the creation. A throne that can take you anywhere if you sleep in it.

This whole creation was planned for years by the carpenter family. Each family member focused on their individual desired part of the creation. Unfortunately, the family never got the chance to create this together, but when they were reunited in the afterlife, they created the entire being from scratch. They wanted this creation to represent their way of thinking.

The Brothchild family took one more moment to celebrate their brainchild. Four palms all resting firmly on the cheeks of the wooden head, a beloved being coming to life. Just as they were showing their affection, they felt a vibration emitting from the body of their creation. They quickly withdrew their hands, worrying that they might have triggered something.

The bells began ringing creating a euphony. The family were blown away by the dramatic collection of ringing sounds. Out of the oil lamp emerged the shadow figure. The shadow figure was holding a long wooden stick, like a cane. It waved the stick at the chandelier, and a swarm of eight-winged inner demon bats rushed in. The shadow figure waved the stick to the left, and the bats moved to the left side of the warehouse. The shadow figure waved the stick to the right, the bats moved to the right side of the warehouse. The shadow figure waved the stick in a circular motion, the bats formed a mobile ring. The family of carpenters were terrified by these bats, they flinched every time the bats got too close to them. The shadow figure dismissed the bats by waving towards the open door. The shadow figure then shook the stick at the light crown and candle teeth in a flickering motion before fading away. The Brothchild family continued to admire their creation until the lights on the light crown started flashing, the warehouse lit up, then darkness. The family covered their faces with their hands to protect themselves from the lighting. This flashing continued until the last flash created a bright white light that engulfed the surroundings. Pvormlu was heading for earth!

Introduction of Alexander Sommervale

Alexander Sommervale is an introverted atypical individual who is psychologically lost and finds it difficult forming relationships with people. He is very private and keeps many things to himself. He also struggles sometimes with asserting himself, leaving him vulnerable to being undermined. But underneath the unsociable, unrelatable exterior lies a sleeping giant inside waiting to be awakened.

After the death of his mother, he was grief-stricken and became unapproachable and withdrawn. Alexander's procrastinating leads to people worrying about him, but without support how is he going to move on? That's the goal and challenge for Pvormlu. Pvormlu can read minds and is particularly fascinated by Alexander's intellect and pattern of thought.

Rothschild family introduction

The Rothchilds were a family of carpenters who owned a furniture store in the 1800s. It was a family business called Oaktopia. The family were always experimenting with furniture creations which made their store popular. The family included the husband, wife, son and daughter, who were all trained carpenters.

In 1890, the last of the family members went to the afterlife. The spirits of the family members reunited and planned to build one last creation that would haunt the world. The husband created the body, the wife created the clock eyes, the daughter created the candle teeth, and the son created paranormal energy and called to Pvormlu.

Pvormlu is rumoured to haunt the mansion in the Cotswolds where the family lived. It has the power to move objects and teleport possessions and can walk through walls, but when it makes an appearance, it will look like physical furniture, however you can't touch Pvormlu unless it wants you to.

The First Encounter, 8th September 2019

Alexander was lounging around on his couch, eating chocolate and drinking coke, as he would normally do at 12:30am, lost in a daze of unawareness and inattentiveness that was now his life. Feelings of loneliness and detachment were welling up inside of him. He felt as though he was being cornered by life, stuck in a place where only lassitude can exist. He spaced out in his living room, feeling completely aloof.

Just for a moment, he raised his head and realised that it was now 12:30am. A resting silence... a sudden strange feeling... earth-shattering bells blasted through the silence. Cataclysmic shockwaves blasted through his body with a force that felt like it came from Krakatoa, causing him to shake like a pendulum on a possessed clock, swaying back and forth like a tree in the middle of a storm, then the overwhelming panic set in making him feel like a monkey swinging through a burning forest.

Alexander was fixated on his wall clock, the lights went out, but he didn't even notice, he was oblivious to the fact that his living room was being transformed into a large, bare Victorian mansion room with two large wooden doors and no ceiling lights. This mysterious room had two sliding sash windows at the front and back. These windows had white blinds which were half-closed. After the bells finished ringing, he immediately turned his head to the front window to see where the noise had come from.

Through the unclosed blinds Alexander could see two clock eyes staring at him with all the intent of the sun, its hypnotic swirling void spinning his eyes into an oblivion. The 12:30 expression became engraved into his mind. His mind was spinning around like a clock out of control. Alexander could feel his anxiety moving all around his body. His heart was racing as if it was running a marathon. Alexander started hyper-focusing on the numbers, he kept counting one to twelve in his head as a way of making sense with what he was seeing. His head was so consumed with time and numbers that he felt like he had just witnessed the end of time itself.

Then two rows of candles appeared, the upper row of candles facing down and the lower row of candles facing up. All the candles were lit. Glowing candle teeth burned through Alexander's outer solitude and igniting thoughts from his deepest conscious. Feelings of mournful remembrance mixed with the feelings of horror and guilt, every emotion he had ever felt, the ever-present thoughts all lined up in his head, waiting for his full attention. The memories; every birthday, every Christmas, every person, every place, every time, a million thoughts all in front of him shining brightly.

The next thing he saw was five old-fashioned lights shining. Alexander's eyes felt sore staring at all these bright glaring lights in the dark, so he decided to close his eyes and take one long blink.

After this long blink Alexander nearly jumped out of his skin when this furniture creation appeared right in front of him. The clock expression was 12:30. The bells began ringing together again but this time Alexander could stand still without flinching or shaking. The clock expression changed to one o'clock, flames were shooting out of the candles, Alexander managed to form a subtle smile on his face. The clock expression changed to two o'clock. The candle flames emerged together to form a wide smile; a wide fiery cartoonish smile that made Alexander feel like erupting with laughter. The clock expression changed to three o'clock. The flames turned green and released a green fire cloud, and he stared at the cloud fearing the worst. At four o'clock, the flames turned blue, the flames expanded into blazing drills, determined to meet their targets. Alexander stared at these flames feeling a passion for hard work. At five o'clock, the flames turned green again; these frames retreated backwards into the wooden mouth as if they didn't want to be seen. He covered his head with his hands, trying to hide from the world. At six o'clock the green candle flames from the upper and lower rows met and formed a row of lines resembling a prison cage. Alexander covered his face with his arms as if he was trying to create his own prison. At seven o'clock the flames turned blue, and candles released fiery bubbles which were popping in front of Alexander's face, giving him intriguing ideas. At eight o'clock the blue candles fused together and created two fiery hands which were connected to fiery arms. These fiery arms looped around Alexander and gave him a tight hug; instead of burning through his flesh the fiery hands made him feel warm inside. At nine o'clock the flames turned back to their original colour and increased in brightness. A bright circle that symbolised the sun was created. Alexander had to stare at this bright circle as if he was a hawk watching its prey. At 10 o'clock the candle flames began flashing, causing his heartbeat to increase at the same pace as the flashing. At 11 o'clock the flames turned purple; a fountain of purple flames was pouring out. Alexander touched this fountain with his hands, he felt his hands being blown around as if they were inside a high-powered air dryer. At 12 o'clock the flames shot out like fireworks then exploded, forming purple stars. Alexander stared at these exploding stars in amazement.

So far Alexander was mesmerised by the stunning beauty and power of this mysterious furniture being. The Victorian streetlight started shining. A ray of light was sent to his forehead forming a linear subliminal connection. He closed his eyes and waited for the subliminal message. "Come on, Alexander, you can do it." He could hear his entire family each saying this phrase, they then chanted this together. Alexander had no idea what they were chanting about, but he still appreciated it greatly. The oil lamp released an ethereal mist, out of this mist emerged a 3D projection of Alexander wearing pyjamas. The projection held its hand out. Alexander, not knowing what else to do, shook the hand of his apparition reflection. Maybe this was a sign that Alexander needed to wake up and change his ways.

The lantern projected an image on the wall showing himself sitting on his couch, looking like he had no motivation to try anything out. Also projected from this lantern were words that read, *I am not a lost cause, I am just having a rest.* He stared at this reflection in utter bewilderment, he had no idea how to process this phrase.

What am I even doing with my life? he thought to himself. The desk lamp began to shine brightly. He could see his many memorable photos spinning around, creating a loop, even photos that he didn't remember taking were appearing. He touched this desk lamp with both his hands, he could feel these memories as if they were happening right now. This made him realise how important the past was and to never stop remembering. The chandelier pulled Alexander's right hand forward using a magnetic pulse. He could feel the light bending around his hand. A shadow was cast in one of the corners of the room, it was a shadow of himself sulking. He responded to this by shaking his head. The ceiling was now covered in shadows of a sulking Alexander. He stared up at the ceiling in disbelief, shaking his head again and again.

He turned to stare at the wall. He waved his finger around, trying to work out what the meaning of this display was. He turned back round to see the clock eyes turning in rapid clockwise cycles, he then turned his head to observe the wall clock of his living room. Alexander was yet again oblivious to the fact that he was returning to his own reality in his living room. When Alexander turned his head around to see what this mighty Victorian furniture being was going to do next, he was surprised to find that he had returned to his living room. *Maybe that was just a dream*, he said to himself. The time on the wall clock was 1am, meaning that he had 'been away' for 30 minutes. Alexander stumbled to bed like a zombie with a hangover, without turning his living room light off or brushing his teeth, something that he would often do since he lacked the urgency to carry out even the most mundane of tasks. He fell asleep, feeling exhausted from the encounter.

The Backstory of the Sommervale Family

In his sleep he kept hearing the word 'Pvormlu'. It sounded like a word from another language. Alexander had no idea what language this would be, Aztec, Russian, Hindi, Hebrew? Maybe even an alien language. He could not work out which language it could have originated from as he had never heard of the creature before. But using his linguistic intellectual prowess he was able to decipher the word as having two separate syllables Pvor and Mlu – the first part meaning furniture and the second meaning 'being' or 'creation'. Alexander spent most of the night trying to work out where this furniture being could have originated from. Alexander was having a subconscious discussion with himself, but he felt as if he was fully awake.

Someone must have created it, but who? He recognised the furniture as being from the Victorian era. *Someone must have created it, someone with carpentry skills from the Victorian period. But why would they name their creation Pvormlu? That's not even an English name. I think that Pvormlu is a time travelling creation, maybe it is a language that was spoken in the past or maybe in the future. This creature reminds me of Big Ben, but it also reminds me of the Tardis. And why is this creation visiting me, the last time I checked I'm not a Time Lord or the Doctor.* Alexander was curious about why he was the chosen one.

Whilst he was writing on his walls, trying to solve all the problems that he had in his head, an unfamiliar older sounding male voice started talking to him. "Who is that? Where are you?"

"You cannot see me now, but I am always with you."

"Um... OK, I wasn't aware that I had a stalker."

"You are stalking me just as much as I am stalking you."

"Uh, OK, that sounds kind of romantic, but OK, whatever."

"You may not know who I am but you might understand these phrases. If you seek nothing, nothing will become of you. Forget life and life will forget you. In the ever-present pitfall of doom, you only need to find the way up."

Alexander froze when he heard these words; the phrases fascinated him. Alexander decided to repeat the phrases back to the mysterious voice. "If you seek nothing, nothing will become of you. Forget life and life will forget you. In the ever-present pitfall of doom,you only need to find the way out."

"Very good. You are a great listener, Alexander. I must be off now."

"One last question."

"Yes, Alexander?"

"That encounter that I had at 12:30am... Is Pvormlu the name of the furniture creation?"

"That is correct, Alexander, but from which language it originates, I do not know."

He woke up later that morning at 9am, which was three hours earlier than usual. He wondered why he had woken up so early. He spent the morning trying to recreate what he had witnessed. Using many pens and pencils and pieces of paper, he created his own interpretation of what he had witnessed. The lights were a particular fascination of his, he spent hours researching different lights and managed to find the exact types that he had seen. He printed them off and attached them to his walls like posters. He also researched the history behind them but found nothing linking it to Pvormlu. The thought of telling everyone what he had seen did cross his mind many times, but he was afraid that if he told anyone the furniture being would disappear. Alexander wanted to have a second encounter so he could learn more about this awe-inspiring creation.

Over the next few days, white letters began appearing. The first one was discovered under his pillow, it read, '*Seek nothing and nothing will become of you*'. Alexander knew that he had to start planning on ways to improve this lonely existence that he called a life, but how to improve remained a mystery for him. Another letter was found under a cushion in his living room. '*Forget life and life will forget you*'.

Reading made Alexander want to become someone who was well known by other people. *How am I going to get people to remember me?* he thought to himself. *Maybe it's time for me to make new friends, it seems that my old friends have forgotten all about me. But how am I going to make new friends, even a five-minute conversation is a challenge for me.*

Another letter was found on his door mat. It read, '*In the ever-present pitfall of doom, you only need to find the way out.*

How am I going to find the way out? I can't even find the way out of a shopping centre.

Alexander decided to look at his family album. The first photograph was of his deceased mother, Rose Sommervale. She was born in a small village in Shropshire in March 1965, she had two sisters and one brother. She was very meticulous; everything was always spot-on whenever she did it. She was also a very kind and considerate person who became a nurse. He picked this photo up and took a closer look. This photo showed Rose wearing a light pink dress. In her right hand was a rose, she was standing in their garden with a welcoming smile on her face. Her wide ocean-blue eyes reflected her kind and honest nature. Her light brown hair rested modestly on her open shoulders. Behind her lay a collection of different flowers: roses, of course, were directly behind her, to the right poppies and to the left corn marigold. He picked this photo up and took a closer look. All the memories came flooding back. Being the most attentive, caring and loving person, they had ever known, Alexander's mind was rich with memories of her.

Memories of breakfast time. Rose would have two different breakfast types, the regular type which was for most days – this included turkey dinosaurs with baked beans slopped on top and maybe a few peas or chips. The other type was reserved for good behaviour or good test results, this included a luxury omelette. Alexander, William and Anna could decide to have whatever they wanted in their exquisite omelette. Rose would use leftovers or prepare small boxes with possible options such as a curry omelette or a risotto omelette, maybe even a fish and chips omelette.

Birthday and Christmas presents for Alexander were different from most other children; he would often prefer his parents to create something entertaining for him as opposed to cheap common material gifts. One example of this would be instead of asking his mum and dad to each buy him a different toy, he would ask one parent to buy him a toy and the other would draw his favourite fictional character. Sometimes his parents would enjoy this as they could save money, other times they would wish that Alexander would just ask for a gift or even just money. Alexander would enjoy seeing his parents attempting to recreate character scenes that they had never even heard of. Alexander and his mother had many ways of bonding together, one thing that Alexander enjoyed doing was starting a story or poem, then asking his mother to complete the other half.

There were many other activities that Alexander, William and Anna would participate in, such as karate, jogging and swimming. Alexander enjoyed reading out verse and prose at speech and language exams. William enjoyed playing competitive sports and Anna loved going to the zoo and watching Disney cartoons. One thing that Alexander remembered about his mum was her ability to communicate messages. She wasn't the type of mother who would always be screaming and shouting at her kids to get their attention, she could get their attention just by writing messages onto a piece of paper, then sticking it to their bedroom's walls. This would be a way of getting across important messages, such as warning for them to improve their behaviour, or even warnings about changes that they would be facing.

A sense of intense numbness and enclosed weariness was weighing on his mind, just wanting to see her again but being forever denied. She always had to be involved with everything, a wonderful control freak. Every birthday, every Christmas was always special; she would always treat the family even though she didn't have much money. She was quite quiet and introverted but never lied about anything and always showed an interest in everything that her children did.

The news of her terminal cancer shook the Sommervale family to the core, within a matter of months she went from a confident healthy woman to someone who was always pale and needed assistance with everything. Witnessing her gradual deterioration caused the family to vacate their previous family humdrum lifestyle and become a family of lacklustre chickens. This new family of chickens just aimlessly wandering around, no harmony, no vibe. Seeking shelter and bits of food but no bond, all trapped in a pen where only the mundane lifeless monotony of today existed, as well as the fear of more inevitable doom hanging off their shoulders. No one communicated to each other properly, just awkwardly paced around each other, muttering to themselves.

Birthdays, a reminder of her demise, Christmas, a forced celebration with little meaning. The irony of her photos hanging, and achievements being presented only after her death. Alexander's biggest regret was not opening to her and trying to impress her. It seems that only after death many people can start living. He carefully placed this photo back into the photo album.

Alexander then looked at a photo of his younger self. Alexander was born in November 1997. This photo showed him as a 12-year-old; it was a snowy winter and Alexander; William and Anna had decided to build a snowman. Alexander wasn't satisfied by the snowman since it didn't have any originality, he wanted to remember this snowman, so he came up with a plan to make it memorable. He decided to add a small hole using a shovel, and he inserted upper and lower candle teeth into this hole. He took out two small wooden alarm clocks and inserted them as eyes. He borrowed a small handbell from his grandma and used this to represent a collar. You might be thinking that this was way too much just for a Mr Frosty, but Alexander thought that it wasn't enough for his Mr Frosty. He took out his desk lamp, which had a white lampshade, and slotted it into the head of the snowman; this resembled a hat. Alexander decided that this snowman needed a finishing touch – cobwebs. Alexander searched around the garage for cobwebs, collecting them using a dust-removal brush. He then took the brush outside and collected the dust with his hands and stuck the dust above the alarm clock eyes. This was one of Alexander's finest creations.

Anna congratulated him for creating something so interesting.

William said, "What on earth is that?" Then he laughed his head off.

Rose said, "That looks wonderful, where did you get the inspiration from?"

Alexander replied by saying that he wanted to make the snowman look as extravagant as possible so that he could remember it.

Tony made up a story of how this snowman reminded him of when he was Alexander's age, even though Tony had never built a snowman before.

Alexander crouched down and smiled for the photo. This photo had striking similarities to Pvormlu.

This photo did two things for Alexander. The first thing it did was remind him of his sweet childhood, the second thing it did was remind him of the extent of his grief. Most of his memories were tied up in a joint account with his mother. He wanted to have a separate account where he could remember things that he didn't associate with grief, but he didn't have the emotional understanding to know how to separate grief from his positive memories, so it felt as if he was mourning his entire history. Alexander got up and stared at himself in the mirror. What did he see? That is something that even he did not understand.

His childhood was normal, but he never had many friends, a bit of an outcast but he was always very aware of who he was. Despite not being very academic and having concentration issues, he liked to possess unique knowledge, almost like a spy who knew things that others didn't. His head had always been a minefield of knowledge, vast minerals of intelligence stored away. A minefield that only he knew about, a minefield that he wanted to keep hidden from the outer world.

Alexander never had the social skills to be popular at school, but there was one friend who he always had a great friendship with. His name was Mick. Mick was a troublemaker; he had learning difficulties and behavioural difficulties, but Alexander didn't care about that. Mick was quick to react and very impulsive and he got excluded from school on many occasions. He also frequently got Alexander into lots of trouble. He couldn't understand people or follow rules. They were always together and conjured up the most embarrassingly terrible plans, mostly orchestrated by Mick, such as plans to escape school via the underground sewage pipes. Another hairbrained scheme was to escape by digging under a school gate.

With a lot of persuasion, their parents relented and allowed them to go to the same secondary school which really set them apart. They were still close friends, but while Alexander was able to improve his grades, Mick got into fights and struggled to make any progress. Alexander was able to make new friends, but this was a struggle because the school was divided amongst different youthful interests such as football, social media, video games and antisocial behaviour. However, Alexander had no interest in any of those topics, so he could only manage brief and temporary friendships. Alexander tried to keep Mick at arm's length by making up excuses for why he couldn't hang out with him, but the troublemaking Mick wasn't having any of it. Most of Mick`s troublemaking altercations didn't involve Alexander but, on a few occasions, Alexander would get detention for being involved in one of Mick`s insane plans, such as breaking into the headmaster's office to steal an incriminating report, or the crazy plan to follow a 'grass' home and force this little grass to withdraw their statement. Luckily none of these plans ever came to fruition, mostly because of Mick's total incompetence and because no one took him seriously. Despite the significant differences in their abilities, they never stopped being friends. They would often go travelling together in different parts of the country and they enjoyed spending time together on the weekends.

Alexander lost contact with Mick when he went to college. This is when his introversion period began; he couldn't make any real friends, sitting alone all the time and he wasn't able to focus on his studies. Alexander finished college and wasn't sure whether he wanted to go to uni or not. A few months later his mum was diagnosed with lung cancer. This caused the family to become deeply upset and terrified about the future. After seven months of battling lung cancer, she unfortunately passed away. Time froze for the next few months.

Alexander had inherited a flat from his grandparents shortly before his mother died. The family home was in Whitehill, Stroud and Alexander's flat was located near Stratford Park, also in Stroud. This park would be a place that Alexander would visit every day as it would provide him with an opportunity to collect his thoughts and to connect with nature. William and Anna also inherited flats in different parts of Stroud which they spent time in during their university breaks.

Alexander used to be a member in a chess club, his rating was 1800, so he was able to progress to the 'A' team. Alexander enjoyed being an active member in this club for three years. Even though the pressure of playing in tournaments made him feel uncomfortable, the constant persuasion from his parents to keep going made him persevere. A few weeks into his mum's diagnosis, the life pressure got to him, so he decided to quit the chess club under the pretence that he was too busy doing other things.

At age 16, Alexander was diagnosed with depression. This was due to his lack of motivation to socialise and make decisions about what he wanted to do. Weekends were always hit and miss; some weekends he could be busy doing homework, socialising and indulging in his hobbies, other weekends were wasted by Alexander not wanting to do anything apart from reading writings on his walls and sleeping. This raised concerns from his family, so he had several appointments with a psychologist, which resulted in his depression and anxiety diagnosis. Not only did Alexander experience problems with motivation and expressing himself but he also had problems with anxiety. His hands would often shake uncontrollably when he was forced to meet someone. Alexander would sometimes take medication to calm himself, Antidepressants and sleeping pills helped him the most.

He used to socialise most weeks; his mother would introduce him to members of the community, which gave him an opportunity to make friends and to live a somewhat productive and meaningful life. Alexander participated in various jobs and activities at the community centre such as making tea and coffee for over 50s. He would enjoy doing the washing up, not so much cleaning toilets. Probably the most challenging aspect of these jobs was the social communication side. Alexander enjoyed participating in conversation but igniting that flame was always the most challenging part. He was also part of a youth club, which helped him mingle with people his own age since Alexander rarely used social media and hated friendship groups. The struggle with seeing his mother suffering made him lose interest in his local community. Even when his mother was ill and suffering, she tried her best to encourage Alexander not to give up on his life. Shortly after her passing, Alexander decided to have a break from everything. The Covid pandemic created a level of depression that made him want to start life from scratch.

He flicked through the next page and saw a photo of Anna holding a straw basket with a black cat napping inside. Nestled on each side of this cat were two kittens. His younger sister, Anna Sommervale, was born in July 1998. She was very studious and hardworking. She was a tall ginger-haired woman with blue eyes. Despite being socially awkward she had a contagious smile and enjoyed socialising with all sorts of people. Her biggest interests were animals, small, cute animals. Her main goal in life was to become a vet, but she also wanted to have an animal family. She imagined having a grandma and grandpa tortoise, aunt parrot, uncle budgerigar, cousin hedgehog, daddy hare, mummy goose, sister hamster and a brother ferret. The only thing she might struggle with was controlling her nerves. She never got into any trouble and had a wonderful personality. At this time, she was studying veterinary biology at Oxford University and made occasional visits to see her family. During Rose's cancer treatment, Anna delayed her application to Oxford so that she could be there for Rose.

Alexander turned to look at a photo of William sitting in an armchair, which was located at the top of a staircase. This was typical of William – being showboat-y about everything, he always had to be number one. William Sommervale was born in October 2001, a snotty competitive academic who always did well at everything. He was studying law at Cambridge University. He wanted to become the flashiest lawyer in Stroud. He studied criminal law because he enjoyed watching horror movies. He was constantly banging on about his endless achievements, even going as far as to write a terrible song about his exaggerated achievements, then proceeding to sing it using a loudspeaker and sounding completely out of tune. He would often taunt Alexander and Anna by doing irritating things such as creating posters of himself and putting them up all over the house. One such poster included a photoshopped picture of himself with a cigar in his mouth and a heading saying, 'you can be like me'.

The siblings shared a lot of common interests but, of course, William liked to believe that he was better at everything, constantly recording his scores in everything. As you might expect from three siblings, they took it in turns to fall out and to bond with each other. Anna would often prefer hanging out with her parents as opposed to hanging out with Alexander and William. They mostly bonded over long walks and watching movies but when it came to doing house chores, it was every man for himself. Whenever Alexander had something that William did not have, he would moan to God about it. They would often play sports and video games together, but William would always take these things too seriously. Underneath the cocky supercilious exterior lay a shy passionate person who just wanted to do well. William massively stepped up during his mum's illness and showed a lot of support, which surprised the family as he had never shown support to anyone before.

Alexander lifted out a photo of Tony (their dad). This photo was taken when he was at the pub; he was wearing a shirt saying, 'If found please return to the pub'. He had a full pint of beer in his right hand, and he was pulling an amusing facial expression with his mouth open and eyes half-open, pointing in different directions. Tony was born in August 1960. He was brought up in a small village in Herefordshire, he had two sisters and a brother. Many people would consider him a jack-of-all-trades since he had done so many different jobs in his lifetime. In his younger days, he worked as a rubbish collector – he would take no crap from anyone. He worked in the Wild Boar pub as a barman – he never missed an opportunity to have a pint. He worked in a chicken factory – he never forgot to 'chick in' in the morning or 'chick out' in the evening. Not the most 'eggsiting' job in the world, he used to say. After doing these menial jobs for many years, he decided that he wanted a career change. One of the things that Tony enjoyed doing was walking around with his clipboard, trying to draw things or make notes. This clipboard mentality led him to become a building inspector; he enjoyed this job at first, but his interest started to fade away, so he studied to become a detective. His colleagues used to tease him a lot calling him Mr Clipboard. He used to joke that he was a 'Sherlock in training'. This clipboard mentality rubbed off on his children as he would often walk around the house with a clipboard making sure that the siblings had completed the household chores.

The Sommervale family

In Autumn 2020, during the Covid pandemic, Alexander was living in a flat in Whiteshill near Stroud. After a few months of grief, he had decided to isolate himself and the pandemic provided him an excuse to stay at home and not participate in the local community. He filled his days by analysing chess positions. He was quite a proud chess player. He had many chess sets; wooden, glass Gothic, paper, pop-up and even clay and mosaic sets. Around 20 in total, he had a room for storing them all.

Sometimes he would discover a position that would fascinate him and then recreate the position on a chessboard, he would often have up to five chessboards at one time. These boards were positioning that Alexander had memorised. He watched *The Queen's Gambit* which inspired him to prove his true capability, seeing someone showing off their raw talent and defying the odds. Alexander had seen himself like that in many ways; when he was in a group of people, his presence was drowned out by mundane chatter.

This was a recurring problem that Alexander had always experienced. People going about their daily lives – everyone around him – seemed to have a connection but he only had a primeval bond with other people. He had the feeling of people talking over him and not taking his opinions and beliefs into consideration. A common assumption of atypical people is that they might not be aware of scenarios or commonly used methods. Feeling the frustration of not being listened to or taken seriously caused Alexander to feel a slight resentment or distaste towards people. He saw himself as a natural force only understood by himself. He had a golden sense of inner pride but not overconfident and deluded, forever wanting to take a long stride towards the rainbow of success. A battle of a lifetime, a battle of identity, not wanting to be drowned out by the stereotypical conformist ideology, wanting to be understood for what he was. Fed up with being underestimated by people who had a stereotypical perception of him, judging him according to their standards.

The chance for Alexander to reveal his true identity and to explain himself for what he was, was what he secretly longed for. He dreamt of a successful future where his unique ideas would make a difference. Nobody understood him, thinking that his inability to socialise was a result of a personality disorder or possible drug misuse. When in actual fact he was just developing differently. This notion caused him to become trapped in his own ideas.

He felt like he was drowning in a sea of ubiquitousness, not being able to synchronise with the people around him, being disdainfully ignored by mainstream society. The constant rejection from job interviews started to wear him down. Of course, there was no real prejudice, and you always had yourself to blame, however if the opportunities weren't there then no real progress could be made.

These thoughts were weighing down on his mind every day. Having the ability to speak multiple languages, memorise chess positions, draw maps from memory and memorise historical dates from throughout history but lacking social prowess and charisma and social confidence to apply himself to real life situations made him ever fearful of the future. The eternal torment of the future beating down on his shoulders like an impatient drummer commanding Alexander's attention. The simplicity of monotonous habits distracting him from setting out to conquer the real world.

Alexander had previously volunteered in kitchens and community centres; one of the main issues he faced was his lack of concentration. He was definitely considered a hard-working person, but he would get distracted sometimes by people, other times by his surroundings. Alexander was quite sensitive to people, easily getting frustrated or upset by other people's behaviour. He also struggled with commitment and sticking with one thing over a period.

So as hours turned into days and days into weeks, and vice versa, twiddling his fingers constantly, he paced around endlessly trying to rectify his problems. Alexander decided that he would come up with a list of goals that he wanted to achieve. These goals were going to change his life and help him reconnect with the world. The chance to be normal seemed ambitious to him but he was willing to try. The haunting notion of the words that he had seen in his sleep made him want to fulfil his potential.

He concocted a masterplan to achieve his desires. He thought about what he wanted to do. The sense of intimate desolation and sexual curiosity made him eager to start dating. He knew nothing about women, but he knew that he needed love, so it was worth a try.

Another feeling he felt was a lack of self-accomplishment and he felt like a bit of a waste of space. He felt like he was ready to enter the world of work. He wanted to prove himself. Which job should he apply for? It didn't seem like an easy choice, but he needed to move on. Joining a social group was something that he believed would help him to become an active member of his community. The desire to have human interaction was an insatiable thrust that he wanted to devour. He was able to come up with eight main ideas of things that he wanted to focus on, he wrote them down.

My Plan
Get a job
Get a girlfriend
Cycle to Gloucester
Join a social group
Go to a gym
Learn how to wear a suit
Write up a CV
Find a course to start

With his new masterplan set in motion, Alexander was looking forward to his new lease of life. He set about googling different jobs, dating websites, and social groups in his local area. It took him several hours of persistent searching and scrolling to find a job that he wanted. He first had the challenge of writing a CV.

After 30 minutes of blankly staring at the screen, he finger-prodded a few sentences about courses that he had been on and qualifications that he had. This seemed like an arduous task to him, his head barely above the keyboard.This was typical of Alexander's ethos. He had all the curiosity of Sherlock Holmes, but the competence of Tom from *Tom and Jerry*. He applied for a few cleaning jobs and retail assistant jobs, not expecting any results.

His next priority was dating. This was a completely foreign concept to him. What he knew about dating could fit on the back of his hand. He browsed different sites – none of them appealed to him, so he chose Tinder. After half an hour of automatically swiping right, he concluded that it was a waste of time since he had received no likes in return. He decided to stop bothering. Although the lingering prospect of having a partner secretly excited him, the unyielding apathy was making him feel disconcerted about trying this out.

His next goal was to make friends. Alexander had previously developed disinterest in this goal. His frustration with people not taking him seriously had enabled this lone wolf mentality that caused him to isolate himself. He found a meet-up group for young people and decided to join it.

After a couple of days, Alexander was receiving messages back from the jobs that he had applied for. He contacted the manager back about a retail assistant job that he had applied for. The feeling of excitement was battling with his feelings of cynicism. They arranged for 9am the next morning. Alexander was feeling nervous about the interview since he had not been successful in one before. He went to bed early and prepared himself. The only problem was he had forgotten to set his alarm! Alexander had a pleasant sleep, slept like a log. He awoke the next day if he had woken up before his alarm clock had gone off. Feeling optimistic, he picked up his phone, but what he saw infuriated him. It was 10am!

"What the fuck!" he yelled to himself.

He picked up his phone and whacked it against his pillow like something out of *Fawlty Towers*. He couldn't believe that this had happened to him again. He spent the next 20 minutes having a full-on tantrum, throwing bed sheets around and doing manic arm gestures as if his favourite football team had lost the World Cup, arms flailing about, pacing back and forth, wandering what the hell was going on. He then picked up his alarm clock and opened a window – he was about to throw it out but decided not to. There had been missed calls. Alexander had no idea what to do. Should he ghost the manager, or should he apologise and attempt to rearrange the interview?

Of course, Alexander realised that he wouldn't get the job, so he decided to ignore the manager. Naturally, Alexander felt disappointed in himself, however, the lesson hadn't been learnt yet. He needed urgently to change his ways. His usual phlegmatic response wouldn't cut it this time. Alexander scanned it 20 times with his eyes, each time his cornea getting bigger, and the words seemed to get bigger as well. The feeling of disappointment was eating away at him. *How can I cock up again?* He then proceeded to fold himself from where he was standing, then face-planted his bed like a bored child. However, this was not out of boredom but out of dread. He lay in this position with the light on for about 20 minutes until he went to bed properly. Alexander did not feel like doing anything for the rest of the day.

First Date, September 20th, 2019

The next day he planned to give the dating app another goes. Just as he switched on his phone, he noticed a message. The message read, *hi there, my name is Jennifer, nice to meet you*. Alexander was initially awe-struck at this discovery. Within ten minutes of nervously finger-tapping on his desk, a response slid down from his mind.

Hi Jennifer, my name is Alexander, nice to meet you too. They chatted amiably on and off for about half an hour. They conversed intently about life plans, pleasantries and jokes. They decided to exchange contact details and meet up the following day. They agreed to meet at a local park at midday and then decided where to take their possible relationship. Alexander expectedly was over the moon about this, he even sent her 50 'kisses' and told her how beautiful she looked. After sending the final text he hopped around the house, cheering to himself, he couldn't believe his luck. For the next few hours all he could think about was her. He stared at her photos unceasingly.

When the day came, he woke up at 10am, which was early for him, fully prepared. He spent so long perfecting his appearance that he almost became lost in the mirror. He had invented many of his own tactics, such as spraying at least half a small can of deodorant over his entire body which made him choke relentlessly. He even practised walking poses to make himself appear more attractive.

It was 11:30 and he cycled towards the park – at least to where he thought the park was. The park was about five miles away and he had just enough time to make it, however, he had never really been out travelling by himself before. He was so blindsided by his adrenaline that he hadn't worked out where exactly it was. He decided to chance his trip, hoping that he wouldn't get lost like he normally did. After 20 minutes of cycling, he believed that the destination was nearby. It turned out that he had taken the completely wrong turn and had ended up on the other side of Stroud. A wave of unmistakable panic had swept across him, quickly followed by a wave of anger which completely engulfed his mind. A surge of terror was rising inside of him. Five, four, three, two, one – a tsunami of frustration was unleashed. He found a spot where nobody was, picked up his phone and frantically gestured at it as if it was the phone's fault that he was lost. He whispered in a frustrated tone, "What the fuck, where the fuck am I?" This was indicative of Alexander's poor forward-planning and sense of direction.

It was already 12:30 and he was miles away! He was devastated that he had let her down. He sent her a message apologising and reassuring her he would be with her soon. He checked with Google Maps and headed towards the location. About ten minutes later he felt his bike getting rough and bumpy and appearing to slow down. He stopped and realised that he had a flat rear tyre. Upon realising this, his face twisted and twisted, forming a horrifying grimace. It was as if his face had been ripped off then scrunched like a piece of paper then unfolded and stuck back on his head. The frantic whispering, swearing and gesturing continued; he felt as if the gods were trying to teach him a lesson. At this point he was starting to doubt whether he should have agreed to this at all.

Alexander proceeded to find the place on foot. Most ordinary people would have by now admitted that they needed help and would have spilled the beans about what was really going on. But he wanted to impress her. He soon realised that he was half an hour late and might have to cancel the date.

Eventually he managed to find the park, but not without making Jennifer wait 45 minutes and appearing with mud on his trainers. The infatuation was taking hold of Alexander and taking him into a place where everything seemed to be happening in slow motion. He took a couple of steps into the park and a friendly face was waving at him. Alexander ran towards her with a monumental grin on his inexperienced face, his eyes fixated on this real-life goddess. His eyes were so attracted to her that it felt as if they were trying to escape from their sockets and bounce around Jennifer like two obsessive bugs. This was a spectacular woman who he really wanted to impress. She was standing before his very eyes, happy to see him. They were a metre apart when an awkward pause fell upon them. Alexander quickly worked out that he had to initiate the conversation.

His first words were, "Hello, I'm Alexander."

Her first words were, "Nice to meet you, I'm Jennifer. How was your journey?"

"Oh, it was difficult... long... difficult journey. Sorry for being late, I had bike problems."

"It's okay," she replied softly, however, sounding slightly insincere.

The conversation started flowing, with them both describing their life experiences and ambitions. Although the slight irregularity gave a slightly awkward vibe. Jennifer asked, "Are you working at the moment?"

Alexander replied with... yeah... I'm doing stuff, you know... lots of things." "So what jobs are you working at?"

"In kitchens, community centres, wherever I can find work," Alexander replied carefully.

After the conversation they went to the café. "The brownie and hot chocolate are my favourite," remarked Jennifer.

"Mine too," Alexander replied automatically.

"I can get this for you," Jennifer offered.

"Oh, it's fine, I can buy everything," Alexander insisted.

The cashier announced, "That's £12.60 please."

Alexander opened his bag and proceeded to search for his wallet. Then the feeling struck him again. *Not again!* he thought. He kept opening and closing his bag, hoping to find something, trying to rationalise the situation.

"Maybe it's in your jacket," Jennifer suggested. Alexander, feeling hopeful, unzipped his jacket pockets. Nothing again. No trace of his wallet. It was as if it had vanished into thin air. "It's okay, it's okay," Jennifer reassured him but to no avail.

"Don't worry I'll find it, I'll find it," persisted Alexander with passion and eagerness to solve this mystery, acting as if he was Sherlock Holmes on steroids. Alexander continued to open and close all his pockets.

Jennifer had to console him by putting her hand on his shoulder. She reassured him that he needed to stop otherwise he would have been blankly searching for the rest of the day. The look of disappointment and shock was painted all over his face. The confused cashier was looking back and forth, wondering what on earth was going on.

She paid for both of their snacks. Alexander persisted to apologise and came up with stories about how he had it with him but must have worn the wrong jacket or how there was a ghost that would sometimes appear and move his possessions around. Alexander concocted a theory that someone must have stolen his wallet to go shopping. Jennifer was twitching her eyes around, trying to think of a way of normalising the conversation. At the end of Alexander's hairbrained theories about what must have happened to his wallet, Jennifer burst out laughing, which pleased Alexander. However, this pleasure was short-lived as Alexander's social fuel tank quickly ran out and there was no fuel anywhere nearby.

After the awkward banter, Alexander attempted to make small talk but after ten minutes he ran out of ideas. But luckily, he had a back-up plan, he had printed a piece of paper that had a list of jokes that he could read. Alexander read out the Christmas cracker jokes and managed to extract some modest laughter out of Jennifer. The conversation then took a turn where they were sharing their experiences working and studying (Alexander made up a lot of stories about his studying and work experience as he expected Jennifer to be making up stories too). Everything appeared to be going well until Alexander's body felt a need to express itself. The yawns kept coming.

"Are you feeling tired, Alexander?"

"I had a busy day yesterday," he replied, trying to excuse himself.

The problem was Alexander had very little sleep due to the stress of having to prepare himself for a date. But Alexander was yawning in a way that made it seem that he was getting bored of Jennifer. All this yawning was followed up by a discreet but audible fart, which Jennifer heard and smelt. This uninvited release of gas was the nail in the coffin for the disastrous date. Alexander ran out of conversational ideas, so he decided to stare at the table and come up with a plan of how to further the conversation. Jennifer was looking at her phone, texting her friends (which is usually a sign that the date has gone wrong) but Alexander couldn't tell what she was thinking. The feeling he felt was like he had just done an exam and was sitting nervously awaiting the results. But Jennifer wasn't reviewing Alexander's performance, she was chatting to alternative dates!

Alexander kept peering at her, wondering what he should say or do. So, he decided to play Temple Run on his phone. The problem with this was that Alexander normally went wild when playing video games. The drive to better his score and the desire to be the best player caused him to completely program himself into the game as if he himself was the main character. He would shake the phone incessantly and vigorously and move his fingers a million miles per hour, his finger moving like bullets coming out of a machine gun. As usual, this did not register as a concern to Alexander.

He clicked on the Temple Run icon and began playing. At first it was just casual playing but not long into this gaming session, his reflexes became fully activated. His reflexes spiralled out of control. His face was becoming more and more engaged with the phone; if his face was any closer then he would literally be glued to this screen. His eyes were just centimetres from the screen. Then strange noises started coming out of his mouth. One of the noises sounded as if he was constipated whilst waiting for his favourite football team to score the winning goal. The other noise sounded like a paranoid old man who was about to sneeze. His mouth kept involuntarily blurting out his score. Jennifer knew exactly what score he had because he was blurting it out so loudly, but she pretended like she couldn't hear him. His facial expressions were becoming hysterical as if he was a racing driver two times over the drink limit just about to win the world championship. He was within spitting distance breaking his former record but just a finger-slip and it would be all over.

It was out of sheer shock that Alexander dropped his phone on the table, followed by a natural reflex of him swinging his hand backwards resulting in Alexander gently knocking Jennifer's hot chocolate and spilling some on her shirt. It was only a small spillage, but it made Alexander completely shocked. He suddenly held his hand out to apologise, with a trembling voice almost as if Jennifer had a gun to his head. He wanted Jennifer to know how remorseful he was and how he had no intention of causing the accident.

Jennifer replied with, "It's OK," but her tone was evidence that she was growing weary of Alexander's bad habits.

The next 20 minutes went by with minimal chatter. Even Alexander could sense that she was wanting to leave. They agreed to end the date and return to their homes. Jennifer offered to drive Alexander home, which he accepted. When the car arrived at Alexander's flat, he offered to invite her in but, unfortunately, she declined and said that she was busy. They both thanked each other for the date. Alexander asked her if they could meet again, and she said that they could. Just before she left, Alexander asked her for a hug, and she agreed. He was a little bit put off by her loose arms and open hands. So, he could only give her half a hug. They said bye to each other and parted ways. Alexander walked through his front door feeling slightly bemused, not knowing what to think of the day's events.

Half an hour later, after thinking over what had happened, Alexander decided to send Jennifer a message, but he was horrified to find that Jennifer had blocked him. Alexander was fully aware that he had messed up again but for him to be blocked, this couldn't be happening. An eruption of rage came out of him; he circled his living room by going round and round with his arms held in a tense position. He was distraught. He looked at photos that he had sent her, then started waving his middle finger at them. Bringing his finger up and down hitting the screen. After that he put both hands over his face and stood there trying to forget everything. He then noticed the flowers that he had forgotten to bring. He picked them up then smashed them against the dining table. He started yelling, "You cow, how can you do this to me? Bloody timewaster!" For most people they could easily move on and think nothing of it. But for Alexander this was going to be another steep learning curve.

Bedtime was approaching for Alexander, but before going to bed he thought about a familiar phrase: 'forget life and life will forget you'. Alexander was feeling as if the gods were trying to make a last-ditch effort to get through to him. From a feckless sulky exterior, Alexander was sensing a humble transformation within himself, feeling the passion to change although not being ready. His face may have been washed but the spots remained.

Five days later, Alexander had another task that he wanted to complete. He had received an invite from a local youth club. It was a social group for young people who wanted to meet people. He received an invite for 1pm the next day. This was an opportunity that was very valuable to Alexander; he was eagerly looking forward to meeting people his own age.

During the last couple of years, Alexander had isolated himself from mainstream society, unable to connect with people. He had a very limited social life, virgin status and had only volunteered in small kitchens and community centres and done a few odd jobs. He had also lost interest in academic work which meant that his job prospects were limited. His fascination with chess, languages and travelling had distracted him from real life affairs, which enabled his long-term procrastination. He longed to meet someone whom he could relate to but lacked the social capability to do so.

The next day, Alexander prepared himself for a social event that was for young people; it was connected to a meet-up group for young people. This would be Alexander's chance to mingle with people his own age – who knew who he might encounter at this event. At this time, he would only meet up with distant friends once a month if he was lucky, and his love life was non-existent.

This event was held in a former community centre, and a fitness class was taking place at the same time. Alexander managed to get to the location on time via a bus, but he was feeling incredibly anxious. He slowly and cautiously walked towards the community centre, not wanting any surprises to unsettle him. Just before he was about to enter the building, he heard a loud woman bellowing out instructions. "Arm up, legs out!"

He saw a big strong fitness instructor giving commands to a fitness class. *Wrong building*, he thought to himself. After taking a small peak at the group, he stood around the doorway, wondering if he should go in or not. He peered through the door and realised that no one was on reception. Alexander did not want to return home without meeting people from the group. He decided to have a small walk around the area to come up with a strategy of how to handle this situation. *Google Maps says that the building with the loud fitness instructor is same building where the social event is being held, should I just go back and confirm with the receptionist that it is the correct building?* Alexander thought to himself. He returned to the building to make another attempt to join the group. But this time he saw a couple having a loud conversation in front of the doorway. *It's fine, I can just ask them to move out of my way*, Alexander thought. Before he approached the couple to politely ask them to move out of his way, he looked at his watch and realised that he had already missed ten minutes of the event. *Ten minutes doesn't matter; the event goes on for two hours. But wait, have I put my name on the visitors list?* After checking the email, it occurred to him that he had forgotten to put his name down on the guest list. *Oh shit, so they don't even know that I'm coming.* Alexander decided to do another walk around the block to figure out his next plan. *I can just explain that I forgot to register for this event. What's the worst that can happen, I must try if I want to get somewhere in life.* Alexander returned to try yet again to enter the 'forbidden' community centre. He saw a young woman who reminded him of Jennifer. *Oh shit! That could be Jennifer or one of her friends or maybe even her sister.* The memories of the challenging experience that had happened a week ago were still eating away at his confidence. *What if Jennifer is at that group event, anyone could be there, what if they don't accept me because I'm late and I haven't put my name down?* All these questions were overwhelming him, so he decided to walk home.

He spent the rest of the day trying to answer these phrases: 'if you seek nothing, nothing will become of you' and 'forget life and life will forget you'. He began writing ideas on his whiteboard. *What do I seek? I seek a job, I seek a girlfriend, I seek friends, I also seek a holiday abroad somewhere.* Alexander wrote all these ideas down on his whiteboard. He then asked himself the next question, *how are people going to remember me? The guy who is good at playing chess with himself, the guy who is good at having conversations with himself in different languages, the guy who is good at creating things that only he can understand. There must be something missing – other people, the value and significance of other beings.*

He left his bedroom and went to sit on his coach. The time was 11pm when he did this. His mind quickly gave way, and his body followed. The light was still on when he woke up at 12:30am. He fixed his gaze upon his wall clock, and suddenly, the lights went off. A power cut, he thought. Then the familiar sound of bells ringing emerged.

Second Encounter, September 30th, 2019

Alexander knew that it was Pvormlu. He turned his head to look through the half-closed blinds. This time he could see all Pvormlu's head and body. *I wonder what sort of entrance I should expect this time*, Alexander thought to himself. The Victorian sliding sash windows opened out like castle gates, the wall folded out along with the windows that seemed to be slotted together as opposed to being traditionally fitted, creating a retro futuristic vision that impressed and confused Alexander at the same time. Outside there was a gravel path that Alexander hadn't seen before. Pvormlu slowly skated with its wagon wheels over to the Victorian living room. Alexander was standing still waiting to greet this furniture king, feeling like a servant. The time on the clock eyes was 12:30.

The clock expression changed to 3 o'clock. The candle flames turned green; this flame colour represented toxicity, a need for things to change. The sliding sash window gate closed behind the furniture being. Alexander felt guilty for screwing up; he wanted to apologise to Pvormlu but instead he stood there silently, observing this mighty creation.

Pvormlu sent a telepathic signal via the streetlight. Alexander closed his eyes and waited for the message.

He could smell Jennifer's perfume and hear her voice. "Thank you for the date, Alexander, do you want to go on a second date?" Alexander tried not to let this get to him. "Oh yeah, I remember, you screwed up our date, so we won't have to bother meeting up again. Good luck with your single life, Alexander." Hearing this really rattled his cage, but he did not want to make a show of himself in front of his sacred Victorian mentor, so he kept quiet. When Alexander opened his eyes, the furniture being turned to its side then revealed its mysterious body. The curtains were slowly drawn, revealing its entire body. A Victorian wall mirror in the middle on the left, in the middle a large wardrobe with two rails. On the right, a chest of three drawers. He was blown away by this discovery; it was like his dream childhood bed had become a symbolic creature.

The clock eyes changed to 5 o'clock. He walked up to the mirror and saw his reflection. Alexander blinked and could see himself lying in bed with documents piling on top of him. Bank loans, eviction notices, contracts that hadn't been signed, there seemed to be a whole heap of them. The documents were then blown over his sleeping head. He saw himself trying to get up, but the documents were stuck to his face, and he saw himself not trying to remove them instead just going back to bed. Alexander took another long blink, now witnessing himself staring out of his bedroom window. This time he saw his three siblings, they all looked a bit older, but they had children of their own, partners, and were smiling away, enjoying themselves whilst he was standing there looking depressed and lonely.

Alexander took another hard blink. This time he noticed a photo album and saw himself picking it up then looking inside. Page after page of empty pockets. He then saw himself picking up dozens of letters addressed to himself and dumping them in the bin. Alexander then opened the wardrobe to find out what was inside. He saw all his clothes hung up the way they normally would be. He checked the clothes individually and was horrified to find that they had been spraypainted with *loser, weirdo, loner*. He instantly closed the doors, then reopened them, hoping to find something better. The second time he opened, nothing appeared. "Where have all my clothes gone?" He closed the door again. He pulled the doors open to discover that all his clothes were hanging upside down. "What on earth is going on here?" Alexander said. "Is this how other people see me? Is this my future?"

The clock eyes changed to 6 o'clock. He opened the top drawer and found a letter. This letter wasn't addressed to Alexander but to Jennifer. "That's strange. Why would I write Jennifer a letter?" He opened it and was shocked to find out that it was an apology letter.

Dear Jennifer

I wanted to apologise for my inappropriate behaviour; it was my first date, I wanted to make a good impression but lacked the knowledge to do so. If I had better forward-thinking skills, then I would have arrived on time and I would have my money with me.

I am sorry for the hot chocolate stain that I caused. If I had better conversational skills, then it would not have happened.

Please can you forgive me?
Alexander

"Who on earth wrote this letter? I bet Jennifer wrote this letter to spite me. I want to find who wrote this letter so I can kick their ass." Alexander was infuriated that someone would mock him like this; he clearly had no intention of apologising for the disastrous date. "Why would I apologise to someone who blocked me?" This letter horrified Alexander. The unfortunate events had demonstrated to Alexander that life is much harder than what he imagined it to be. An undesirable outcome would be inevitable if he continued along this path of isolating himself from the real world but also from reality. Alexander did not want to accept this. He shook his head at the furniture body, he shook his hands, he turned his back to the furniture body. Alexander closed his eyes, not wanting to witness anymore of this. The furniture being exited out of the sliding sash gate, realising that Alexander was not in the mood to continue this encounter.

Alexander opened his eyes; the lights came back on. He found himself staring at his wall, looking lost. His walls were covered in writing, any thoughts he had about anything could be written on his walls. He had diagrams, posters, and photographs. Anyone visiting him would think that he was some kind of super detective. He would often pace around his flat reading information in order to stimulate his brain. On many occasions he would pretend that he was a professor and would talk to himself about various topics such as literature, astronomy, foreign languages, art and various other topics that he could learn about. This was a form of entertainment as he did not know how to handle other people and follow their rules and reach their expectations, so he would enter his own world where everything was different, and he could make up the rules and follow his own expectations. He went to bed feeling exhausted. He decided that he was going to work out how to deal with these issues in the morning.

When Alexander awoke the next day, he was feeling haggard. He wrestled his way out of bed then stared at himself in the mirror, imagining himself stuck there forever, nothing ever changing. Alexander needed order; it was time to build his empire. Throughout every corner of his flat he sensed Pvormlu's presence. He decided to leave his flat to go on a long walk. The weather was sunny outside, birds were chirping. He started walking through his neighbourhood; every house had a different personality in his mind. He entered a trail that led into the Cotswolds.

The first part of the trail was covered in mud with stinging nettles on each side. He carefully trod through the mud one step at a time. He reached halfway, then he had a strong instinct to stay still, his body suddenly froze in place as if he was an animal. His feet appeared to be sinking and felt like they were being pulled down. His feet were completely covered in mud and frozen into place. Alexander didn't try to free himself even though he knew that this wasn't quicksand. Instead, he calmly waited to see what was causing him to have this reaction.

Unusual sounds were coming from different directions, he could hear some high-pitched squeaking noises. Every few seconds a bat would fly over him and disappear into the trees. Alexander's nerves were steady and firm. No fear, just curiosity. When his feet were released, it took him a few minutes to decide to carry on walking. When he reached the end of this muddy trail he heard the same squeaking noises as before. This time he noticed a ring of bats above him, they were about 100 metres away, but he could still see them very clearly. These bats had eight wings and were making high-pitched cackling noises like that of a witch. They seemed to be perpetually following each other around in a circle. It was like they were trying to create harmony, but the dizzying sight appeared to be more of a trance than a show. The bats drifted elegantly then began speeding up until it appeared that they were racing each other or possibly chasing each other. After a while of witnessing this phenomenon, the bats vanished into thin air.

Alexander was dazed, trying to make sense of what this encounter could possibly mean. He decided to take photos of the surroundings to see if there were any hidden messages that he could decipher. After taking the photos he returned home. On the way back he was debating in his mind, *should I get married? Should I live abroad?* He pondered to himself. Now, just getting himself out of the flat was a challenge. He needed a lifeline, a chance to live.

Meeting Martha, October 18th, 2019

When he arrived back in his flat, sitting by himself, he thought about the fact that he was always alone. The realisation of his apathy was becoming more and more noticeable to him. A recommendation popped up on his phone, it was another meet-up group. The group was for different ages, and Alexander wanted to give it a try. This was a community club that met up on a weekend to participate in social and leisure activities. Alexander spent much of the evening sitting around imagining himself living the life of a normal person. He also imagined having social independence.

The prospect of meeting someone excited Alexander to his very core. Visions of himself lying on a beach with a girl his own age holding him in her arms and pressing her beautiful face against his chest and picturing himself and his future girlfriend muttering and giggling away in hush tones. He had belief that things could get better and would get better. An unemployed genius, a hopeless romantic who dreamt of love, a whole new Alexander was going to emerge.

The next day Alexander made his way to the community centre, feeling nervous and uneasy but willing to face the music. He reached the community centre and spent a few minutes preparing himself.

He walked into the community centre, searching cautiously for the meeting room. A petite Asian woman around 50 spotted Alexander heading towards the meeting room. She had a wide smile on her face and introduced herself as Martha from the Philippines and said that she went to the club every week. They both shook hands and went inside.

The room was filled with all sorts of people, and there was a generally friendly, hospitable vibe. Most of them were chatting, some were listening to music, others were eating, and some were even playing chess. Martha introduced Alexander to other club members, despite the loose handshakes and awkward hellos, Alexander was starting to feel comfortable. This was his chance to belong to something.

Alexander and Martha chatted for a while, opening about everything. She was separated, had two adult children and was a nurse by profession. She explained that the group helped her with socialising, and she was able to enjoy herself. Martha reassured Alexander that he would be fine in the group and that he would always have friends there. Martha then asked Alexander what he wanted to do; he looked around then said that he would like to play chess. They both sat down next to the chessboard. Martha scanned her eyes around for people who could play, she asked around but unfortunately for her the only two people who could play had gone home. "Do you want to learn how to play chess?" Alexander asked.

She relented and he had managed to convince her to leave her comfort zone. He began by explaining how the pieces move then he showed her tactics. Martha was astounded and intrigued by the game as well as Alexander's methodical insight. Alexander was impressed by her amiability and willingness to spend time with him. After the community session, Martha promised to spend some time with him outside of the group and they exchanged contact details. Martha also invited Alexander to a WhatsApp group where he could meet older Asian women, just as friends, of course.

It was an immense sense of achievement, making friends. The age gap wasn't a problem since Martha was a trustworthy person, a nurse, a former carer, and she wanted to take the role of being a close friend to Alexander which was all he needed at that time.

Alexander went to his dad's house and told him about meeting Martha. His father seemed worried about him; his face was quivering around. But after a while he started smiling and was glad that Alexander was willing to make friends again. They had tea together and shared memories of Rose Sommervale. Tony's favourite memory was when he drove her 50 miles so they could stay with her parents. Only when they had arrived, they noticed that she had left her mobile phone and makeup bag back at the house. Tony was trying to convince her to make do without it and to wait until their stay was over. But Rose being the woman she persisted until Tony relented. So, they had to travel all the way back to their house. They made 150 miles out of a 50-mile trip. Alexander couldn't stop laughing when he heard this, he didn't even doubt this, knowing his mum.

Then, when Alexander had collected himself, he told his story. When he and his siblings were on a road trip to Cirencester. During the car journey to Cirencester there became a point where Rose became lost. Instead of using a satnav, she relied on using the passenger next to her (who was Alexander) to read an A-to-Z map. At this time, Alexander was ten and he had no clue how to read maps. Alexander zoned out whilst reading the map and led her down a side road full of potholes. After the bumpy ordeal came a problem that none of them were prepared for. They all noticed that the car felt bumpy even though the ground was smooth. Alexander got out of the car to investigate. He realised that one of the front tyres had been punctured by the potholes. A massive debate began to ensue; one of the biggest problems was that nobody knew where they were. They decided to keep on driving until they reached another road. He said that Rose called the breakdown service. Meanwhile, they all sat around blaming each other. The breakdown service took 30 minutes to arrive. Alexander and his dad were laughing together hysterically, something which they had rarely done.

They had a few drinks together and decided to watch a film. After the film was over, they both thanked each other for the occasion. Tony recommended that they do something as a family. Alexander asked his dad what he had in mind. Tony replied, “We could go to Gloucester.”

“Then we could fight over which crappy film to watch,” Alexander replied slyly.

This was a chance to rekindle the spirit of the family.

Day out in Gloucester, November 21st, 2019

The Sommervale family sat around the dining table and discussed what they wanted to do that day. Alexander suggested they go for a meal to which they all agreed. William suggested that they go to the cinema as well. Tony was slightly reluctant at this idea but quickly relented. It took them 30 long minutes of unremitting debating for them to finally come to a consensus on what to watch. The expostulation sent Alexander to sleep. It seemed that there were far more films that they didn't want to watch than films that they did want to watch. Even after the bickering ceasefire they were still not in complete agreement. The film they wanted to watch was *Avengers*. Of course, most of them didn't really want to watch this film but they agreed to it anyway.

Their father was going to drive them to a cinema in Gloucester. When they arrived at the Sherborne cinema, they each took in some popcorn and went to watch the film. Even just the opening credits were painful enough; constant rattling of popcorn, Tony sighing loudly every two minutes. When the movie finally started to play, Alexander's eyes were flickering like a broken light bulb on Halloween. The contrast of light was messing with his eyesight. And every five minutes, they could all sense

William's ravening presence, waiting for his opportunity to steal popcorn. They already knew what he was up to and could see perfectly clearly out of their peripheral vision but chose to turn yet another blind eye, not because the movie was so exhilarating but because they had no interest in William's mannerisms anymore. In fact, most of the popcorn of the four of them was gobbled by William, with his irritating intentional crunching sounds and his mouth – a mouth foaming with popcorn and two hands slithering beneath their eyes. They all started to feel annoyed.

Tony was starting to get restless and was muttering to himself, "Oh yeah, this is ridiculous, what time is it?"

On the seat in front of him was a six-foot-five man with an afro, so Tony had to turn his head left and right constantly to see what was happening. By this time, Alexander had already fallen asleep. Anna was the only one who was still throughout the entire film, with a pleasant smile on her face, not letting the fidgeting trio bother her.

When the two-hour-long unintentional torture experiment was over, Alexander pulled himself up out of his seat, feeling like a decrepit old man. William leapt out of his seat in his usual irritating fashion. Tony quickly got up and started shaking his legs with a face that looked like he had forcibly woken up. He also started bending his neck and loosening it with his hand as if he was a chiropractor. When they exited the venue, Anna asked them all what their favourite parts of the film were. Alexander said that he couldn't remember because he was asleep. William said he couldn't remember because he was busy eating popcorn. Tony said he couldn't see anything because his vision was obstructed. Anna said that her favourite part was when Wanda subdued Banner with haunting visions. Of course, none of them knew what she was talking about.

They decided to go to Wetherforks to have dinner. They sat down and decided what to eat. Alexander ordered a curry, William ordered fish and chips, Tony ordered a beef steak and Anna ordered chicken and chips. Whilst they were waiting, Anna valiantly attempted to strike up a conversation. "So have we got any plans?"

Tony replied, "Are you asking me about my love life?"

Anna said, "Have you thought about that?"

"I have downloaded a dating app, but don't hold out any hope."

"You should keep trying," Anna said gingerly.

The two sons didn't feel like discussing this topic, but Anna was always the best at difficult and awkward subjects. Alexander was observing people around him, seeing what people were eating, what they were wearing and their body sizes. He counted that 12 people were wearing jeans, eight had a coat with them. He also had a fascination with people's body sizes; he spotted five skinny people, five average-sized people and 15 proportionately large people.

The sight of people walking past was far more entertaining than their table conversation. William was meanwhile playing on his phone. When the food did arrive, William wanted extra mushy peas, and everyone knew why. Tony wanted a medium steak. The conversation drifted between Anna`s studying and Tony's holiday plans. Within minutes of being served, William was already doing his signature dining move – crushing peas with his fingers. He had been told many times not to do this, but this time the family tried to ignore it. He did this because he had a thrill of winding people up. The others were doing their best to ignore him. Tony was flicking through his phone in a restless manor and Anna was just enjoying her meal, she didn't let other people bother her.

After a couple of bites of his steak, Tony realised that the steak was a bit raw in the middle, so he decided to inform the waiter about this. The French waiter looked at the steak with one eye open as if he was looking through a telescope. He said, "I don't see a raw steak."

Tony's blood was starting to boil by this point. He didn't like this waiter's attitude, so he picked up the steak with his bare hands and waved it in the arrogant waiter's face. "See it now?" Tony shouted.

The waiter tried arguing that his brother's steaks were always perfect and that the steaks always look like that. The red-faced waiter finally agreed to send it back.

Despite the unyielding chaos that seemed to follow the family around, they always found a way to enjoy themselves. Alexander shared the news about meeting Martha, Anna told him that she was glad that he was making new friends. William kept mentioning how hot his current girlfriend was and how he managed to woo her on his first attempt. This series of events seemed suspicious to the family as they had never seen William woo a hot babe before. Anna told him that making friends is always important as it can help you find out where you belong and the type of people that you want to share your life with. The family wanted to meet Martha as they were curious about Asians. They also were keen to find out the type of connection that Alexander and Martha had.

Cotswolds Cycling Adventure, April 27th, 2020

Alexander was cycling vigorously through the bare Cotswolds roads. Following his satnav, he navigated across various roads and terrains. Everything was going well until he went down a narrow country lane; this lane didn't seem to go anywhere. An exhausted Alexander dismounted his bike and noticed a turnstile. He decided to go through the turnstile to investigate what was on the other side. It was just another grass field, however Alexander had urges based on previous encounters to explore and see what was waiting for him.

He slowly walked down the field and spotted a small footbridge which led to another field. He carefully walked over the footbridge and found himself in a similar field, but this one felt very different, despite looking the same. Alexander lifted his head up to see what was ahead of him. In complete astonishment he saw a shadow figure standing on top of a wooden staircase that did not lead anywhere. Above the stick figure were dozens of eight-winged bats. With bated breath, Alexander observed what was happening. The shadow figure was waving a stick around and the bats were moving accordingly. It was like an orchestra of horror. The shadow figure waved the stick up – the bats went up. The shadow figure waved the stick down and the bats went down.

The shadow figure waved the stick to the right and the bats went to the right. The shadow figure waved the stick to the left and the bats went left. After this, the figure pointed the stick directly at Alexander, then the bats all turned to face him. Alexander was nervously glancing at the shadow figure. The bats were positioned strategically like aircraft that were locked in on their target.

The shadow figure then waved the stick towards itself as if telling Alexander to come closer. "It brings me much delight to see you today," it said in a deep mysterious voice. "We are here to test your soul, to see what you are truly capable of."

Alexander nodded with intense awkwardness. Even just him interacting with a woman was difficult enough, never mind being forced to interact with a shadow figure. The uncontrollable urge to go to the toilet was constantly on his mind. His bladder was shaking as much as he was.

Alexander was getting used to being put on the spot, although he felt that something was different with this shadow figure. With Pvormlu it was as if he had become possessed and had become completely interconnected with Pvormlu's spirit. But with this shadow figure, he felt as if he was in the presence of a real person. The next thing the shadow figure said really got to Alexander. "Wherever you go your shadow will always follow, don't expect your shadow to hide. We have no choice as to whether we want to have demon bats, but the choice we have is whether or not we want to control them or let them control us." After announcing these phrases, the shadow figure silently stared at Alexander with the bats poised in an aggressive position like bulldogs that were waiting to attack.

Alexander had no idea how to respond to this, he had no idea why the shadow figure had stopped talking, he didn't remember the shadow figure asking him a question. He felt like lasers were being pointed at him. "Is that all?" Alexander could not think of what else to say.

"Is that all?" the shadow figure responded.

"Sorry, I don't follow you," Alexander responded.

"Is that all you have got?"

"Umm, I have my backpack here. I have a sandwich that I have made, I have my phone."

"Just show me something, just put on a show for once." Alexander had absolutely no idea what the shadow figure wanted from him. He decided to run around in a circle like a child. "More!" the shadow figure commanded. Alexander started jumping whilst running around in a circle. "Even more," the shadow figure commanded. Alexander waved his arms around, he started shouting, singing, pulling faces, going as wild as he possibly could. "You can stop now, Alexander. How does that feel Alexander? How does it feel?"

"Uh, it feels like I have finally done some exercise apart from cycling and walking."

"You started off as an emotional and social log, but now you are becoming a boat that can sail down the river until you meet an estuary where new opportunities will lie in wait. What are you like with bees, Alexander?

"Bees? Um, I like them, I think they are cool and important for the environment."

"What about guard dogs?"

"Guard dogs? Um, I don't like them very much, but I understand why people need them."

The shadow figure pointed the stick at Alexander then thrusted its shadow arm forward, commanding an attack. As soon as he saw the bats charging towards him in a line formation, he ran around the field like a schoolboy being chased by older kids. "Lesson number one: never run away from bees or guard dogs, they will just chase you."

Alexander stopped. The bats were breathing heavily on his shoulders, he could hear loud cackling, he was unable to turn around to face the bats. One, two, three, he turned around to be bombarded by a wall of eight-winged demon bats. Alexander fell on the ground, covered in these bats like a swarm of locusts.

"Get back on your feet, Alexander," the shadow figure commanded.

He managed to pull himself up to his feet despite being blinded by these ferocious bats from hell. He frantically shook his arms and legs to remove the swarm of eight-winged pests.

"Well done, Alexander, you did not run away. How possessive is you?"

"How possessive am I? Um, I don't know what you mean."

"How much do you value your possessions?"

"They are important to me; I don't want to lose them. I panic when I lose my stuff, which happens all the time, so I am panicking all the time."

The shadow figure told Alexander to turn around, and he showed his back. The shadow figure secretly pointed at the bag then raised the stick. When Alexander turned back around, he was asked, "Did you lock your bike up?"

"Of course I did, I locked it to the gate."

The shadow figure waved the stick, forming two small circles, then lifted the stick in the air once more.

The shadow bats swarmed around him, then lifted his backpack in the air.

"Oi, give that back!" Alexander shouted. He leaped in the air, but the bats were too high for him. To add to his horror, he saw his bike being lifted in the air by the bats. "How the hell? I locked the fucking bike up! This isn't funny, you know!" Alexander had had enough of this nonsense, he charged towards the bats like Usain Bolt then did a running jump to let out his frustration, but the wind produced by the bats sucked him in and he was able to grab hold of his bag. Alexander was grabbing tightly onto the straps of his bag. He felt motion sickness causing him to shut his eyes to calm himself down. The two swarm of bats were lapping around the field. Alexander noticed that the swarm of bats with his bike were in sync with the bats that were carrying his backpack, the bats carrying his bike would sometimes fly very close to him then stretch out. Alexander came up with an idea to use his feet to grab the bike to create a body bridge that would slow the bats down. He waited for the 'bike swarm' to get closer to him. When they came closer, he used the bag straps to pull himself up, he then swung his body around, his feet were pointing upwards acting as a wedge that was connecting his two possessions together. The pressure was really getting to him, he had no idea how to rescue his possessions. Alexander fell asleep and allowed his body weight to sink causing the bats to be pulled down. When Alexander opened his eyes, he discovered that he had in fact saved his belongings from the evil clutches of the demon bats. His bag and bike were piled over his resting body.

"That was remarkable, Alexander, you have tremendous potential."

Alexander locked his bike and bag together on a nearby gate, hoping that no one would steal them this time. When he returned to the middle of the field, the shadow figure waved the stick in a clockwise motion, stopping 12 times as if the stick was a clock hand. A shadow of a clock surrounded him, he found himself right in the middle.

"This is your time to master the art of time." Alexander could see the shadowy outline of a clock, and two shadowy clock hands that read 12 o'clock. He looked around the clock, counting all the shadow numerals. "Your challenge is to keep up with the motion of the minute hand, it's your turn to show what you are made of. Off you go."

Alexander stood on the arrow of the shadowy minute hand. He followed the pace, the sudden swinging followed by the sudden halt made him feel dizzy, but he was determined to not let the flow of time beat him. Alexander repeated this action but this time he stepped backwards in the counterclockwise direction.

"Your next challenge is to show me your energy. I will call out a time and you will show me your own personal inner and outer expression. Three o'clock." Alexander responded to this by staring at the shadow figure with a worried expression on his face, his body as still as a statue. "Six o'clock." Alexander stared at his shoes, his head bent down, he closed his eyes looking as sad and depressed as he possibly could. "Nine o'clock." Alexander stared at the blank face of the shadow figure with a deadly serious, menacing facial expression. "Twelve o'clock." Alexander gazed up at the blue sky, he stretched his arms out as if he was trying to grab the sun and take the sun home with him. "You have done remarkably well, Alexander, demonstrating that you do have a lot of energy inside of you."

"Do I get a medal or something, or is this just entertainment for you?"

"You get the medal of life. Farewell, Alexander."

"Um, OK, 'the medal of life' it is. Farewell, shadow figure."

He headed back, not even caring that he had failed to reach his destination. He cycled back feeling the wind pushing him forwards and conquering the hills.

Third Encounter, June 6th, 2020

Alexander was sitting on his couch staring at the blank screen of his tv wondering what he should do next. He stood up and watched his wall clock, it was 30 seconds until 12:30am. He pressed his finger against the clock, then moved his finger in sync with the second hand until it reached 12:30am. The familiar sound of bells ringing could be heard, the lights went out as expected. Alexander could feel a strong draft blowing in, he thought that the windows might be open. He turned to see where the breeze was coming from. The entire wall was missing. Pvormlu entered through this space. The clock expression changed to 7 o'clock. This meant that the furniture being was starting to have faith in Alexander. He could sense that new ideas were on the horizon. Alexander ran circles using his index fingers whilst staring at the clock eyes. Pvormlu's lantern started shining, an image was projected onto the wall. A caption read: *Who do you want to be?* Two images were reflected, one showed a man alone in his bedroom writing in his notepad, the other showed a man digging a hole in the ground alongside other men wearing rags, they were all digging holes in the ground. Alexander pressed his finger on the option that showed a man writing alone on his notepad. The next projection showed a man surrounded by women; the other one showed a man holding hands with a woman. Alexander pressed the second option. The next projection showed a room full of people, the other one was an empty room. He chose the empty room. The final projection showed a man sitting on a white floor in a white room staring at a blank piece of white paper, the other option showed a man surrounded by his family, smiling and having fun. He chose the second option. The personality quiz made Alexander realise that there were decisions that he could make that would change his circumstances.

The candle flames turned blue, fiery bubbles were floating around the room. Alexander popped the bubbles with his fingers, each time he popped the bubbles his fingers would turn blue. The more bubbles he burst the bluer his skin turned. Alexander knew that this represented opportunities that were at his fingertips. He blew some of the bubbles, they burst into raging blue flames. The feeling he got made his stomach feel like a hot air balloon.

The chandelier cast a shadow on the ceiling. This shadow was reaching for the corners of the room, feet and arms stretched out looking as if it was flying. Alexander looked back down at the clock eyes – the clock expression changed to 9 o'clock. Alexander stared intently at the clock eyes showing Pvormlu that he was ready for what was ahead of him. "I'm ready, Pvormlu," he said.

Alexander turned to look at his wall clock; this time he felt like he wanted the time to go by fast so that he could experience everything. *It's time to live a day of years not a year of days*, Alexander said to himself.

This new phrase means that every day would be a day to remember as opposed to every day being the same until a year is over. This phrase became Alexander's mantra. The furniture being reversed out, making sure that Alexander was feeling confident in himself.

Volunteering, July 18th, 2020

Alexander had applied to start volunteering at the community centre. This would be a way for him to start gradually rebuilding his life, and he hoped that it would eventually lead to him finding employment. He had not developed a work ethic yet and was only willing to do ten hours a week volunteering, but this was still progress at this time. He had arranged a meeting to start his first volunteering shift. When he turned up, the receptionist took him to a room where four people in their mid- to late-60s were waiting for him. Even though these were just a pack of unassuming old codgers, the social awkwardness and unpredictability was starting to take its toll. Even just a few minutes sitting down with one stranger was a challenge, never mind four strangers all waiting to strike. The group consisted of four siblings, two brothers and two sisters. The twins, Sophie and Sophia were former health care workers. Matt was a retired firefighter. Rick was a retired medic. Matt was health and safety mad; he would patrol around constantly searching for things to fix that he saw as hazardous. Rick was a very talkative bloke, he would always be talking to someone about something, one minute it could be his childhood memories, the next it would be what was on tv, or even politics.

Despite Rick being a paramedic, he was usually late whenever you decided with him. But if he has an ulterior motive he would be there in a flash. The twin sisters, Sophie and Sophia, were very similar in appearance and personality. They were both hoarders who would shop every week at second hand stores and markets. They were also bossy know-it-alls who wanted their opinion to be the be-all and end-all. The only difference between them was that one had their husband on a tight leash, and the other had their husband running for the hills.

There were a multitude of different roles that Alexander had. In the community centres many projects were run. These were projects helping people from disadvantaged backgrounds. The jobs that they wanted Alexander to do varied from collecting rubbish to taking disabled people on guided community walks. Sometimes he would have to teach elderly people how to use smartphones.

Community Guided Walk Event, September 14th, 2020

The five had planned a community guided walk event. They were going to take a group of elderly and disabled people on a long walk around the Cotswolds. Alexander's job was to help them travel the distance. As planned, Alexander and the five met up at Sophie and Sophia's house. Alexander was aware that they were hoarders, but he had no idea what the house was like. When they entered the house, they could only half-open the front door; they all had to squeeze through. Upon realising that this was going to be the meeting place, Alexander was stunned. He asked how 15 elderly and disabled people could meet in a house barely fit for one. Their response was that Matt and Rick had too many dogs. How to describe the place? The best way to describe the place was an antique market, a China store, a warehouse and a charity shop full of old women's clothes that had all mated with the house and had left their babies behind. The front door wouldn't open because cardboard boxes were behind the door. Racks of old shoes were cluttered everywhere. Obsolete phone books were stacked on top of each other and dotted around the dining room table which resembled a city of phone books. Their walls were plastered in ornaments, ropes and hooks and shelves everywhere, as well as paintings hanging around everywhere. It was like you were stuck in a trance just being in the house.

Sophia took them into what resembled a living room. In the living room there were two sofas, sofa A and sofa B. Sofa A was covered in cats and Sofa B was covered in dogs. Sophia asked Alexander which sofa he wanted to sit on. Alexander chose sofa A. He was awkwardly slumped between cats. The house was so overloaded and bombarded with junk that the view out of the window was limited. Half an hour later the minibus arrived. One thing to point out was that Rick still hasn't arrived, which was typical of him. It was Alexander and Matt's job to invite the group members in.

They managed to squeeze ten people through the door until a wheelchair user appeared. Alexander and Matt looked at each other, wondering what on earth to do. They thought about making room by removing junk that was blocking the doorway but then realised that they didn't have all day. So, they decided to take the wheelchair past the side gate and through the back door. They managed to get the wheelchair up the back door ramp and into the cluttered dining room. Matt was growing frustrated with the day's events. He asked Sophie in a frustrated tone to move the books away, but she snapped right back at him. She ironically said that someone needed to make the tea and entertain the guests. Matt was about to grab the nugatory Yellow Pages and throw them at Sophie when a considerate guest walked over and offered to move the Yellow Pages, followed by another considerate guest.

Matt and Alexander were super grateful for the help from the guests and made sure to scowl at Sophie. They managed to get him into the living room but there was no room for him so he slotted himself into the crowd, stuck behind a wall of standing guests. Out of the 15 guests, only four were able to sit down. The dining room chairs were covered in heavy ornaments and were fused together in a corner, buried in cardboard boxes. There were cats and dogs roaming around creating even less space. The downstairs was appearing more like something out of India, with people standing around everywhere unable to move. The scene also appeared more like a teenage house party, with rubbish everywhere and people queuing up, waiting to join in the action.

Sophie and Sophia then commanded Alexander and Matt to collect the tea orders. This was going to be a monumental challenge, but they came up with an ingenious idea. They would ask the group who wanted tea and who wanted coffee. Alexander would call out a type of tea then ask the guests to raise their hand if they wanted it, then he would ask them if they wanted sugar or milk. The next challenge was delivering the tea or coffee to the guests. This was going to be like a military operation. Matt and Alexander felt like they were part of the Salvation Army. Alexander and Matt decided to operate on the different queues, Alexander would focus on the queue that led from the doorway to the living room, meanwhile Matt would focus on the crowd inside the living room.

When the tea-drinking palaver was over, they evacuated the group members out and helped them get into the minibus. At this time, Rick still hasn't arrived, he had sent text messages stating that he was sorting stuff out and would be there soon, but soon never came. The four got into Matt's car and were fully prepared to leave without Rick. Just when they were about to leave, Rick came to the house on his bike. Infuriated by this, Sophia had an argument with him. Rick then parked his bike up and got into the car and they started the journey.

Whilst in the car there was a big argument between the twin sisters and Rick. Sophia waved her phone in Rick's face, Rick then ranted about all the paperwork that he had to deal with. They arrived at a car park that was where their separate trails would begin. Sophie and Sophia would lead one trail whilst Alexander, Matt and Rick would lead the other. They both set off in different directions, Alexander's trail was slightly more remote and challenging. Sophie and Sophia's trail was mostly a shared path.

The journey was going smoothly until a turnstile appeared. Amazingly, the so-called professional volunteers had not thought of this. So they decided to reroute and go a different route. Further along the journey, a steep hill appeared, but this particular hill was covered in mud and deep puddles. The crew spent ten minutes debating what they should do. Alexander came up with a hairbrained solution. His idea was to carry the elderly and disabled members over the hill. It seemed like a ludicrous idea at first but observing all the potential hazards, they agreed that this would probably be the best idea. They decided that they would help the people up the hill by pulling them along the hill. There was one section where a few muddy puddles were blocking the path. Alexander, Matt and Rick would lift them up and carry each member on their shoulders. This took 30 minutes to do. By the time this was finished, they were all absolutely knackered. The rest of the journey went by without too many problems.

They arrived at the Hungry Dog, expecting to see Sophie and Sophia. But to their surprise they were nowhere in sight. Matt tried calling them, but they were unreachable. They all debated what to do. “Maybe we should go back the house and see if they are there,” suggested Rick.

“I’m not sure if they will be there, maybe they got lost,” replied Matt.

“I think that we should wait to see if they turn up,” suggested Alexander.

Matt kept trying their phone and eventually managed to get through, but the reception he got from Sophie and Sophia was even worse than the phone reception. It turned out that Sophie and Sophia had forgotten the name of the pub which they all agreed to meet up at, and they also didn’t know the planned route. They looked at a map and thought that the Hungry Lion was the pub that they were supposed to meet at. Sophia and Sophie were blindly insisting that the Hungry Lion was where they were supposed to be meeting. After the long unapologetic argument on the phone, Matt arranged for the minibus to pick them up then pick up the other half of the group at the Hungry Lion. Luckily, the group members praised the crew’s efforts rather than moaning or whining about the mishaps. But what lingered amongst the crew was far from fine and dandy.

Forest of Dean Journey, April 15th, 2021

Alexander dismounted his bike, finding himself in the middle of wilderness. To most people this was just a hiking trail, but to Alexander it was a euphoria of hidden spectacles. Bluebells sprawled out like the purple fire of mysticism. Every individual petal stood out to him, forming a unique personality and characteristic. A world of purple micro-aliens dancing with each other. The daffodils were proudly lined up in a crowd formation to salute their god, the sun. Their petals were roaring with beauty. He had a fascination with wildlife such as deer and pine martens. It wouldn't be uncommon for him to spend three hours searching for a deer, losing himself in the vibrancy.

Just as he was soaking in the natural wonders, familiar bell chimes started ringing in his ear. He knew that it was Pvormlu trying to communicate with him again. He felt his body lighting up like a candle, his mind spinning round and round like a ceiling fan. Images appeared in his mind, this time completely unfamiliar, cackling, jeering and taunting him relentlessly. Feeling completely bewildered; Alexander was trying to work out what was going on but could only get lost in the ominous haze that was filling his mind. Images of eight-winged bats were filling his head. The bats, this time, had developed outlandish smiles and human teeth, it was like they were taking on the human form.

Eventually Alexander was able to think clearly again. Alexander decided to carry on through the forest, but a wave of unease was following him around as if he was being watched. A small cave came into view. Alexander paused and observed the surroundings as if checking the coast was clear. He then proceeded to take ten steps towards the cave. One; a flurry of ravens emerged from the trees then disappeared into the forest. Two; an adder quickly scuttled up a tree. Three; a wild boar darted out in front of him. Four; a deer frantically ran horizontally behind him. Five; a crow swooped down and nearly struck Alexander. Six; a rain cloud briefly appeared. Seven; an owl hooted. Eight; a horse galloped past. Ninel a gunshot was heard. Ten; other footsteps were heard.

Alexander stopped again, sensing a recurring feeling. A wall of bats appeared in front of him and another wall of bats appeared behind him. The same thing happened when he looked to his right, then his left. Soon a square of eight-winged bat demons was surrounding him. This square began to close in on him, trapping him like a net. Alexander's eyes darted around desperately searching for a way out. As the bats drew closer, Alexander focused his attention on the cave. With a tsunami of adrenaline building up inside of him, he dived forwards, straight over the walls of bats. His hands heroically flailed around as if he was a professional goalkeeper. His body aimed for the leaves right outside the cave, and he landed on his hands then his body followed, creating a crash-landing.

He laid motionless on the ground for a few seconds before turning his head. The first thing he saw was the cave entrance, a chamber of stalagmites, a fortress of granite, a tunnel of darkness. He then turned to face the bats, but they were all gone. Still lying on the ground, feeling slightly inebriated by what was happening, Alexander felt a few droplets of water which was strange to him as he knew that the weather was supposed to be sunny. Even though the weather in the UK was as unpredictable as your cat's or dog's behaviour, he knew that raindrops shouldn't be appearing. Not quite believing what was starting to happen, he slithered his way up and noticed that the sky was completely grey. Not wanting to waste another second lying down, Alexander quickly jumped to his feet. The rain started pouring more and more violently. Alexander realised that the cave was going to be his only form of solace from the rain. Alexander decided to enter the cave.

The sight of this cave filled him with inspiration, he could feel the weight of the cave on his shoulders, he could hear his footsteps reverberating around the cave walls like a musical instrument. He could see light trickling through the cracks in the cave, this seemed superficial and unnatural because it was raining outside; Alexander expected to see raindrops. The light seeping in appeared to be following Alexander around the cave; this reminded him of the streetlight of the furniture being. Alexander calmly ventured through the cave passage. He could see the same light following him through the cave as if he was the Messiah. After a few steps, the light went out, only darkness prevailed. Alexander heard strange unrecognisable high-pitched voices.

"Carry on wandering through this cave, weirdo, you will never find your future." This unfamiliar voice echoed throughout the cave.

Alexander became aware that he was being taunted, but with the mentality that 'the only way is forward' stuck in his mind, he desperately wanted to find the source of this mockery so he could teach it a lesson. He quickly stepped through the narrow passage; at times he had to walk sideways to fit through. He eventually made it to a large corridor; this corridor had three exits, Exit A, Exit B and Exit C. The exits had wooden doors, these wooden doors each had engravings on them. Exit A was of a shovel, Exit B was of a rope and Exit C was of a chandelier. Alexander thought long and hard about which one it would likely be. He thought about option A, a shovel. *What use would a shovel be?* he thought to himself. He then thought about option B, a rope. *Where would I tie a rope?* he thought. Of course, the third option seemed even more useless than the others, but he thought about the darkness in the tunnel, and he needed to find his bearings. So, he chose Exit C.

He walked up to the wooden door and jangled the doorknob with his right hand but it wouldn't budge. He had an idea to look up to see if he could see the chandelier. He cocked his head up and saw the chandelier levitating two metres above him, a constant flurry of pearly white luminescent lights orbiting the chandelier, stretching into the ceiling of the cave. The door then opened by itself. Alexander could see his shadow bearing down on him, a tall figure standing like a god, a feeling of judgement flowing through his veins. He decided it was time to enter.

The corridor had several chandeliers placed on the ceiling; the passage seemed straightforward to cross. Just then the cave walls began to shudder. Alexander could feel his body being swayed side to side like a tree in a tropical storm. Alexander had to take heavy footsteps to stay on the ground; his pace appeared to be getting faster and faster to the point where his feet were sliding towards the passage exit. He skidded through the narrow points like a racing driver. Even though he couldn't stop himself, he still had his hands out to protect himself. He carried on skating until he was thrown off his feet and landed on his hands. Alexander was stuck in a crawl position, but he felt like a lion ready to pounce. Right in front of him lay a staircase made of rocks that led to another chandelier. The staircase was carved into the cave wall. There were just five steps, but each step was coated in a layer that appeared hazardous to walk on. The first step was covered in cement. The second step was covered in thick mud. The third step was covered in oil, the fourth step was covered in ice, then the fifth step was covered in quicksand. These steps were carved into the cave wall. The steps led to a ledge, and above this ledge was the chandelier. Alexander was released from his crawl position, and he walked towards the staircase and braced himself for the climb up the hazardous stairs.

Alexander lifted his right leg up to take the first step and before he was able to unbend his leg and place his foot down, a swarm of bats came flooding in. They were surrounding him from behind. They did it with such stealth and professionalism that Alexander felt as if he was being pursued by the FBI. The bats just lingered behind him, tormenting Alexander with their disparaging presence. They then began their high-pitched cackling and chanting. "Mind the gap, you already have one foot in the grave, tread carefully." These horribly distorted wailing voices were echoing.

With his knee raised in the air, aching from keeping it steady for so long, he decided to start his journey up this staircase of doom. He firmly planted his foot in the cement on the first step, he did this the same way that king Arthur stuck his sword in the stone. As soon as he stuck his foot in the cement, it hardened and turned into concrete. Alexander was left with one foot stuck in the concrete, and the background taunting continued. "How are you going to get your way out of this?" Alexander raised his left leg in the air then, with all his might, stamped onto the concrete. At first nothing, but then cracks were appearing – after a few minutes the concrete split apart and his feet were now free again.

The next step was covered in mud. Alexander lifted his right foot up again and pressed it into the muddy step. This was followed by his left foot. The cackling continued. "Remember to clean your muddy boots." This was the cue that he needed, he swivelled his feet in the mud as if wiping his feet on the doormat. He felt the mud disappear from his feet.

The next step was covered in oil. He carefully dipped his feet into the oil; the gut-wrenching fear of what was ahead of him was ripping into him. The pious bats were relishing in Alexander's fear, like mosquitos sucking fear out of him. "Highly flammable," the bats were chanting. This was starting to worry Alexander as the only fire exit was behind him. Fire, fire, fire." The bats were goading a fire to take place. Alexander was under the belief that the bats were just trying to scare him. The oil began to bubble, then he felt heat rising, steam was rising all around him. Suddenly a flame appeared, and he closed his eyes and expected to find himself in hell. The intensity of the heat was causing Alexander to sweat profusely. But the flames were not touching Alexander. A ring of fire was forming around him. "Burn, burn, burn." The bats were flapping their wings trying to spread the fire. Just then smoke started billowing, and it wasn't long until all Alexander could see was thick, acrid smoke. He began coughing and choking and put both hands over his mouth. Alexander had no idea how to defeat this fire. Minutes went by and choking and coughing continued, he was now fighting for his life. "Suffocate the fire, remove the oxygen." He came up with the idea that the fire was feeding off his energy, so he decided to remove his own energy to smother the fire. He held his breath, hoping that this would weaken the fire. To his surprise, the fire weakened, and the smoke disappeared; he could now see what him was around. He then breathed out, releasing all his tension and a white spray was unleashed, whitewashing the whole of the cave. Alexander had just defeated the fire! The fog subsided and revealed that he still had two more steps to climb.

The next step was covered in ice. Alexander carefully placed his right foot on this step and stepped very carefully then slowly stood up, trying not to slip. The temperature of the cave suddenly plummeted. Alexander's feet were frozen in place, his hands were shaking, and his breath was visible. The temperature continued to plummet; Alexander was only dressed for a British spring not a Russian winter. Then strong arctic blasts surged throughout the cave and Alexander's fingers became bullets, his spine became a lamppost. His arms became branches, frozen in place. At this point Alexander was unable to move. He realised that the only thing he could do was control his breath and move his eyeballs around.

He withdrew his breath then closed his eyes. He did this for two minutes but had no idea why he chose to do this (probably to access a meditative state). He knew that he had to find the key somewhere. Alexander reopened his eyes and this time his eyes were pointing directly at the chandelier. The chandelier lit up; this time the lightbulb was emitting a glowing red which was radiating throughout the entire cave. Alexander could feel his body again, his hands were now moveable, his feet were now free. The bright red aura was filling Alexander with motivation and his blood was now flowing with vigour.

The final step was quicksand. Alexander carefully placed his feet in the quicksand. His feet sunk straight away, followed by his legs and his torso. His body was now literally at one with the cave. Being stuck in the cave, Alexander only had the use of his head and arms. The bats were now swarming around his head like flies. "Looks like you have found yourself in a sticky situation." All Alexander could see was a swarm of bats buzzing around him. "We haven't eaten today, look what's on the menu." The bats were gawping at Alexander, salivating, with their long dog-like tongues stuck out, licking his face and biting his arms. Alexander was constantly swatting the bats with his hands, but they wouldn't stop attacking him. He reached his hand out, not knowing what he was trying to grab – maybe a bat for breakfast, Alexander got so fed up with the bats taunting him that he told them he would rip them apart and make a 'batwurst' out of them.

"Batwurst?" the bats squealed in a German accent. "Das hort sich lecker an," the bats replied.

"Oh great, German-speaking bats. Ich meine es ernst, ich werde eine Batwurst aus dir machen!" Alexander yelled at the bats.

The bats responded to this by releasing evil, high-pitched German laughter. "Ha ha, Ja, klar," the bats shrieked sarcastically.

He reached out as far as he could. The bats were licking his face. His right arm was aching from being overstretched. Just when Alexander thought he couldn't hold his arm out any further, he felt his body being lifted out of the quicksand. He felt like a child who was being carried by their father. He was placed on the ledge. He could see that the chandelier was within jumping distance. He heard a loud thud and looked down to discover that a black hole had swallowed the ground. Alexander realised that he had to jump and reach for the chandelier. He had to make the leap of faith!

On the count of three; one, legs bending in preparation; two, Alexander braving himself for the leap; three, he launched himself up like a dog after a bone. He managed to grab the bottom of the chandelier. His weight caused the chandelier to rock side to side, his body was swaying side to side like Tarzan. The weight of his body was going to be too much for the loosely placed chandelier. Plus, he wasn't going to be able to hold on for much longer. The bats surrounded the chandelier and created a vortex that was orbiting the chandelier. One moment Alexander was fixating his worried expression on the wobbling chandelier, the next moment he looked down and the only thing he could see was a massive hole. This hole was filled with darkness, the depth of this pit was immeasurable. The speed of the chandelier shaking was increasing alongside the bat's vortex of speed. The chandelier's light was flickering as if it was being unplugged. Alexander had a choice; should he let go of the chandelier and free fall into the unknown, or should he keep holding on risking more damage to his arms? Alexander didn't have time to make that decision as the chandelier finally broke loose and came hurtling towards the empty abyss. The speed of the fall suddenly decreased, and Alexander felt like he was holding onto a parachute. The speed was almost coming to a complete stop and Alexander was slowly drifting down. The only sound he could hear was a cascading intonation as if he was directly above a giant waterfall. The bats abandoned the chandelier and disappeared into the abyss. Alexander went further and further into the darkness until he woke up again outside by his bike. Alexander was wondering if all this had just been a dream. But the vivid details toiled with his mind, making him beg to differ.

Fourth Encounter, May 21st, 2021

Alexander was having a midnight stroll along the Ruscombe brook. This was a common thing for him to be doing since he often felt restless during the night. He used a small torch to light his way. After walking for around 15 minutes, he turned on his phone screen and noticed that it was 12:30am. He turned his head to the right and noticed a small footbridge, and as he came closer to the footbridge, a ticking noise started sounding. As he was standing next to the bridge, two clock eyes appeared, the expression was 12:30. A small breeze came drifting through. The breeze was blowing from behind him, making his jacket blow forward but the leaves around him remained perfectly still. It was as if there was a cooling fan right behind him. Alexander decided not to turn around. He instead looked up and noticed a letter drifting down slowly, which he caught in midair. On the letter a date was written, 8/8/2019, it was the date that his mum had passed away. Alexander analysed the date, and all the memories came flooding back. He opened the letter and saw the last photo of them both. The photo showed them both sitting together in a cafe, drinking tea and having biscuits. They were both smiling but the haunting inevitability was putting a slight downward expression on the photo, their smiles seemed genuine, but the horror created a hidden expression that Alexander felt every time he glanced at the photo.

After reflecting on the photo, Alexander felt the letter pulling upwards as if it wanted to be free. Even though Alexander wanted to let go of the photo, his hands remained closed. Eventually Alexander allowed himself to let go of the letter. He watched as the letter slowly drifted in the night sky until it was no longer visible. He then felt a cold hand resting on his shoulder (this, of course, was the shadow figure) but Alexander chose not to look behind himself. Another letter drifted down; this time the letter had no writing on it. He opened the letter and found a blank piece of paper, inside the piece of paper was a pen. Alexander picked up the pen and wrote one last message.

Dear Mum,

I know we'll never meet again, at least not in my lifetime, but I hope to meet someone someday who will have all the qualities that you have. I hope to someday experience the passion and love that made you the person you were. To inherit half of your soul is more than enough for me to continue living this life. I'm not going to pretend that there is a way out of this terminal void but I will try to make myself at home in this new world that I live in. I will try to find a place for you, a place that will never be forgotten. I just wanted to write down my belated farewell, hope to see you again in another life.

He carefully folded the letter then held it close to his face, then breathed out a long-awaited sigh of relief.

One last kiss was given to the letter before he attempted to release it. He then said, "This final kiss is for you." He slowly let go of the letter, he gradually raised his hand then unfolded his fingers, loosening his grip so that the letter could drift away. The letter was being held by two fingers; Alexander had his arm stretched as high as it would go with his fingers holding onto the bottom of the letter. After a few seconds of desperately holding on he decided to let the letter float away. He watched as the letter slowly drifted away. He stood in wait, hoping that the letter would reach her.

Alexander turned around to see the furniture being and the shadow figure. The clock expression changed to 12 o'clock. Alexander gazed up at the stars. When he looked back down, he noticed that the flames on the candle teeth were different colours. He walked up to the candles and felt every one; the feeling was of many mixed emotions. Each candle gave him a different sensation. Some candles gave him a shock of euphoria, others made him feel sorrow. When he was done touching the candles, he stood back and formed a prayer. But this was a special prayer. He made a cup out of his hands then placed them in front of his face. He formed a pyramid with his hands, he then peeked through the hole in his hands. This was a spontaneous prayer that helped connect Alexander with his lost mother. After the prayer was over, Pvormlu released the candles, all at once. Incandescent lights floating into the night sky, a thousand wishes, remaining lit. The rising of hope, a revolution of hope.

Brecon Beacons trip, June 28th, 2021

It was a sunny day in June. The family had decided to do a hiking tour around the Brecon Beacons. This was a 12-mile-round walk that Tony had prepared. This time it wasn't just going to be the five of them, Alexander's friend, Martha, was going to join the fun. Plus, Tony had finally found a date, her name was Samantha. Samantha was a former office manager; she was very punctual, but her organisational skills were up for debate. She had a habit of moving objects around and using them for unconventional purposes.

It was 9:30am, Tony was pedantically pacing around the house, back and forth, making sure that everything was prepared. Meanwhile, William was prattling around pretending to be Bear Grylls. He was walking around the house with a compass and binoculars, making no effort to be useful. Anna was helping their dad with organising everything as if she was his secretary. Alexander was trying to memorise the GPS coordinates for the trip, which was also incredibly useless, but he had no idea how to assist his father, so he chose to indulge in his long-time hobby instead.

It was now 10am which was the original time they agreed to embark on their journey but there was still no sign of Martha or Samantha. This, of course, put

Tony on edge. The response that Tony received from Samantha was that she was on her way, but this was little reassurance as there appeared to be no definitive meaning of 'on my way'.

During the first five minutes of waiting Tony was peering through the window, whilst counting the minutes on his fingers, as if he was giving an indirect non-verbal warning to Samantha for being late. During the second five minutes, Tony proceeded to stand by the front door and gesture with his hands in the air as if there was a slow car in front of him. Then, five minutes later... he was at boiling point. So, he went outside and stood on his driveway with a scowl as big as a rotten apple. He was also huffing and puffing so much that you could probably fit an apple in his mouth. By the time Samantha`s car came into view, Tony was waiting for her like a disgruntled chauffeur. He stuck out a forced smile with a half-polished grin. Samantha gave Tony a hug, then took out two bags of belongings. One bag was full of snacks, another was full of old map books and contained binoculars, dog waste bags and a compass.

What on earth do you need that for? Tony was probably wondering. But instead of complaining, he offered to carry the bags. Samantha wasn't done yet; she opened the boot of her car and had an umbrella with her. This was too much for his tolerance level. Tony asked her why she needed all this junk. "What is the purpose of all this?" he asked begrudgingly.

"You never know what we might need, it's better to be safe than sorry," she countered.

"Why would we need dog waste bags?"

"Isn't that obvious?" Samantha replied.

"Do you think we will be shitting in the woods?" Tony said in a sarcastic tone.

"One of us might," she replied.

"What's the umbrella for?"

"You never know when it might rain."

"It's forecasted to be sunny all day," Tony replied.

But Tony's common logic was no match for Samantha`s charisma. Tony used a large backpack and stuffed it with one jug of coffee, one jug of water, two packets of Mars bars, a map book, plastic cups, as well as sandwiches which they had made. Samantha also felt the need to bring insect spray, sun lotion, and a bug zapper. These items went in the second backpack.

Eventually Martha arrived, but instead of making up for her absence she instead decided to start a video call with her Filipino friends, recording a disgruntled Tony and restless Alexander. Samantha was endlessly digging through her stuff as if she was looking for something. And William was prattling around with his binoculars, sombrero hat and a compass. Tony was at his wits' end again!

"Can we all just get in the cars and stop wasting time!" he said in drill sergeant's voice.

The next task they faced was deciding who would go in which car. There were two cars: Samantha's and Tony's. It was going to be a challenge deciding who would go in each car; so, the two captains, Tony and Samantha, would decide who they would nominate to be on their team. Tony chose Anna, then Samantha chose Martha. Tony chose Alexander then William went in Samantha's car.

They all set off heading to Crickowel. The car journey went smoothly for Tony and Samantha, but after they arrived all hell broke loose again. Tony and

Samantha both opened their car boots to reveal even more stuff that they had brought with them. A picnic blanket, metal detector and even a selfie stick! The last two objects were Samantha's. Samantha and Martha dived into her car boot like two bees collecting honey whilst the Somervales just stood there wondering what on earth they were doing. Despite Tony's persistent pleas for Samantha to abandon her extra belongings, Samantha insisted that it was all essential. Alexander offered to carry one of the bags on his back. For some strange reason, Tony decided to bring a clipboard. This was to hold all the documents that he thought he would need for the trip.

The walking formation was quite bizarre. Tony was the self-appointed leader of the group, and Anna was walking next to Tony assisting him. Alexander nominated himself as the first person to carry Tony's backpack. Anna was delicately carrying the picnic mat as if it was a baby. William offered to carry the metal detector (probably just to see how he could annoy people with it). Martha was waving the selfie stick around trying to get a memorable shot of themselves posing like cartoon characters. Martha and Samantha were walking quite far behind the rest of the group, they were busy laughing and chatting, a far cry from the captain's tight militaristic demeanour. Tony marched ahead as if he was a business inspector on a tight schedule. They made their way through Crickowel and started walking across the Brecon Beacons.

Their plan was to get to Table Mountain, following the path. Tony's plan was to go around the trail then return. But the crew members had other plans. William wanted to locate wildlife. Samantha wanted to explore further, and Alexander wanted to go home. They started off by walking around Crickhowell castle. Martha made the group pose in front of the castle ten times, in various outlandish poses. Tony was busy flicking through his clipboard. Samantha and Martha were going around the castle pointing at every little detail, it was like they were stuck in a perpetual orbit. They were tugging at each other's arms like schoolgirls observing a designer handbag.

The walk around the Table Mountain was enjoyable and the group had the opportunity to mingle amongst themselves. Samantha and Martha were buzzing away like two bees in endless conversation. Alexander was trying to keep up with their flow, but their current was too fast for him. So, he awkwardly chipped in and mentioned what he was doing with his life. Alexander attempted to socialise with the pair but there was only so much shoulder-grabbing and nose-pinching that he could take. So, he decided to mingle with William. However, the conversation was not much longer. William kept rambling on about coordinates and how to use binoculars. Alexander tried on William's binoculars but not without William taunting Alexander about how to wear the binoculars.

"You must crouch down and only keep your right eye open. Make sure you keep it completely still. Grip it tightly so it doesn't slip.

Alexander became fed up very quickly with this vexing humdrum. William then whipped out his high-resolution camera and told Alexander to take a photo of him. Alexander reluctantly agreed. Alexander took two photos of William posing like an arrogant twat. William then viewed the photos; he had a look of disbelief on his face.

"Can you explain to me why half the background is missing and why you haven't zoomed into my face?"

Alexander felt like dropping the £400 camera on the ground. "Find another slave, you ignorant twat," Alexander said in response.

"Can you just take a proper photo?" he pleaded in a boisterous tone.

"That's a resounding never," Alexander replied.

They had reached their picnic spot. Tony laid out the picnic mat. Anna handed out the sandwiches, and Martha gave everyone their water. For a moment it seemed like everything was just how it should be. That was until Samantha knocked over the jug of water which caused a large spillage to flood the picnic mat and created soggy sandwiches.

"Uh-oh, I'm so sorry!" she wailed in an over-apologetic voice.

Tony's eyes rolled back in disbelief before he grabbed the picnic blanket and started persistently shaking it as if trying to bring the fainted blanket back to life.

"No need to worry," Anna said reassuringly.

"My sandwiches are worried," remarked William.

"How are we going to dry everything?" Tony said in a panicked voice.

Anna then came up with the idea that everyone would carry the wet items in their hands, including Tony's clipboard, Martha's diary and William's camera.

The group marched on until they reached the peak. Martha insisted that they take a group selfie. The group kept reshuffling themselves according to Martha's specifications. Martha was holding her phone out whilst the rest of the group crouched down into their poses.

Alexander turned and noticed fog approaching his direction. This was unusual as the day's forecast was sunny. Alexander wanted to investigate this fog, so he excused himself and said that he was going to have a pee. He wandered closer and closer to the fog until he was in the fog. A few steps in and he realised that this was no ordinary fog. The shadow figure suddenly appeared, standing at the top of a wooden staircase shrouded in the mist.

"Greetings, Alexander," the shadow figure said. "You must navigate your way through the foggy maze and find the lost items then place them on the stone table. You will need to find a compass, a mirror, an old map and an oil lamp. You must discover where these objects are to restore the natural working order which will unblock your mind." The shadow figure then disappeared as if it had never been there.

Alexander cautiously stepped through the fog. He had no idea about where to go since all he could see was thick mist. So, he took a few steps in one direction then turned and took a few steps in another direction. He noticed dark lines flickering around him. It became clearer and resembled a shadow maze.

The maze wasn't a physical barrier but more of a psychological one. The maze kept vanishing and reappearing. The maze would change its dimensions creating confusion. Alexander noticed the outline of a letter suspended in midair – the letter was 'U'. He had no idea what the U was supposed to mean, but then he remembered the first item that he needed to find was a compass. The letter U does not appear on a compass. Alexander was exhausting his brainpower by thinking of relatable words such as *underground, universe, umbrella* but he was none the wiser. He then pictured the U upside down and he saw an 'N'. *This N must signify north*, he thought. He worked out which direction was north. He discovered another letter suspended in the air. It was the letter 'M'. Using his previous logic, Alexander flipped this letter to the side revealing the letter 'E'. This read east. The outline of a square appeared in front of him, inside the letter were a series of instructions. *North 5, East 7, South 3.* Alexander worked out that the numbers meant steps, so he took five steps north, seven steps east then three steps south. A shining compass appeared on a wooden table. Alexander picked this compass up; he then walked down the shadow corridor and placed this compass on the stone table.

The next object that he had to find was the oval wall mirror. Alexander re-entered the shadow maze, this time he noticed that there were black arrows pointing in different directions. The first arrow was pointing towards him, this confused Alexander because behind him was the shadow corridor, but then he realised that this was a mirror that he was searching for, so the arrows were going to be in mirror reverse. He proceeded straight on only to find another arrow. This arrow was pointing right (so Alexander knew that it was actually pointing left). He turned left but then saw two arrows facing away from each other, one was pointing straight on, the other was pointing backwards.

How on earth am I supposed to know where to go? This is just like following Google Maps, Alexander thought to himself.

Just then, the idea dawned upon him. He imagined two mirrors both facing away from each other, it would be impossible to look into two mirrors at the same time. So Alexander came up with an idea to search in both directions until he found something conclusive. He quickly paced forwards and backwards as if he was trying to catch a thief until he spotted a narrow passageway on the left arrow side, he slowly ventured through this passageway. In the distant corner he spotted two more arrows, however, this time instead of pointing away from each other they were pointing towards each other. This created an image in Alexander's mind of two mirrors facing each other. He decided to stand in the middle of the arrows whilst moving his head back and forth to see which direction became clearer. Alexander was looking left when he noticed that his shadow had been cast in this direction. He quickly turned around and an oval mirror levitated in the congealed mist waiting to be taken home. Alexander picked up this oval mirror and placed it carefully on the stone table.

The next object that he had to find was the map. When he entered the shadow maze for the third time, he saw a wooden table filled with blank pieces of paper and it contained an old quill pen with a long white feather attached to it. He picked up the pen and an old brown piece of paper and thought about what to write. Whilst he was thinking, the layout of the shadow maze was constantly changing, one minute it appeared like a labyrinth the next it appeared like a fortress with high shadow walls surrounding the area. The next minute, shadowy hills were dominating the background, a shadowy Brecon Beacons. The minute after that nothing apart from the dense white fog. Alexander had no idea what to write – should he draw everything that he could see, or should he draw a map of the Brecon Beacons? He decided that this was one big personality test to see who he was. He stared at this piece of paper for a while before drawing himself as a stick man who was staring at shadowy hills in the distance surrounded by a shadow fortress. He was standing on a ledge overlooking the surrounding area but below him was the labyrinth, a maze that made no sense to him. He drew all this in black ink, imagining what his life would look like on paper. The hills would represent where he should be, but this was too far away and steep for him to climb. The shadow fortress represented his confined lifestyle and inability to break down barriers. And the labyrinth represented his constant confusion with where his life is heading. After completing this drawing, he held it in the air as if revealing an answer to someone. Suddenly, a swarm of eight-winged demon bats grabbed the map and took it to the stone table. Even though the constant plumes of the fog were nauseating and were causing intense dizziness, Alexander's willpower to succeed was making everything as clear as day in his mind. His thoughts were not affected by the blinding mist.

Now, the final object – the handheld lantern. Alexander was slowly tiptoeing through the dark passageways searching for the next riddle. A luminescent ray of light slowly crept in, and he followed it. This light kept bending round, and Alexander found himself going around in circles, a never-ending ring of light bending around the forlorn maze. Just when Alexander thought he was wasting his time, a large stone pillar arose from the centre of this shadowy luminous ring. Alexander squinted his twitchy eyes at this large grey monument and noticed that there was writing on it but under the current lighting conditions it was barely visible. *There is a...* He could just about make out a few words but then the rest of the letters faded into the darkness. Alexander kept looking from different angles to try to work out what the missing letters were. He could only make out an 'L'. Alexander quickly worked out that this stood for *light. There is a light... at the end of the tunnel.* Alexander wondered where the end of this tunnel was. If where he came in was the start of the tunnel, then the deepest part of the maze would reveal the end of the tunnel. Alexander pushed on through the winding shadow maze having no idea where he was going. He kept walking in different directions until he came across three streams of light connecting to three passageways. *How am I supposed to know which one to take?* he thought. But then he thought of labelling these tunnels Tunnel A, Tunnel B and Tunnel C. After a short while of sticking his right hand out in a chopping motion and lightly chopping towards each tunnel, one at a time, a bit like he was preparing to slice a delicate cake, he renamed the tunnels: Tunnel A as 'past tunnel', Tunnel B as 'present tunnel' and Tunnel C as the 'future tunnel'. *Which tunnel should I enter?* he thought.

After a while of deciding between present and future, he decided that it was going to be the future that was the most important. He entered the future tunnel and followed the glowing light until he was able to identify the source of the light. He discovered the hand-held lantern, picked it up and placed it on the stone table. When he looked up from the stone table, he witnessed the shadow figure standing on the wooden steps like a tribal leader waving his stick around as if trying to command attention from a large audience.

"Greetings again, Alexander, I am here to send you another message."

These words instantly commanded Alexander's attention. The shadow figure walked towards the stone table, picked up the compass then returned to the top of the wooden stairs. This compass was held high in the air like a gold medal, the shadow figure started waving the compass in the air to take the place of his wooden stick. The figure turned around and stretched his sinewy elastic arm out with the compass wedged between the long pointy spider-like fingers. This arm was stretched out high and the gesture was done in the same fashion of an air stewardess – slow, calm and instructional. This was followed by a command, "To the north." This gesture was succeeded by the shadow figure turning around to his right then slowly lowering his raised arm like a lever. Then followed the phrase, "By the east." The shadow figure then turned to face Alexander, dropped his arm down in the same manner as a veteran showing respect at a memorial, then uttered the phrase, "In the south." The final compass gesture involved the shadow figure turning to his right then making a robotic dance gesture with his bent arm stuck out, followed by the final phrase, "For the west."

These riddles would always mystify Alexander's mind, yet he felt like the answer to these riddles was always interpretational for his mind, a world full of colour not just black and white. The shadow figure then picked up the oval wall mirror and held it like it was a trophy. "What do you see?" the figure asked whilst pointing the mirror at Alexander.

"I see someone who is lost and trapped in a never-ending maze," Alexander sheepishly but honestly answered.

"I see someone who has already found the way out of their never-ending maze." This was a very conflicting yet honourable comment from the shadow figure. This was said with fatherly compassion like a father telling his son that he had done well and not to worry.

The shadow figure then picked up the map that Alexander had drawn and held it with both shadow hands, one hand at each end. This was held in a patriotic fashion as if it was a flag. A long pointy shadowy finger was raised then aimed at the hills on the map. This was done in a way that was like a teacher pointing to a painting done by a small child – a friendly yet very formal way of communicating. "Those hills are the hills that you will conquer." This finger was now aimed at the shadow walls. "These walls are merely shadows; you can walk through them – don't let spiders kick you out of your own house." These words were said in a deep but light tone. The same finger pointed at the labyrinth. "You are free, this labyrinth has no power over you, you will find your way out of this maze." The shadow figure then lifted the map high into the air; a mysterious breeze was causing this map to wave in the air. The shadow figure then released this map causing it to drift over to Alexander. He held this identity map in the air admiring, his own creation.

The hand-held lantern was the last object to be lifted. The shadow figure had the resemblance of a miner who was searching desperately for a way out. After a short while of holding the lantern still, the shadow figure started slowly swinging the lantern like a pendulum on a grandfather clock. This light was becoming hypnotic to the point where the surroundings were completely changing day-night, night-day, clouds were forming, clouds were dissipating. "Your emotions are like night and day, constantly changing, from one opposite to the next. Your emotions are as predictable as British weather." After saying these phrases the shadow figure stretched his arm out and held the lantern at a position where it was almost touching Alexander's face; this dazzling sensation sent his senses into overdrive. Alexander felt as though he was about to have an epileptic fit, he closed his eyes as tight as he could.

A flash! He slowly turned around with his eyes shut. When he opened his eyes, he saw that he was with his family again and had just finished peeing in the bush. "That's a long piss," his dad commented. It turned out that Alexander had been absent from the group for around ten minutes, even though he felt like he had been gone for hours.

"I just had some things to sort out," Alexander replied, completely missing the social cue to just say nothing and get on with the rest of his day.

"Busy doing what?" his dad asked, deliberately trying to get a reaction out of his son.

"Bird watching," Alexander replied.

The journey back was calmer and more enjoyable than the journey there. The group appeared more cohesive and relaxed, Tony had stopped panicking and was laughing with Martha and Samantha. Alexander and William were having an intelligent conversation instead of trying to wind each other up. Anna was busy giving compliments about how nice the weather was and how wonderful the trip had been. This was an experience that would be remembered for a very long time, a journey of inner symbolism, this ability to enjoy the outside world instead of hiding from it.

Fifth Encounter, September 12th, 2021

Alexander had been applying for numerous jobs in the hope that he could better himself; gardening jobs, retail jobs, waitering jobs, cleaning jobs, and now he had applied to be a receptionist at The First Inn. It was a cool September evening; Alexander was sitting alone in his bedroom staring out the window with a feeling of impending doom. Was this just going to be another flop or would he be thrown straight into the deep end and have to work with people he had never met before? He didn't have any hopes but still the impulsive feeling of dread – walking the plank then having to jump straight into murky water. His phone rang. It was from First Inn.

Alexander slowly picked up the phone and waited for the caller to introduce themselves. "Hello, is this Alexander?" the caller asked.

"Yes, I'm Alexander," he replied, feeling incredibly uncomfortable.

The call didn't last long, but Alexander was able to arrange. This arrangement was for him to be at the interview in two days' time at 1pm. This should have been wonderful news for him but the fear and anxiety of having to work with other people and having to force himself to appear professional and normal in front of customers was causing knots in his stomach. This was so much so that he ended up throwing up in the toilet three times that evening. He couldn't eat much, he couldn't play video games or watch TV, he just sat in silence trying to prepare himself mentally for this interview and for the possibility of entering the terrifying world of work.

The clock was ticking; it was already midnight again; the past few hours were consumed by doubtful thinking and Alexander's routine of walking back and forth from his kitchen to his front door to clear his congested thoughts and feelings. He laid down on his couch and started staring at his wall clock as if trying to seek advice. The nerves that Alexander was feeling were amplified by the constant ticking of the wall clock. The whole sensation of a ticking clock staring back at him with charming foxiness combined with the never-ending ticking noises created intense havoc inside Alexander's mind. There was no way of blocking it all out. He just stared into the expressionless face of the clock, feeling numb and having no idea what to do.

The clock ticked on; 12:20… 12:25… 12:30… The echoing sound of school bells all simultaneously rang at once. Alexander's living room transformed into a bare hallway with an office at the other end. Alexander detracted his glare from the wall clock and discovered that he was sitting on a chair behind a desk. The desk was cluttered with interview forms and there was a chair on the other side, but no one was sitting in it. Alexander turned his head to look at where his living room windows used to be and discovered that in its place was an office door with a square window. There appeared to be a light emitting from the door but there was nothing visible from inside the mysterious room.

Alexander stood up and slowly walked towards this door. Just as his trembling hands were about to touch the mysterious doorknob, the wooden face appeared. The wooden clock eyes were ticking at an immense speed, the bright glare of the light crown of the furniture being caused Alexander to look away to avoid damaging his eyes. The bells were ringing riotously, creating a feeling of dread and panic to surge from inside him. Alexander looked away in fear. He walked over to the mysterious desk with his head down as if he was too ashamed to show his face. He pressed his head against the desk with his eyes shut, not knowing how to handle this pressure, having no idea why he felt this way. The constant ringing of the bells caused him to put a finger in each ear, trying desperately to survive the immense fear. The ringing stopped. Alexander pulled his fingers out of his ears and slowly lifted himself up. He turned around to notice that there were now two large office doors that had the shape and format of a castle gate. These doors boldly opened, revealing Pvormlu as the interviewer!

This was no ordinary Pvormlu – this was an office version! White blinds were in place of white curtains. Behind these white blinds were a series of shelves filled with folders. Instead of wooden table legs, Pvormlu had six large office chairs with large wheels. Instead of a bed, Pvormlu had a reception counter at the top of its body. Instead of the light crown, Pvormlu had a screen projector attached to a black metal pole which was inserted into the top of the wooden head. The clock eyes had a very large pair of glasses covering them. Beneath the wooden neck hung a tie.

Pvormlu slowly shifted around Alexander with the sound of heavy wheels vibrating on the creaky wooden floor. Pvormlu was slowly pacing around Alexander with an authoritarian and slightly creepy demeanour. The giant old-fashioned teacher's glasses were putting Alexander on edge with an intense historic glare. The screen projector displayed a presentation. The presentation was just a series of flashing charts comparing employee progress and listing endless company policies. These presentations were wreaking havoc on Alexander's visual senses. The brightness kept changing from dim to maximum brightness. The different slideshows were flashing at an alarming speed. Some slideshows contained essays-worth of information; others were just white flashes. The filing cabinet compartments were being organised by poltergeist activity. The constant rearranging of files and inspections made Alexander feel dizzy. He had no idea what was being recorded and why it was being recorded. Above the filing cabinet compartment lay a reception desk, which was cluttered with files and documents – a sight of complete disarray.

To make matters worse there was a long queue of eight-winged demon bats behind him. *Maybe these are the customers*, he thought to himself.

The bats were flapping their wings peevishly showing disapproval. In their high-pitched voices they were chanting, "Hurry up, stop wasting our time, we will just go somewhere else."

This pandemonium was causing Alexander's body to shiver as if he was in the Arctic. He couldn't hear himself think, he was unable to form a response. The impatient bats then swarmed over the desk and started tearing the documents up in rage. Alexander had no clue as to why Pvormlu was showing this to him – how was this going to help? Alexander felt like he had had enough, so he put his hands over his ears then closed his eyes, doing his best to block everything out. After the shrieking bats finally stopped terrorising him, he slowly opened his eyes, took a few deep breaths then sat down on the interviewee chair. Pvormlu slowly skated to the other end of the interview table. It lowered its body then stared at Alexander directly. The direct eye contact was burning into Alexander's corneas, as if he was staring into direct sunlight. Alexander kept briefly breaking eye contact to maintain focus. Pvormlu used the projector flag to communicate messages. The first instruction was for Alexander to fill out a form. Pvormlu stared at Alexander with a 1 o'clock expression. One of its candles was released and it levitated towards him then sat upright. To write on he was given a plank of wood.

Alexander picked up the candle then turned it upside down and held it in the air for a few seconds, deciding what to write. He then glanced up at the projector flag:

Title:
Name:
Date of Birth:
Address:
Phone Number:

Alexander pressed the candle flame against the wooden board and wrote his name using the flame as though it was a pen. The letters were burned onto the piece of wood creating a thick black sooty print. He wrote this fluently as if he was used to using candles as pens. The next question appeared on the projector flag read:

How would you describe yourself?

Alexander froze and stared at this question. How was he supposed to answer it? He had no idea how to describe himself because he was himself. He was struggling immensely with finding adjectives that would describe his personality. He thought about describing his physical features: 5-foot-9, slim, blue eyes but then he realised that this description would have no relevance to a job interview question. He pondered over this for a while as if it was a maths question. Alexander knew that this was an open-ended question based around subjective opinions. The purpose behind this question was to see how well employees could script whilst being put on the spot. But Alexander had no idea how to script when talking about himself. He thought of a few adjectives: intelligent, sophisticated, fast and strong. He wrote these adjectives down.

Where do you see yourself in five years' time?

This next open-ended question was arguably even harder since Alexander didn't own a crystal ball. *I see myself not working here in five years' time*, he thought to himself. He had no idea how to approach such a hypothetical question. He decided to write 'the CEO of First Inn'. This, of course, was an ambitious answer yet there was no other answer that Alexander could come up with.

What would you do if a customer was unsure about what to ask you and there was a queue forming behind you?

Are these questions going to get any easier or just remain at this level of difficulty? he thought. This was yet another tough question for Alexander. *Should I tell the customer to hurry up? Or maybe I should just wait for the confused customer to finish their question.* 'I'll explain to the customer that they have approximately 30 seconds to finish their question, or they'll have to leave'. This was a very confused answer that showed how socially unaware he was.

Interviewer Pvormlu then revealed suitable answers for these questions. Alexander had no idea how he was supposed to have guessed this; he thought that he would stand a better chance winning the lottery than getting the answer to this question right. Alexander lifted the wooden board and presented it, waiting for Pvormlu's approval.

Pvormlu's clock expression changed to 8 o'clock – a sign of approval. Alexander got up out of his chair and walked up to Pvormlu. Pvormlu's house bell was extended out, waiting for Alexander to shake it. He stretched his arm out and grabbed the clapper, shaking it slowly but firmly. Pvormlu's candle teeth retracted then the broomstick was extended out as another handshake gesture. Alexander grabbed the broomstick brush and shook it with pleasure.

All that remained was for Alexander to open one final door. This lead to the First Inn interview room. Alexander stared intensely at the door as if the door was staring back at him. He made his way, one step at a time, towards the door. Eventually his hand was touching the doorknob. He put both hands on the doorknob for reassurance and took a few deep breaths. Then he opened the door.

Job Interview, September 15th, 2021

Alexander walked towards the First Inn. His stomach was all tangled and jumping up and down. His insides felt like a box containing puppies that were all trying to escape. His dad and aunt had driven him to the interview to make sure that he arrived on time. Alexander wanted to take a few minutes to gather himself before walking straight in, but his dad and aunt's irksome faces and hand gestures made it impossible for him to regulate himself. He walked straight into the First Inn feeling totally unprepared. His head was so low that it was almost dangling from his neck. His lips quivering and uneven footsteps made him appear almost suspicious. The perceived impending fate was eating away at him, creating dread. The expectation that the interview was going to be a massive flop and another blow to his chances of being normal was weighing him down.

He awkwardly made his way to the reception desk and asked to see Mr Goddard who was the general manager. The interview went well, just a typical, normal conversation, nothing like the torture session that his aunt and Samantha had concocted. The manager seemed impressed by Alexander's determination to change. The interview went by without a hitch. In fact, Mr Goddard was impressed that Alexander had even bothered to turn up since he was the only one out of eight applicants who had made an appearance. Despite Alexander's restless, fidgety behaviour and wobbly voice, he was able to coordinate himself very well.

In preparation for this interview, his family had forced him to participate in role-playing games. They had also written a script and told Alexander to memorise it, but Alexander could not remember a word of the rehearsed script and he didn't need to because he only had to represent himself and he could do that perfectly well without the help of his family.

Trial shift,
September 20th, 2021

Fortunately, Alexander was offered a trial shift, but his ordeal was far from over. It was the morning of the trial shift and Alexander had spent hours studying hotels and trying to memorise everything. This time he was able to spend ten minutes gathering himself before entering the building. These unnerving ten minutes were spent pacing around the building and walking around in circles, doing everything he can to remember what he had researched. After he had finished doing this bizarre preparation ritual, he was determined that he could now proceed to his quest of wage slavery. He entered the First Inn feeling that he was a knight in shining armour. Ready to fight a battle, a battle for his future!

He entered the building (this time with his head held up) only to be greeted by an older dishevelled man who had the most repulsive facial expression he had ever seen, he looked like he hadn't slept in a week. He stood there, leaning against the wall with a cigar in his mouth.

"All right, mate, what have you come here for?" he said in a hoarse voice.

Alexander awkwardly looked into the man's sore eyes, trying his best to come with a one-liner that could help him escape this cringeworthy situation. "Uh... receptionist... trial shift," he stuttered awkwardly.

The man looked at Alexander with half a smirk and patted him on the back then disappeared somewhere.

Who the hell was that guy? Alexander thought. He walked over to the receptionist and told her that this was his trial shift. He was taken into a small office and briefed about the job. He had to fill out a company policy form then he was introduced to the manager who was going to shadow him. Her name was Chloe, and she was the assistant manager.

Alexander was very much looking forward to being supported by experienced members of staff. He tried his best to mask his agoraphobia and pretend like he had done this job 100 times before. He forced a smile which stretched nearly to the point of snapping and his eyeballs were hyper-fixated on every detail, making him look a bit like a cat. Alexander pushed through the trial shift, unaware that there is only so far that he could travel as a neurotypical poser.

Chloe started by explaining how they operated and showed him how to use their computers. Next, Alexander was given was a hotel tour. The tour was quite lengthy and was too long, considering that Alexander had many things that he needed to learn about. She pointed out the fire exits and spent half the tour chatting to the cleaning staff. Alexander had developed an absorbent mindset that made him believe that he could soak in information like a sponge but his sponge was full of holes and the information was pouring straight through him in a torrential storm of madness.

After the tours and explanation was over, then came the customer service, the part that Alexander was dreading the most. Although the first customers were friendly, the discomfort he was feeling was causing his body language to freeze and every attempt to interact was a strain on his body. He felt like a penguin alone in Antarctica shivering in the bitter winds.

Chloe had a very different demeanour to Alexander; she was very outgoing and knew exactly how to exert herself in a social setting. She was unapologetic and would say whatever she wanted to say. She was now in the mood to test Alexander in front of the guests (this, of course, was without warning).

A customer asked, "How many floors are there?"

Then Chloe asked Alexander, "How many floors are there, Alexander?"

He felt a wave of confusion hitting him. "Uh... five, no, six," he replied feeling uneasy.

"It's six, remember, why did you forget?"

Alexander just stood there blankly, not knowing how to respond.

Chloe, being the neurotypical moody manager, decided that she wasn't done humiliating Alexander on his first day. She then dared to ask Alexander another question. "Tell the customer what time we start breakfast."

"Uh... six... seven... eight?" Alexander was erupting inside like a volcano.

"See, he doesn't listen, what am I meant to do with him? I'm meant to be training him." The customer then gave an awkward laugh. Alexander was unable to understand what was going on and felt like leaving the building. "It's 6:30am," she said in a loud, condescending voice.

When the long four-hour shift was finally over, Alexander was relieved and headed out the door. But as he came out of the exit, a gang of middle-aged women with tattoos started talking in a loud manner to Alexander.

"That's the new one," one of the women said.

"What's your name?" another one of the women asked in a grunty tone.

Alexander was about to try to introduce himself when Chloe appeared out of nowhere and said, "Alexander. He doesn't normally speak much."

Alexander was standing still with his feet twitching back and forth, trying to find a way to get out of the situation. There was a moment of silence when they stopped talking. Alexander had no idea what to say or do so he just said hi and started slowly making his way back home. He could tell that the women were laughing at him. Alexander slowly shifted past, avoiding eye contact. This behaviour was something that Alexander had become accustomed to. Alexander was relieved to finally be heading home but the lingering anxiety of the upcoming day was weighing heavily on his mind.

First Part-time Shift, 22nd September 2021

Although only being a 12-6pm shift, the fear and anxiety was shaking throughout Alexander's entire body causing time to slow down for him. His exposed nerves were reacting to every sound, every voice. Alexander had become a work robot – he was programmed to only focus on getting the job done then leaving. He had no manoeuvrability to endeavour in social matters. He turned up ten minutes early and, in his mind, raring to go. He greeted a few friendly coworkers then proceeded to start his shift. The first thing he had to do was log into his computer then start with the guest bookings. He tried to log in but realised that the information on his slip wasn't working. Alexander had a quick idea to start looking around to see if he could find the information but just when he was in the middle of rummaging around, he heard a familiar voice shouting at him from the other side of the room. Alexander looked up and with a horrified expression, realised that there was a queue of three people and then he saw Chloe walking towards him in an aggressive manner.

"I told you yesterday, go to my office to get your password, why haven't you done it and what are you looking for, can't you see that there are customers waiting?"

This sudden intrusion made Alexander feel incredibly uncomfortable. He just stood there trying to process what was happening around him. Chloe then disappeared without saying anything, Alexander was left standing there, having idea what was going on, no idea what to do. He was standing still, frantically looking around, just trying to work out what to do. *Why did she shout at me? What am I supposed to do now? Where did she go? Is she waiting for me? Should I wait for her?* All these questions were echoing in his mind. The customers were looking confused but also slightly annoyed. Alexander decided that after 20 seconds of staring at the door, that he should find Chloe. Alexander opened the door but at the same time Chloe walked in from a different door.

"Where are you going?" she asked in a demeaning voice.

"Uh…" was all Alexander could respond with.

Chloe then asked Alexander directly, "Have you apologised to the customers?"

Alexander wanted to say yes but he thought that the customer would rat him out so he said no. Chloe then made him apologise to the customer for wasting their time. Alexander felt so embarrassed doing this. Chloe then logged him in.

"Do I have to do everything for you?" She then decided to go for overkill on embarrassing Alexander and asked him to explain the problem to the customer.

Alexander felt too uncomfortable to look directly at the customer and his voice was shaking so he could only mutter. He looked like a child who was upset from being told off by the teacher. "Uh… I'm having problems with the computer."

Chloe, not satisfied with this answer, explained to the customer what Alexander had done wrong, creating the impression that Alexander was a naughty little schoolboy and the customers were the parents. "This new one forgot to ask me for the new login details."

To make matters even worse, the guest was a regular and was friends with Chloe. "You can't find good ones anymore," the guest said in a patronising tone.

The rest of the day went by with Alexander being constantly taunted by the people around him, his robotic mental processing creating a cold atmosphere. Finally, Alexander had a break – this was going to be his 30-minute break. Stephanie, another middle-aged woman manager, told Alexander that he could go on his break. Alexander was so relieved to have this break that he went straight to the toilet and spent the next ten minutes trying to understand what was going on and what he needed to do. After this, he went to the staff room and spent a further ten minutes working out what he should spend his break doing. Alexander thought that he had a one-hour break, he had forgotten what Chloe had told him. Alexander nervously sat down in the canteen, deciding whether or not he had an appetite. Another ten minutes had gone by and his break was now over.

Alexander decided that he wanted a hot chocolate and muffin. Whilst he stood in line waiting, Stephanie noticed that he was still on his break. "Alexander! Your break has finished, why are you still here? You have had 35 minutes already."

Alexander stood watching her, not knowing how to respond. She slowly walked towards Alexander and asked him about what he was doing. Stephanie agreed to let Alexander have a one-hour break but told him that it would come out of his pay if he wanted another break extension.

This first week was very physically draining for Alexander. At the end of the shift, he returned to his desk to log out but noticed a letter that had his name on.

Dear Alexander

MY TARGETS!
LISTEN TO WHAT PEOPLE TELL ME!
I MUST TAKE ONLY 30 MINUTES FOR MY BREAK!
I MUST SMILE WHEN GUESTS ARE TALKING TO ME!
I MUST SAY HELLO TO GUESTS AND MY COWORKERS!
I MUST ALSO REMEMBER TO LOG OUT

This message sent Alexander into a state of shock. He had no idea why someone would leave such a message for him. He felt his world disappearing before his very eyes. This first week of working he had done everything that he could have done yet this was the feedback that he was getting. He shoved the letter in his bag and made his way to the staff toilets. He closed the toilet door and did his business. But before he thought about flushing, the thought of that letter was causing his mind to spin like never before. He picked up the letter and went over and over it. *Is this what people really think of me?* he thought. After ten minutes of staring at this letter he ripped it into pieces then dropped the pieces in the toilet. He spent the next few minutes feeling like flushing himself down the toilet. When he eventually flushed the toilet, the urge to get home as soon as possible was bursting through his veins.

The evening was meant to be a joyous celebratory occasion, but all Alexander could think about was how he would be able to survive another shift.

Now you have experienced what it's like to be in the world of work. You now know how I feel," Tony said, feeling relieved.

"Six hours is a good start, but try doing ten hours," William replied slyly.

"I can't remember the last time you worked ten hours," Tony fired back at him.

"I work as much as i can," William replied.

"I think this is a great opportunity," Anna said with optimism.

When the meal was over, Alexander went to the toilet. He felt a wave of intense nausea and anxiety and vomited half his meal into the toilet. The thought of having to do that job day-in and day-out was making Alexander feel physically sick. Alexander went to sit down on the bottom of the stairs, looking like he had the world on his shoulders. Anna went to see if he was all right.

She sat next to him and said, "The first week will be the most difficult, the change of environment, the challenging coworkers, mean bosses and hectic schedule. The more you deal with it, the less of a burden it becomes. I know you can deal with the pressure; it will help you become more independent." Anna was doing her best to reassure Alexander.

"I wasn't aware that it would be so difficult to fit in," Alexander said with a lost expression.

"I don't fit in either," Anna said. "All I do is mask, pretend, I don't care about my annoying coworkers, I don't care about my mundane job, but what I do care about is succeeding in life. This job won't last forever, you will find what's waiting for you soon enough. Mum would be proud of you; she would be proud of all of us. What that thing that she always used to say?"

"Preparation is the key to everything." Alexander quoted their mum's most common mantra.

"She certainly did say that," Anna replied gleefully.

Alexander also pondered on his own motto: 'live a day of years, not a year of days'. At that point in time, he felt like he was living a year of very long and exhausting days. The day that would come along that would represent years-worth of achievements was yet to come.

Horse Riding Journey, October 2021

After weeks of tirelessly working at the First Inn, Alexander's sympathetic aunt offered to take him horse riding. Alexander found a weekend where he would be available and agreed to spend the weekend with his aunt and uncle.

He decided to take the train to Hereford station. This was a short and easy journey for him. When he met his aunt and uncle, they gave him a hug and asked how his job was.

He told them that he was enjoying his job, and it was a great experience for him. His aunt kept telling him how great he was doing. Inside, Alexander was feeling intense exhaustion and was dreading another week at the grind. But he wanted to give a positive impression of himself so that people wouldn't be concerned about him.

Alexander sat down with his aunt and uncle and had a lengthy conversation (75% was his aunt's input, 20% was his uncle complaining about his aunt's comments and 5% was Alexander pretending to agree with everything that his aunt was saying). After 30 minutes of being soaked from his aunt's torrential downpour of waffle, his uncle mentioned about the charity bags that his aunt had bought for Alexander. This was going to be the next act of the Aunt Berta show. She had prepared two bags of stuff that she wanted Alexander to have.

"Could you fetch the two charity bags, Tim." Aunt Bertha had another errand for his uncle to run.

"Don't you have another slave?" his uncle replied sarcastically.

"I did but I fired them." His uncle reluctantly got up and asked where the bags were. "They might be upstairs... no, they are probably downstairs," his aunt replied, unsure of where she put the bags.

"Upstairs or downstairs?" his uncle asked in a frustrated tone.

"You must have seen them," she replied.

"I haven't seen them!" his uncle fired back.

"Why don't you find out," his aunt replied in a bossy tone.

Alexander quickly devised a plan. He would search downstairs whilst his uncle searched upstairs. They all thought that this was a brilliant idea. The two detectives set out to search for the missing charity bags. Ten minutes went by... every corner, every cupboard, still no sign.

"Have you found it yet?" his aunt called out.

"No, we bloody haven't," his uncle said back.

His aunt was busy video calling her friends whilst her slaves were slaving away. "I think I might have left it in my car, could you have a look?"

"You only just remembered now," his uncle said in a frustrated tone.

"You could have thought of it," his aunt unapologetically replied.

Uncle and Alexander checked the car. They managed to find the charity bags. Both bags were completely full.

"Look to see if there is anything that you might need."

Inside was an odd glove, a Bible that looked like it had been sitting around for 30 years, a book about fashion from the 1970s, a green knitted hat and black trousers that were fit for a giant and, of course, her car keys.

"That's where your car keys were, so I went on a ten-minute ramble around the house for nothing," Tim snarled. "What about the scarf and bike gloves that you bought for him?" his uncle asked.

"Oh yeah, you should have reminded me earlier," Aunt replied. Aunt told uncle that she left it in her handbag.

"Where have you left your handbag?" his uncle asked in a tiresome, worn-out tone.

"It might be upstairs," his unt said in a confused voice.

"Maybe it's under your chair," Alexander suggested. Aunt Bertha moved her legs and discovered that Alexander was right.

Alexander was very grateful for the garments and wore them as much as he could.

Aunt Bertha had a meal planned for the evening. She wanted to cook a stew. She allocated Alexander the role of chopping and preparing the potatoes and carrots. She was going to be the head chef and his uncle's job was to be useful. However, his uncle took it upon himself to be the chief health and safety inspector, constantly reminding Aunt Bertha that she was creating an unsafe work environment and posing a health and safety risk. "You might chop your fingers off. Those shoes are not suitable for the kitchen. There are not enough chopping boards, we might have an E coli outbreak." This of course absolutely enraged his aunt, who fired his uncle for disruptive behaviour.

His uncle went upstairs to continue watching the news. Alexander and Bertha finished their meal in peace. "Looks fabuloso," his aunt commented. "Dinner's ready!" his aunt shrieked at the top of her lungs, nearly waking the dead from their slumber.

"Don't yell!", his uncle yelled back.

They all enjoyed their meal. "Compliments to the chef!" Aunt applauded Alexander for his help.

The next morning, his aunt had a treat planned for Alexander. She had a horse-riding experience planned. They needed to be at the barn by noon. They had plenty of time to prepare for the event. But Aunt Bertha was preoccupied with video calling her friends and watching *Bargain Hunt* on demand. His uncle was busy watching the news, and Alexander was busy playing online chess. So, who was going to be the timekeeper?

Soon, 10am turned into 10:30am. They all had breakfast but were oblivious to the time. Then 11am arrived and still no one was counting the clock. At 11:30am, Aunt Bertha noticed the clock. "Why has no one reminded me!"

"That's your job not my job!" his uncle yelled back.

Aunt Bertha sprang out of her seat as if she was on an emergency drill. One of the things that Aunt Bertha hated the most was being late, if she thought that she might be late then she activated her moody cow persona. Alexander was going to have his first ever horse-riding experience but also, he was going to be driven there by a moody cow. What a day he had ahead of him!

Just as they were leaving, his uncle was wiping the windows. "Tim, you could have reminded me."

"Sorry I'm your window cleaner today, tomorrow I will be your alarm clock."

Aunt Bertha was now in panic mode. The journey to the farm was like a rollercoaster, flying past blind bends, wrestling with the steering wheel. "Where do I need to turn, where do I need to turn?" she was frantically yelling. A tractor came into view. "Oh shit!" She spent the next few minutes weaving around the road, trying to get past the tractor. His aunt was trying desperately to find out when she should take her next turn.

"In 200 yards turn left then take the next right." Alexander was her talking sat nav. But this information only fell on deaf ears. His aunt abruptly flung her car to the left and straight into the disabled parking, nearly causing the car to stall in the process. Alexander tried telling his aunt that she had taken the wrong turn, but she was adamant that she saw the sign. What mysterious sign she saw, Alexander would never know.

Just then, a scruffy yard worker approached the car and asked what they were parked there for. Aunt wasn't best pleased with this scruffy yard worker, so she started yelling, "Is this Yew Tree Farm?"

"No, this is a scrap yard."

"Why are we in a scrap yard?" his aunt asked Alexander.

"Because you made the wrong turn," Alexander replied.

"Why are you blaming me?" his aunt replied in an argumentative tone.

"I'm not blaming you," Alexander replied.

"You are now arguing," his aunt said.

Alexander managed to convince his aunt that she had taken the wrong turn and showed her where she should have turned. She hurriedly shot out of the car park, causing a reaction from another one of the scrap yard workers. “Oi!” the other scrap yard worker shouted, because his aunt was driving too fast.

When the pair finally did arrive, it turned out that the horse rider hadn’t even arrived yet. Aunt Bertha’s demeanour changed like a switch when she realised that she wasn’t going to be late. She was very friendly and sociable. Meanwhile, Alexander was standing there, waiting for his turn to say something. She spent the next ten minutes rambling about her experiences growing up in the countryside. She went on about winning a donkey derby.

When the instructor finally did arrive, she spent five minutes giving Alexander a health and safety lecture. Alexander made his way onto the back of the horse, feeling like a knight in shining armour. The bumpy journey wasn’t bothering him, and the view was picturesque.

Sixth Encounter, March 3rd, 2022

It was a blooming spring, and Alexander decided to take a walk past the local church. He was walking through a field of daffodils when he heard church bells. He was surprised to hear the bells, one, because it was 12:30pm, and two, because it sounded like two different church bells were ringing at the same time, trying to compete. It sounded like the church bells were being accompanied by the sound of desk bells. He decided to venture through the field until he stumbled across a footbridge. Alexander could see the furniture being waiting for him at the other side of the bridge. He slowly made his way over the bridge, wondering why on earth Pvormlu was here.

The furniture being had a two o'clock expression on its face which was an optimistic expression. Daffodils were raining down like confetti. His body was covered in yellow petals, and he kept brushing them off. After the array of unexpected daffodil rain subsided, the candle flames turned purple. These flames became hearts. Burning purple hearts swarmed around Alexander – the joy of a child popping bubbles, warm soulful energy burning right into Alexander. He stared into the clock eye vortex, trying to find the meaning of this display. After a few seconds of staring into the vortex, he felt a feeling of intense loneliness, missing his potential other half. He had no enthusiasm to find love yet there was a desire to find love. The light crown of the furniture being began flashing mysteriously. The lights became interconnected. All the individual lights released themselves to resemble poltergeist lights that were levitating around the wooden head. The lights began orbiting the wooden head like satellites monitoring the energy emitting from mighty furniture being. Beams of lights became interconnected, forming a sphere. This sphere resembled a model of the Victorian globe – this globe went around and around then transformed into a modern-day coloured globe. Alexander was mesmerised by the globe and pictured himself travelling and meeting different women. A sudden burst of newfound confidence was flourishing from within his desolate soul.

The furniture being turned to its side and opened the poltergeist wardrobe. Inside the wardrobe appeared a collection of foreign carnival dresses. Alexander had never seen these before. These dresses were blowing in the mysterious wind, a special type of dancing, a romantic dance in the aromatic Cotswold field. The Victorian wardrobe doors opened and closed revealing all sorts of exotic clothing. Alampay Filipino dresses, Churidar Hindu dresses, Brazilian sequin feathers. This exotic display captivated Alexander's mind. Pvormlu's poltergeist Victorian cupboards started opening. The top drawer opened, and a rose appeared. Alexander walked up to the cupboard and picked up the rose and sniffed it. The wonderfully aromatic scent inspired him. The next draw opened, and a birthday card appeared. Alexander picked up and opened the card. Inside was a message wishing him a happy birthday, it was signed by your secret lover. This was something that Alexander had never received before. The lower middle draw opened revealing a love letter.

Dear My Future

How I long to see you, how I long to feel you.
Half of me is missing, I long to be whole.
Butterflies in the air by day
Moths orbiting fading lights by night
I want to be free before the net bears down
My future at last, have I found you?

After reading this, Alexander felt a romantic passion from within himself that had remained undiscovered until this time. Alexander came to the realisation that he had only lived half a life, the unrelenting desire to live a whole life was eating away at him. The bottom draw opened, and an engagement ring appeared. Alexander crouched down and picked up the ring, he lifted the ring in the direction of sunlight and marvelled at the beauty of the ring. He stood up, stared directly at the clock eyes and sent a flying kiss. Alexander turned around and made his way back through the fields of splendour.

Alexander's Dating Profile, March 20th, 2022

With a rejuvenated feeling of youthful passion, Alexander skipped through the fields with glee. His mind was spinning like a globe, a world of opportunities was on his horizon. After he returned to his flat, he started researching foreign women and trying to find out as much information as he could. Swedish, Brazilian, Turkish, Zimbabwean, French, Italian, Spanish, Thai, Filipino, Japanese. These were the women that Alexander was researching. They all appeared very interesting to him. But there was a problem, how could he become accustomed with their culture when he didn't understand his own. He already knew lots of information about these countries, but these were just facts, he had no experience with interacting with people in different countries. Even just leaving his flat to meet someone was an inconvenience for him; how was he going to leave his country?

Swedish, Brazilian, Turkish, Zimbabwean, French, Italian, Spanish, Thai, Filipino, Japanese. These words were orbiting Alexander's mind. He got up and started walking around his bedroom in circles and pointing whilst saying the names aloud. Alexander did this a few times with his eyes open, he then closed his eyes. Whichever nationality he said just before he would open his eyes would be the nationality that he would commit himself to. Italian... Spanish... Filipino... His eyes opened, his fingers pointing at the wall clock. He made up his mind, he was going to find a Filipina!

Alexander then started researching websites that would connect him with Filipinos. He discovered Filipino Cupid; this would be the start of discovering his connection with women. Up until this point, he had never felt a connection to women, he had an attraction to them but never had a spark. His first challenge was to create a profile. How should he describe himself?

About myself
Hi, my name is Alexander, I am feeling very much obliged to meet you here. I am known as a respectable gentleman in my local community. I am well acquainted with the art of romance. I, myself, am an aspiring success story. No one is as romantic as me. Getting married is a walk in the park for me. I would consider myself your Excalibur in shining armour.

My Perfect Match is:
Anyone who is beautiful, talented, intelligent, sexy, funny, successful and attractive – you are all mine :)

Alexander felt very proud of his profile, trying his best to impress potential matches. He uploaded pictures of himself wearing smart clothes and smiling at himself in the mirror, he also decided to wear wigs to make himself look impressive. Alexander wanted to make a good impression, to show that he had confidence. He was incredibly excited seeing a catalogue of foreign faces, so many adorable women that he had never heard of.

Forget an Argos catalogue, this catalogue of lovely women would make him dream of a shared Christmas, his first ever romantic Christmas. The more he viewed their profiles, the more he became entranced with these wonderful women whom he had never met before. He spent four hours just viewing their profiles, too afraid to message them, just admiring their photos and profile information. When he did finally find the courage to message them, the conversations were endless, hours and hours went by. He had never had the opportunity to connect with people like this, he wanted to know every inch of these petite ladies' lives. The cultural difference fascinated him. How could these impoverished people have such a positive outlook on life, where did this joyous spirituality come from? These questions were rumbling around in Alexander's mind, creating a whole new way of thinking.

Their connection with God (or known to them as Diyos) gave them an enlightened view of the world, the importance of marriage, the idea that hope was always on its way. They had an optimism to always do what was right, stood by your family no matter what, and always counted themself lucky even if they had nothing. Why couldn't Alexander feel this way? He had a comfortable life; he wasn't stuck in poverty. Why did he feel so empty inside? His encounters with Pvormlu had given him spiritual inspiration but he still felt isolated from reality, maybe he needed to believe in something.

Months on the Grind

The months passed slowly whilst working at the First Inn. The motivation and drive to carry on working there was still outweighing his desire to end this slow torment. This was a battle of sanity; Alexander was fighting a Guerra war with his inner demons. The siege of First Inn. Weeks on top of weeks, nothing ever improving. His experience as a receptionist was horrific. Customers would leave the building because Alexander was unable to explain what was going on, he would zone out whilst listening to a customer who has many requests. Hours and hours of standing behind a computer waiting for uncomfortable and awkward interactions. Plus, the torment of Chloe and her accomplice, always finding ways of embarrassing Alexander often in front of guests and coworkers.

What would appear as 'the real world' to neurotypicals was presented as a never-ending nightmare, a never-ending struggle to Alexander. He would return home and stare at the walls for hours, thinking about what had happened and what he should have done and what the problem was and why this kept happening to him. Even just making friends wasn't easy. He had no idea what to say to people, how to vibe with people or how to socialise. He had no idea if people liked him or not. He could hear idle conversation in the background but had no idea how to respond to it. The only thing he could do was to knuckle down and try to do his job as well as possible. Even just the over-familiar voices of coworkers and the responsibility of having to say hello to all the many guests and coworkers was wearing him out.

After six months of being stuck behind the till, he was offered a job as a hotel cleaner. This was because Alexander's weary face was off-putting for customers. Alexander gladly accepted this because he hated interacting with strangers. But this job was no improvement from the other role, which Alexander found out the hard way. The constant frustration of Chloe and Stephanie inspecting the hotel rooms that he has tidied. Constantly reminding him what he forgot to do. The confusion over which floor he should complete first led him to be cleaning the wrong rooms and being scolded as if he was a child. Sometimes he would be in such a rush to finish a floor after being constantly reminded to move faster that he would enter 'do not disturb' rooms then he would be shouted at to get out and told to open his eyes next time. He also kept leaving belongings in hotel rooms. This was normal for him since he would leave things lying around at home but in this situation, it was seen as something unacceptable. He did this because he was in such a rush and was unable to organise his belongings and work quickly at the same time. He would leave his water bottle, his coffee mug, his phone and even his watch. This was only once or twice a week but enough for Chloe and her minion to catch wind of.

After three months of slogging away at this role, he asked if he could do something else. So his friendly boss offered a kitchen team member role. This sounded like something that Alexander was going to enjoy. Mr Goddard introduced him to the team; everything was fine and well until he remembered who the kitchen manager was. That guy who he had met on his first shift. His name was Gary, he was someone who was very loud and said whatever he wanted to say as well as looking like he had never slept in his life. He was the type of person who you would always hear before you see them. A horrible hoarse voice with a gruff demeanour, also known as being incredibly bossy and rude.

This job ended up being the final straw for Alexander. As if wearing dirty trousers and aprons that didn't fit him, having to rush around and find things to do, doing errands for lazy bossy coworkers and having to ask people to put a bandage on his endless cuts wasn't bad enough, he also had to put up with a first-class bully and dictator. Weeks of being stuck in the kitchen took its toll on Alexander's physical and mental health. He would tell Alexander to stop acting like a pussy and to stand on his own two feet as if he was Alexander's father. He would say this at least once every week. It only took him two weeks to start this behaviour. This systematic bullying would continue, and nobody would do anything about it. Alexander was treated like Gary's slave. Gary would order him around the kitchen to do things like clean up other workers' messes and fetch things for the other workers. Often the kitchen was crowded and Alexander found it difficult navigating around the kitchen, he also didn't know what to do since his roles were often switched and his rota was changed all the time without any warning, leading to him being too late or too early. Plus, the mocking by Chloe and Gary, who would be constantly laughing at him.

Seventh Encounter, August 26th, 2022

Alexander was quietly drinking tea whilst memorising a chess game between Paul Morphy and Adolf Anderssen when a terrifying message popped up on his phone. Naturally, Alexander wouldn't read messages on his phone straight away, so he then received a phone call. *What now?* he thought. He hated being disturbed whilst he was studying things. He eventually relented and picked up the phone only to hear a distressed voice.

"Alexander, Alexander, you need to come to the hospital, it's Anna, she has had an accident."

Before Alexander could get a word in edgeways, the caller hung up abruptly. It was Tony and he was more frantic than ever. Alexander had no idea how to process this information, he didn't know what to do. He sat down panicking, his wrists were flipping and flopping violently like a nervous drummer, his eyes were darting around uncontrollably as if trying to escape his eye sockets.

After 30 minutes, Alexander received another message. It was from Tony. '*Where are you?*'

Alexander had no idea what the message meant, so he replied with, '*I'm at home*'.

Tony responded by ringing his phone. When Alexander picked up the phone, the reception he got wasn't the warmest. "Why are you at home? Didn't you hear what I said to you, your sister is in hospital."

Alexander replied with, "I heard, I heard, I'll be there soon."

When he finally arrived at the hospital he was in a total state of panic, he needed to spend ten minutes outside to prepare himself for what he was going to see. This would only further annoy his family, but he needed the time. Alexander then quickly walked in and tried to get the attention of the receptionist by waving his arms around like a bird that was about to crash.

"Where is Anna Sommervale, where is Anna Sommervale?" Alexander asked, having no idea how to ask the question.

"Is she a patient?"

"She is my sister," Alexander quickly replied without thinking about the question.

"Yes, but is she a patient?"

"Yes, she is," Alexander automatically replied.

"Room 105," the receptionist replied.

Alexander quickly darted off without even knowing where the room was. The receptionist tried to tell him that he was going the wrong way, but Alexander was determined to find her so he raced off in whichever direction he thought she would be. He started pacing around the corridors, pointing his fingers at the doors, trying to work out where 105 might be.

"Are you alright?" a nurse asked him.

"I'm looking for room 105."

"That's the other side of the building," the nurse replied.

Room 105 was now in sight for Alexander. He slowly crept forwards preparing himself for the horrors that he thought were ahead of him. He peered through the window to see Anna in a hospital bed and Tony looking stressed out, with Samantha and William standing around the bed, not knowing what to do. After making these observations, Alexander was able to make his way into the house of horrors. He entered quietly without drawing any attention because the others were facing away from him. He stared at Anna for a few seconds until Tony noticed him.

"Oh, there you are."

"What happened?" he asked.

"She climbed a tree to save a cat then lost her balance and blacked out," William responded in a considerate but also slightly sarcastic tone.

"Is she OK?" Alexander asked.

"What does it look like?" Tony replied in a patronising voice.

Alexander, unphased by his father's sarcasm, asked, "Will she be, OK?"

"We don't know yet," Tony replied.

"Don't worry, Alexander, she will be fine," Samantha said, reassuring him not to worry.

The report from the doctor stated that she had a head concussion and would need time for the swelling on the brain to fade away. After a few hours everyone decided to call it a day and hope for the best. But Alexander wasn't done, he spent another hour standing over her, not knowing what to expect. He then began pacing around the hospital room, trying to get his thoughts under control. He finished by staring out of the hospital window, watching cars go by.

Alexander opened the door to this flat then walked in like a lifeless zombie. He was so lifeless that he left the front door wide open and made a detour around his flat. His hands were rubbing against his walls as if he was trying to connect to something. His footsteps were slow and irregular almost like he was trying to get his footing correct. After a while he began to resemble a train going round and round on the tracks, a train with a passenger door open. The first journey around his flat was a slow train, the second detour was a much faster train, his right hand was rubbing tightly against the walls and against the bathroom and kitchen tiles. After this exhausting train journey, he crashed out and sat on his couch. It was 10pm now and he hadn't even thought about eating. He entered a prolonged daze. By the time Alexander had snapped out of this prolonged daze it was 12:25am. He got up and stared out of the undrawn window. Alexander was still in zombie mode, unable to get himself to do anything. He started to pull on his blinds, opening and closing them in a robotic fashion. He then sat back down on his couch. He gazed up at the ceiling as if trying to call out for God. He then stared at the wooden wall clock; 12:29... 57, 58, 59. The lights went out.

The bells began ringing but this time it was a faint ringing a bit like a toy bell. The sound of church bells moving very slowly, the sound of desk bells being lightly pressed. Alexander's living room transformed into a Victorian hospital ward – bare empty walls, 174 beds lined up but with no people inside them. His living room was now lit up by candles. Pvormlu's clock eyes appeared. The expression was 12 o'clock, this was the comforting expression. The shining white candles appeared, but this time the colour was blue, a burning sign of hope. Then the rest of the body appeared, candles pointing above the white curtains. The appearance of the face was also different; three handheld lanterns had appeared on its face instead of one. Instead of the house bell dangling down from the wooden chin, a lantern was in its place. Instead of an oil lamp, it had two lanterns on the side of its head. Alexander thought that Pvormlu resembled Florence Nightingale with all the lanterns and candles. Pvormlu slowly skated towards Alexander. Then it leaned over towards Alexander, almost touching his face. The wooden fan started to spin warm air next to Alexander's body. This warm air healed Alexander from his shivering fear and anxiety. Then cool air was blasted from this fan. This cool air felt like air conditioning, the uplifting breeze cured Alexander from his sweltering forehead. Next, Pvormlu leaned back. Its white candles mechanically turned to face upwards, these teeth were pointing upwards like missiles. All the individual blue candle lights connected and formed two large blue flame tusks creating desire to fight, a desire to battle for the future. Alexander stared at these raging tusks with sheer admiration. He felt like Muhammed Ali. He held his arms in the air in a boxing position, then clenched his fists. He felt the heat radiating through his shaking body, his arms held as tight as possible like tree branches. Pvormlu's clock eyes changed to an eight o'clock expression. This was a time for Alexander to be proud of himself.

Alexander then touched all three of the furniture being's lanterns with his hands, he rested his face against all of them, doing his best to receive spiritual healing. He then climbed the spiral wooden staircase up onto the bed of the furniture being. He tucked himself into the bed, trying to get as much rest as possible. After twisting and turning for a few minutes he eventually drifted off.

A white mist blanketed the room. Alexander felt a therapeutic wave of enlightenment as he was carried through the sea of mist. The mist subsided. Alexander awoke. He found himself on top of a hill, staring at the Stroud general hospital. Despite the darkness of night, he could clearly see his sister just lying there, still unresponsive. Alexander felt cold, the autumn breeze was making him shiver. Alexander was completely obfuscated as to why the furniture being had brought him here.

As he lay there, gazing up at the wondrous night sky, counting the stars, a large incandescent light lit up the surrounding darkness. It took Alexander a few seconds to realise that this was the glowing white desk lamp. Alexander's face was pulled straight into this mystifying beam of light like a moth admiring a lightbulb. He took a closer look at the lightbulb and saw ghostly holographic visions. Looking into this lightbulb was like looking into a crystal ball except these were visions of the past instead of the future.

Inside this lightbulb were memories of the three siblings playing together. William popping balloons, Alexander jumping on people's backs like a monkey, Anna holding people's hands whilst skipping. Alexander became fixated on these visions. The desk lamp then began levitating in the sky like a fairy before dropping down underneath Pvormlu's furniture undercarriage. Alexander was now activating himself into cat mode. He sprang out of bed and rushed down the steps. He searched for the light but didn't see it. He then felt a warm glow behind him. He turned around to see the levitating desk lamp playfully taunting him. Just then he heard a rumbling coming from inside the wooden mouth. Pvormlu's coffee table chest started rotating backwards, it then slotted out of Pvormlu's wooden body. The table floated like a ghost, then wooden table legs unfolded themselves and assembled underneath the undercarriage of the furniture being. A cup of tea and a saucer with a slice of cake hovered over to the table and placed themselves in one corner as if being served. A Victorian dining chair dropped out of the undercarriage. Then three more chairs followed. *Why are there four chairs here?* Alexander thought.

Alexander took a seat and started sipping the tea. He was enjoying this tea until he heard a familiar voice that made him spit out his tea. It sounded like Anna when she was 12. "Mummy, look what I found." This is the phrase that she would say the most.

The next voice said, "What a wonderful thing to do!" This is something she would say every time someone would do something nice.

The next voice said, "Everything is you, always be the one who decides." This came from an older sounding Anna – maybe a 50-year-old Anna. This phrase was the same phrase that their mum would always use. The meaning behind the phrase was that you could be anything and everything and to always make sure that you had a say in everything that affected you. Hearing this voice made Alexander realise that Anna was the spitting image of their mum, Rose Sommervale.

He then witnessed three holographic ghostly, but spiritual figures make their way to the undercarriage to join Alexander. Three cups of tea followed by three saucers and three biscuits were served for them. It was like a tea party for Alexander and the past, present and future spirits of Anna Sommervale. This was going to be a social experience that Alexander had never had before!

The past spirit of Anna was her 12-year-old self, wearing a pink woollen jumper with white flowers on it. She had the same youthful vibrant expression on her face.

"Hello, Alexander, it's me, Anna, I want you to know that the future version of me will be fine. "Don't lose hope, please don't."

Alexander found himself getting emotional at the sight of this, tears began dripping, pouring, then flooding down his pale face. He had never seen Anna like this before.

The present spirit of Anna was wearing a white hospital gown. She looked a bit delirious but was looking at Alexander with intent. "Don't worry, I will be with you soon, I'm just putting on my makeup and trying to find my handbag." These words made Alexander laugh a bit whilst tears were still slowly sliding down his face. He stretched out his hands to touch her hands, he felt a warm supernatural glow reverberating throughout his body. "It won't be long now, I'll be out soon," she said in a reassuring voice.

"Don't forget your phone," Alexander said as a way of trying to verbalise something. They both smiled at each other.

The future spirit of Anna was wearing a wedding dress. She looked around 30. The spirit of his sister in a wedding dress made him feel such passion for her. "Do you want to meet my husband?"

"Wow, I would love to meet your husband."

"If you keep waiting you will be able to meet him. Me and my husband have decided that we want to have kids."

"Really, how many do you want?"

"As many as we can love."

"That sounds great."

"All this will happen if you just wait, wait for the storm to be over."

"Yes, I will wait, I will wait forever if I have to." Alexander was determined to hold onto the hope that he had in his heart.

Pvormlu then took a glance under its undercarriage and gave Alexander a reassuring look. He took one more glance at the resting Anna, trying to hope for the best.

He then turned round and glanced at the three spirits of Anna, scanning them one by one. The spirits all had optimistic expressions on their faces. They all stuck their arms out as a united good luck gesture. Alexander put his hand on top of their hands, feeling the intense heat emanating from the hands. Alexander then closed his eyes.

Anna Sommervale's Reawakening, August 27th, 2022

When Alexander opened his eyes, he was with Anna in the hospital room. He sat down next to her thinking about those spirits that he had seen, wondering if they were real. The time was now 9am, and Alexander had no idea if he had even had any sleep at all. He just sat there waiting as if he was about to audition for a talent show. Alexander rubbed his tired face with his wobbly hands, feeling absolutely exhausted. Out of the corner of his eye he saw movement. Could this be... Her locked face cracked open revealing a very tired Anna. She looked at Alexander as if she didn't know what was going on. Alexander stood up to greet the revived Anna. He gave her a massive hug then kissed her hand.

"I've missed you so much," she said.

"I missed you too," she replied in a confused voice. "What happened?"

"I was hoping you could answer that," Alexander said, hoping to get a reaction out of her. They both laughed. Alexander could see a salubrious expression rising on her face. "Do you remember how you ended up here?" Alexander asked.

"I... don't know, I obviously hit my head on something and blacked out," Anna replied.

"According to your friends, you fell out of a tree and banged your head on the ground," Alexander told her, trying to keep a straight face.

"Fell out of a tree! What was I doing in a tree in the first place?"

"You tell me," Alexander said, trying to jog her memory.

"I really have no idea what I was doing in a tree, I can't even climb."

"You were trying to save a cat."

"Save a cat? Everyone knows that cats always land on their feet," Anna said, wondering what on earth she was thinking trying to save a cat from a tree.

"I thought you, being a vet, would tell you that this would be a bad idea," Alexander said mockingly.

"Shut up, Alexander, I did this for the greater good."

"The greater good is when you do something bad for a good cause," Alexander replied slyly.

"You always know everything," Anna replied sarcastically.

"I think I always do," Alexander replied in a cocky manner. "And the cat's fine, thanks for asking," Alexander said in a provocative voice.

"Of course the cat's fine, because of my sacrifice," Anna replied persistently. "Or maybe the cat's fine because it has four feet instead of two."

"Do you know what gender the cat might have been?" Alexander asked curiously.

"If I knew what gender the cat was, then I would have remembered the incident," Anna replied.

Anna slowly and cautiously leaned forwards and stretched her legs and planted her feet on the ground as if this was her first time ever walking. Alexander held her hand and helped her onto her feet. "Would you like Earl Grey or yYorkshire, Granny Sommervale?" Alexander said, trying to make light of the situation.

"I'm not too old to give you a hiding," Anna replied, feeling glad to see Alexander full of spirit instead of avoiding life.

Once Anna was able to be discharged, they walked to a pub and sat down together. This was the first time that they have had a chance to have a long conversation. Usually, the manic panic of the Sommervale family would make it impossible for Alexander to have much of a relationship with his family members.

"So how is life at the moment?" she asked.

Alexander was slightly taken aback by this since he wouldn't normally get asked this question. "My, uh, life is going well at the moment." Alexander was still masking, trying to convince neurotypicals that he was doing fine but Anna, his sister, wasn't just some neurotypical who needed to be palmed off, she had a much greater understanding than Alexander could ever imagine.

"What is going well at the moment?" she asked.

This question completely threw Alexander as he had no idea what she meant by this. "I, uh... think that everything is going well," he responded, unsure of what to say.

"Are you really enjoying your new job?"

"Well, it's OK, not the worst job in the world."

"How do they treat you?"

Alexander decided to admit his true thoughts. "Most of them are nice but I find some of the managers very bossy."

"Very bossy, how?"

"The managers are always double-checking everything that I do, they get me to do lots of errands for them."

"Do you feel comfortable working there?"

This question made Alexander realise that he was digging himself a hole by continuing to work there. "I feel tired, stressed out. I feel I have no privacy when I'm working there." Alexander found himself saying things that he wouldn't normally say.

"Do you expect things to be this way?" Anna asked this in an expressionless tone, trying to get Alexander to open to her.

Alexander took a long pause then said something that he had never said before. "This is the way things have always been for me, an outsider looking in through the window at everyone else who appears to be an insider, the whole world is one big conspiracy, nothing makes sense to me. Everywhere I go, normal people exist, but what do I exist as? In a world of ants where does a woodlouse belong?" Alexander was blown away by his sudden outburst of his internal truth, and so was Anna she had never heard much from him but this insight into Alexander's veracity gave her a perception that she had never heard of before.

"Wow, I have never heard all that from you before, I have always known that you were unique and experienced things differently, but this is a whole new side to you. I want to travel with you on this journey of self-discovery, I want to be there for you."

Anna's words evoked a feeling of trust for a very grey and weary Alexander. "A journey to discover where I belong in the world?"

"Yes, exactly, to find out which character of the story you are." This idea of becoming a character in a real-life story created a strong inspirational feeling for him. "So, you see yourself as a woodlouse amongst a world of ants?"

"Yes, I do, always under my rock whilst all the ants are busy doing things."

"Do you want to carry on working at the First Inn?" Anna asked in a curious voice.

Alexander took a short while to think of what to say before replying, "Absolutely not!"

"Good answer," Anna replied. "The best advice is just quit it, fuck those shitty managers, you will be able to get a new job if you try."

"I can't wait to give my managers the middle finger," Alexander said with confidence.

"That's my boy," she said with pride.

This was the perception that Alexander had: the neurodivergent woodlouse amongst a colony of neurotypical ants. He saw himself as someone who spent his entire life under a rock, hiding away from the real world. Everyone else was a neurotypical ant: hardworking, an active member of the colony. These people were always surrounded by each other, helping each out and communicating with each other. These ants were all individuals, yet they moved as one collective unit. There was one thing – knowing what other people did, knowing how people did things was a completely new topic. Alexander being the atypical woodlouse could see perfectly well from his hiding spot what the ants were doing but he had no idea how they were doing it.

"So, what about you?" Alexander asked.

This question caught Anna slightly off guard since Alexander wouldn't normally ask questions about other people. "I'm glad you asked," Anna said before opening up about her experiences. "I am enjoying studying veterinary biology, I can't wait to become a qualified vet."

"That sounds amazing," Alexander said. "So, what about your relationship? Do you want to marry Ethan?"

"Marry Ethan!" Anna said in a repulsed voice. "Of course not!"

"Can I ask why?" Alexander said sheepishly. "I thought you two looked good together."

"I thought that we were good together, but it turns out that he is an absolute arsehole," Anna said with contempt.

"How is he an arsehole, if you don't mind me asking?"

"He drinks and smokes a lot, he doesn't do any house chores and he gets mad when I make small messes. Plus he hasn't even visited me here because working is more important."

"What a prick," Alexander replied. "Don't let him use his money to control you."

"That's really good advice," Anna replied.

They then gave each other a toast. "Good riddance to shit wankers."

This was the time for Alexander to enjoy himself and open up to people. For someone who felt like an outsider observing all the action, the best thing to do was to ring the doorbell and see if anyone would open to you.

Meeting Garcia Online, September 18th, 2022

After weeks of searching online, Alexander finally came across a Filipina who really caught his attention, her name was Garcia Agbayani. Alexander scanned the profile picture intensely, spending no less than five minutes admiring her beauty before even clicking on her profile. Her eyes were two hazel portals, staring with intensity, a whole world lurked inside them. Smoochy lips that had incredible depth to them, the type of lips that you would dream of kissing. Her half-exposed chest shone like a crescent moon against the dark background. Her petite hands were innocently holding the camera to get the angle right. Her long jet-black hair brushed against her tender figure, creating a harmony that he had never witnessed before. Even though she was wearing a juvenile-looking pink shirt with Hello Kitty on it, she still had the most mature body language and facial expression.

He clicked on her profile and gave her a 'like'. 'Hello, my name is Alexander, nice to meet you'. The feeling that he was experiencing was overwhelming but in a positive way. He sent this message feeling like he had just bought a lottery ticket and was waiting to see if the numbers matched.

A heart-pounding two minutes went by. Alexander received a message. 'Hello, nice to meet you too, my name is Garcia, how are you?'

Alexander couldn't believe it! He jumped around his flat waving his arms in the air as if he had just won the lottery. To most people they might just be thinking that she was just another foreign girl that he had met online, and she might just be after his money, but Alexander would not think of that as a possibility in his new love equation. 'Hi, I'm so glad to meet you' Alexander repeated, blissfully unaware of this repetition.

'So, what are you looking for?' she asked.

This was yet another question that would confuse the hell out of Alexander. The question reminded him of the interview with Pvormlu. *Pretty, nice, kind, attractive, fun*, he thought. It took him a while to realise what the question was about. 'I'm looking for… I just need a few minutes to think of the answer'.

'Ah OK,' Garcia messaged him, confused about his answer.

Alexander finally replied with, 'Someone to be with'.

'Me too' she replied.

'So, what does your name mean, if you don't mind me asking?' Alexander typed.

'Agbayani means 'heroic',' she said.

'Wow, you are a hero!' Alexander replied.

'Not yet' she replied with a laugh emoji.

The two then chatted about their life experiences and goals. Garcia wanted to be a fashion designer; she had spent years designing dresses that she liked. She had just one more year of college to contend with. Like Alexander, she had a brother and sister. She was from a poor family, yet she was still able to dream big. It turned out that she does actually have a lot in common with him – her mum was a nurse just like Alexander's mum. Her father used to work as an IT office manager, just like Alexander's father. She also has a sister who is a vet. This was information that Alexander found intriguing – he felt as though he had just found his soulmate. Getting to know Garcia was a great pleasure for Alexander, but when it came to explaining himself, things became incredibly awkward.

'I'm working at this hotel called the First Inn, I am now working in the kitchen'.

'Oh, that sounds good, do you enjoy it?'

This was another question that Alexander hated answering, he felt like there were two truths: the automatic truth which was the truth that you say to please people and the whole truth which was the genuine truth. Questions that involved a definitive answer were seen as real questions to Alexander but questions that were subjective and involved an opinion were seen as fake questions. Alexander decided that he wanted to be truthful and admit his true feelings about things in his life.

'I'm not really enjoying working there, in fact I absolutely hate the bloody place and the people who I have to work with'. This was a truth that Alexander needed to be able to communicate to understand perspective in his life.

'Oh, sorry to hear that, I thought you enjoyed it' Garcia typed back.

'I absolutely despise it, long hours, mean managers, coworkers with whom I have nothing in common, unpredictable schedule, hidden expectations that I am completely blind to, constant shouting and loud noises, weird smells, cluttered chaotic environment and let's not forget the exhausting commute through busy and noisy traffic'.

This long unpredictable message stunned Garcia. Alexander had not realised that mentioning all this was going to give a certain impression of himself to Garcia. He just thought that the whole truth was better than the automatic truth.

'It's just a job isn't it' Garcia replied.

This comment made Alexander feel incredibly confused, he thought that Garcia was going to agree with him and admit that she had had the same experiences, but she came out with just a blunt comment. 'Maybe it's just the job' Alexander wrote back.

'Yes, maybe its is' she replied. 'Do you have any plans for the future?' she asked.

Yet another unanswerable question, how was Alexander to reply to this, should he tell the automatic truth, or should he risk telling the whole truth? After a couple of minutes of debating about how to approach this question, he wrote 'I plan to study and to get a better job'.

'What will you study?' she asked.

'I will study creative writing and art' Alexander replied.

'What do you plan to be?' she asked.

'I hope to become an artist' Alexander wrote back.

The two exchanged contact information. They added each other on WhatsApp. Garcia insisted that they video called. Alexander tried making excuses about how tired he was, but Garcia just wanted five minutes with him. This was always a challenge for him. Smalltalk – how was he supposed to interact, what was he supposed to say? There is no instruction manual on how to chat up a foreign woman who you had met online.

With little warning, Garcia started ringing him, Alexander took a few seconds to prepare for this call. The first moments of this call were interrupted by static. Her shining round face appeared in the dark background, her face was brightly lit up by her camera. Alexander greeted her by timidly waving his hand.

They both stared at each other for a while before Alexander said, "Nice to meet you."

Garcia responded, "A pleasure meeting you too, are you busy?"

"Uh... I am busy chatting to you," he said jokingly.

"Is this your first time on Filipino Cupid?"

"Yes, it is, I joined earlier this year, uh... you are my first real 'like', if that's what you mean."

"Have you had any luck dating?" she asked.

This was one question too many for Alexander. "I... uh, no luck whatsoever, but meeting you here, that's a whole different story, you know." Alexander had no idea what he was saying or the effect that he was having on Garcia, but he had to come out with something to appear normal.

"Sorry, what do you mean?" Garcia asked in a confused tone.

Alexander was starting to feel uncomfortable with all these questions that he didn't know how to answer, and he started stimming. He stared at the ceiling with his mouth wide open like a fish on dry land. "Uh... uh... what do I mean, let me think."

"Are you OK there, are you having a think about something?"

"I'm talking about the weather."

"Uh, what?"

This conversation was becoming excruciating. Alexander had to think fast to recover his script. "Just joking, I was trying to mention that I liked your profile picture."

"Ah OK, I was just lost for a moment there."

"Are you sleeping in a cellar?" Alexander asked, curious about why it was so dark in her bedroom.

"A cellar? No, why would you think that? I'm sleeping in my bedroom."

"I was just wondering about the lighting in there."

"We are poor, that's why," Garcia responded in a slightly annoyed tone.

"Uh... there is nothing wrong with being poor. I mean, I'm poor, not poor as in poor-poor, but I'm poor at certain things such as a poor football player or a poor businessman, not that I am an actual businessman. I'm poor at algebra and poor at conversation with strangers, not that you are a stranger of course." Alexander found this conversation so exhausting that he was almost out of breath.

"Oh OK, I got that," Garcia responded.

"So, how is your clothing designing career?" Alexander asked.

"I'm enjoying it, I design lots of women's clothing for the Philippines. I want to start my own business in the future."

"That sounds great, I hope you enjoy that."

"Thanks, I will, can I see a tour of your home?"

This was probably a mistake on Garcia's part since Alexander's flat was plastered in quirky displays and charts and all sorts of unusual paraphernalia. Alexander gave a tour to Garcia, showing his wild man cave.

The first room he displayed was his living room. This room was full of clothes and chess boards. One of Alexander's habits was to leave things lying around, he also used blue tack to hang documents and letters to the wall. He did this because he was worried that he would lose it unless it was attached to a wall. Alexander was also into symbols and writing; his living room and bedroom were covered in writing. He did of course record information in books and documents, but he often had the urge to write on the walls. Every day Alexander would read his walls to make sure that he had memorised all the information.

The spaces that weren't covered in writing would either be covered with posters or printed out charts and diagrams with facts and statistic that he would try to memorise or he would hang his clothes there to dry, or if there was an occasion where he needed to wear something he would leave the clothes hanging on his living room wall so that he wouldn't forget to wear it. Alexander would also Blu Tack all his post next to his front door so that would remember to read it if it was important. He would also hang his duvet cover over the living room curtain pole; he would do this because he had no balcony. In every room there was a chessboard – whether it be a glass, wooden, travel, paper or light-up, he would always be playing a theoretical game. His bedroom walls were covered in photos of himself and his family, having a photo album wouldn't be enough for Alexander because he wouldn't remember to open it and view his pictures. He also had piles of books in each corner of his flat – he did this so that he would remember to pick up a certain book before leaving the room. The book piles were arranged in a particular order – the corner next to his front door would be journals and diaries, the corners in his living room would be for novels, and corners in his bedroom would be for books about languages and chess. Alexander also had many lamps which had different colours and brightness levels, these helped him focus on reading.

Alexander was enjoying giving a flat tour to Garcia, but he zoned out whilst reading the writing on his wall. He began scanning his own writing and forgot that he was in a live video call. "These are my symbols, that one means divinity, this one mean potence."

"Wow, that's fascinating, have you made these yourself or used symbols from different religions?"

Alexander wasn't in question mode and instead in presentation mode. "That symbol means 'almighty'. What does this one mean? Umm." Alexander had become hyper-fixated by his own wall and was muttering to himself incoherently whilst pointing to his own writing and pacing up and down his living room and bedroom inconsistently, almost as if he was being possessed.

"Hello, Alexander, are you still with me?" Garcia repeated but to no avail.

"I, uh, can't remember writing that one, when must I have written that one?" Alexander said in a mumbled fashion.

"Alexander, hello, hello, I'm still here!"

Alexander suddenly noticed that Garcia was trying to get hold of him. "Uh… I'm so sorry. I was just, umm." Alexander felt mortified at the discovery that he had been ignoring Garcia and just talking to himself.

Garcia had a half-grin, half-gasp facial expression. "I just wanted to know if those were your symbols or you copied them from somewhere."

"Oh, sorry, yes, I copied the symbols on the left wall over them but these symbols on the right wall are my own symbols."

"Can I see your photos?" Garcia asked.

"Sure, I keep them all on my bedroom wall." Alexander pointed at all the photos. Some were of him as a baby, others were family photos. Alexander was able to form a mutual bond with Garcia over these photos.

The remainder of the video call went by smoothly without any more awkward moments. After two hours of chatting, Alexander said goodbye whilst waving, feeling proud of himself that he had managed a two-hour-long conversation online.

That night, Alexander stared at Garcia's profile picture for hours; this brought him much exaltation, not wanting to sleep without her. This was not merely a date or just a quick chat, this was an opportunity for Alexander to turn his life around.

The Final Straw, February 14th, 2023

Alexander was coming closer and closer to complete burnout. The unexpected shift patterns, the bossy behaviour from his managers and annoying coworkers and the constant monotonous crappy grind was taking its toll on him. He was mentally and physically drained, being devoid of personality and feeling like a tired zombie. He was feeling like a shell of his former self. He was reaching boiling point like the potatoes and carrots that he was shouted at for not boiling properly. After nearly a year and a half of having multiple roles in the same company, Alexander was at his wits' end. The constant sensory overload of loud noises and weird smells coupled with constant shouting and temperature changes was bearing down on him. There were times when he would enjoy working there, that would involve chatting with coworkers and sometimes even having the odd night out with them. Some managers were supportive and friendly towards him, such as saying well done to him for working hard. Even though he had financial gain and a chance to interact with people, the whole experience was wearing him down to the point where the only option would be to quit.

It was the 14th of February – a day which Alexander would much rather be spending on a romantic getaway but instead he had to do yet another 10am to 8pm shift. Alexander had no idea why they expected him to do this shift since he only applied for part-time work. Alexander came into work feeling like shit, but this was a normal feeling, so he didn't call in sick. Alexander came in with a worn-out expression on his face, looking sad and regretful. He lightly greeted a few coworkers then made his way to the changing room with the urgency of a tortoise. He opened the staff room door and greeted a few more coworkers. He reluctantly took his clothes off and changed into the only clothes that were left for him which were dirty, wet and smelly and had holes in them. He paused for a few seconds, wondering why he should even put these shitrags on. Alexander also needed to wear a filthy hat. He made his way down the stairs and into the kitchen, looking like the Boy in the Striped Pyjamas, with his matching striped apron and trousers. He was also looking very skinny from the exhaustion. Of course, standing by the doorway of the kitchen were Chloe and head chef, Gary. These two were standing by the door like two school bullies who would wait for certain kids to walk past then jump out at them. They were both slouched by the doorway, chatting as usual. Alexander gave a brief hello to which they responded by jeering at him.

"Oh, look who it is, it's Alexander. Come on, Alexander, get stuck in," said Chloe in her usual extroverted tone.

Gary was quick to follow by saying, "Get stuck in, we are busy today." This was the usual friendly greeting that Alexander had to put up with every time that he had to start work.

He went to his usual section, which was the veg prep, but noticed someone unfamiliar standing there.

It turned out that they were being trained. Alexander stood there for a few seconds, trying to work out what to do.

"Alexander, don't just stand there, get over here," called Pavel, a bossy assistant of Gary.

Pavel was like Gary's minion; he would bark orders on Gary's behalf. Pavel wanted Alexander to sort the pot wash out because the usual kitchen porter wasn't in. To make matters worse, there was already a great big pile that he needed to be sorted out. Alexander was rushing around, trying to simultaneously scrape fat off and get plates through the pot wash.

"What are you doing, what are you doing?" Gary said to Alexander in his usual charming voice.

"I'm doing the pot wash," Alexander said in a lifeless tone.

"Get the plates sorted first then you can wash the trays." This was typical of Gary having to micromanage the kitchen all the time instead of trusting people to manage themselves.

The pungent smell of fat and oil was clogging Alexander's senses. Water and grease were pouring down his already dirty and smelly uniform. Suddenly a plate fell down the side of the pot wash. "Oh fuck," Alexander said to himself, annoyed that this kept happening. All the bits of food from the dirty plates kept blocking the sink and his apron was now covered in baked beans and breakfast grease. Alexander decided to get a paper towel and wipe the muck off his apron. As you would expect, this didn't go down well with working boy, Pavel, who expected people to be working non-stop like a machine.

"Those plates won't wash themselves, Alexander." These constant, second-hand observations from

Pavel and Gary were making it difficult for Alexander to concentrate.

After Alexander had finished on the pot wash section he was called to the meat prep section. Alexander was told to prepare some fish for the lunch service. He did this as he usually would until he noticed Gary's unpleasant scrunched up old face peering at him from around the corner.

"What have I told you before?" he said in his usual condescending tone.

These questions were ones that Alexander hated, was he supposed to guess what Gary's problem was this time? "To work faster?" Alexander said, feeling completely confused.

"No, to tidy up after yourself."

"But that wasn't my mess, I have just started here," Alexander replied just trying to state the facts, but manager Gary didn't care about facts, he only cared about his own agenda.

"I don't care whose mess it was you need to clean it up before preparing fish." This was not enough for Gary, he needed to dish out some more insults. "Come on, I'm not your mum, you wouldn't behave like this at home, get moving."

This shocked Alexander, why would he mention Alexander's mum? Alexander had no response for this insult. He had no idea how to process this. His soul went blank but his body was still working, so he continued working but feeling numb and lifeless inside. *What is that guy's problem with me, why is he such an arsehole? Should I have confronted him? Have I let myself down? Why am I still working here? Is this a normal way for workers to be treated?*

All these questions were going round and round in his head. Mentally he was completely preoccupied and overwhelmed but physically he was showing no signs of emotion.

The next few hours were spent with him just doing what he was told and being helpful to the others. Five hours had passed, and it was now 3pm and Alexander still hadn't had his break. He felt hungry and tired. Breakfast service was particularly busy, so he didn't have a chance to eat anything. He was almost feeling at the point of having a meltdown. Of course, Sergeant Gary and Sergeant Pavel either did not notice or just didn't care because they were tough working boys who could go for 13 hours with no break. This time they were together, the 'pair from hell', in Alexander's experience. He could hear them in the background talking, using vulgar language. They both approached Alexander and then asked him to do a few errands for them.

"Seeing as you are not busy, can you fetch me a box of takeaway boxes and hats from upstairs, a bag of onions from the outside fridge and paper towels from the storage cupboard."

Alexander agreed to this unusual request and went looking for the items. He decided to start off with the takeaway boxes and chef hats. When he returned to give these items, he noticed that Chloe was there chatting with them, which appeared strange to him since today was a busy day. He handed them over, not to be greeted by 'thank you' but 'you need to be moving faster'. Alexander handed two paper towels only to be met with, "How many paper towels does one kitchen need?" This question frustrated the hell out of Alexander because the instructions were not specific. Alexander fetched the other two paper towels to be greeted by, "Why didn't you bring the onions in at the same time, you are just wasting time." Alexander tried to respond to this, but he was ushered out and told to get the bag of onions.

Alexander returned to find that the managers were not there, so he had no idea where to put the bag of onions, so he put them down on the vegetable section and carried on working on the meat section. A few minutes later Alexander heard the familiar voice of Gary. "Alexander! Why have you dumped these onions here?" Before Alexander had a chance to respond, Gary said, "If you need help, just ask, don't put things where they don't belong."

Alexander was reaching the end of his tether; he was not used to being spoken to like this and was getting fed up with being treated like the runt of the litter. His face was glowing red, he could feel magma rising inside of himself. "You are now behind because you have taken too long. What's this? That's not how I showed you to do it."

Alexander could not contain himself any longer. He flew into a rage by waving his hands in the air like an angry bird. He then shouted, "I'm fucking tired of you and this shitty job!"

Gary was completely taken aback; he did not expect timid Alexander to behave like this. Alexander then stuck his middle fingers out at Gary and stormed out of the kitchen.

"Where are you going?" Gary shouted back but Alexander was in no mood to answer. "Fine, fuck off then," Gary continued but Alexander carried on storming off.

As soon as he left the kitchen, Chloe was standing there with an obnoxious smirk written on her face, the same one she had every time Alexander walked past her. Alexander would always ignore this facetious expression on her face but this time he wanted to let Chloe know exactly what he thought of her. "Fuck you, too, Chloe, you cow." Alexander couldn't help himself; he was now a raging bull!

He looked over his shoulder one more time to see Chloe, Pavel and Gary standing behind him, almost laughing at him, as if Alexander was the crazy person. The only person to take Alexander's outburst seriously was Mr Goddard. He was always very professional and courteous towards Alexander. He asked Alexander what was wrong.

Mathew, Mr Goddard's first name, had a chat about what went on. He said that their behaviour was not appropriate, and he thought he were assholes too, he also apologised for not noticing that Alexander was struggling so much. They both shook hands and thanked each other. Alexander went upstairs to change his manky uniform into his usual clothes, but his coworkers were there. They showed empathy towards him and thanked him for his work.

Showing aggression was not something that Alexander was used to doing. He, in fact, was afraid of showing aggression since he did not know how people would react to him, so he would normally bottle up his feelings of frustration and suffer from internal rages that would sometimes last for days. Although this outburst was not something that he would normally be proud of, the cathartic relief from standing up for himself gave him much pleasure and self-satisfaction.

Back to Square One, February 15th, 2023

Even though Alexander was back to square one in the sense that he was now unemployed again, the overwhelming feeling of escapism from not being constricted to a proletarian lifestyle that would grind him down to a shell of a person made him look forward to future endeavours and adventures that he could have. Alexander had many goals which he wanted to achieve.

His main goal was to start a relationship with Garcia. He imagined Garcia as his future wife, someone who would always be there for him no matter what. He had no idea what she thought of him, but he knew it was worth a shot. He had confided in her about his stressful work situation and his need to quit the job, to which she responded by telling him that no job is worth sacrificing your health and sanity for. She also recommended that he should visit the Philippines if he has the chance to. Life at this time consisted of waking up, washing, finding things to eat, overindulging in his special interests then going back to bed again. Although this would seem a solitary lifestyle to most people, for Alexander he felt as if he had all the company in the world whilst chatting to Garcia. His chats with Garcia became more and more frequent until they were chatting for at least one hour every day. At this period of his life, he lived for her, wanting to wake up next to her every day yet not knowing how to even ask her to be his girlfriend.

After months of beating around the bush, it was decided that now was the chance to declare his undying feelings. How was he to do this? After three hours of writing all the possible solutions on his wall, he discovered that the only solution was for him to write a love letter and hope that it would impress her. Alexander wanted to rehearse this love letter to score extra points with Garcia. Alexander wanted to focus on body language as well as facial expressions and tone of voice, since he was aware that he had a monotone voice. *How am I going to rehearse this?* he thought to himself. If I write it down then I will have to bend down to look at it. He needed to come up with an interactive solution that would motivate his memory. Then the idea dawned on him – wear a suit then perform a speech which will win her heart. Alexander set about writing a speech which he rehearsed for several days leading up to his proposal.

Alexander's next plan was to travel to the Philippines. He had researched about all the different places that there were to explore. Remote tropical islands, mysterious brown hills, shining white beaches, volcanic islands. Alexander had never seen such things before but he wanted to experience them now. He desperately wanted to travel to this wonderful archipelago, but he didn't want to travel there without visiting Garcia. He needed someone who would help him manage his travel experience. Visions of crystal-clear waters and exotic foods were filling his mind. There were many questions that Alexander kept going over in regard to this proposed trip. *What would my budget be? What type of insurance would I need? What type of visa would I need? What would happen if I lost my passport? How should I carry my money around?*

Alexander was able to do some research, yet he did not feel that his interpretation was going to be good enough for a successful trip. He decided that it would be best to enlist the help of a family member.

Start of a New Relationship, February 18th, 2023

It was now time for Alexander to start his first official relationship. The prospect of Garcia being the one was keeping him awake at night, she was the heroine that Alexander needed to save his life. With the nerves of a shaking tv show contestant, he picked up his phone. With nerves of steel, he gave Garcia a call that would change both of their lives. The ringing started; shock waves of fear, passion and sheer hope were vibrating through his body, causing him to stand in a motionless position, anxiously waiting for Garcia to answer the phone. When Garcia did answer the phone, Alexander told her that he had a message to give her. She seemed surprised but was eager to find out what the message was.

Alexander was taking this call inside his living room; the phone was placed on a phone holder on his living room table facing his bedroom door. "Are you ready?" he asked Garcia.

"Yes, I am," she replied.

"Close your eyes."

Garcia closed her eyes. Alexander closed his bedroom door and changed into his suit. In his head this seemed like a brilliant idea, but it would make matters more complicated for him. As he tossed and turned in his suit, trying to make himself look presentable, Garcia was calling his name.

"Alexander, where are you, what is going on?"

Alexander decided not to reply as he didn't want to spoil the surprise. "Where is my bloody shoe polish?" Alexander was frantically searching for his shoe polish. After several attempts he managed to get his tie on, but it was loose and not tucked in properly. He looked like a lawyer who had gotten into an altercation with his client.

"Hello, anyone there?" Garcia kept asking.

Alexander finally managed to make himself look half-presentable. He slowly opened his bedroom door, imagining himself as a handsome celebrity such as Leonardo di Caprio or Will Smith. Garcia was feeling incredibly creeped out; she thought that Alexander was trying to scare her. Alexander was wearing sunglasses to try to make himself look cool. He slowly opened the door, revealing a very presentable version of himself. He then delivered a speech which he had rehearsed.

"Dear Garcia Agbayani, your hazel eyes captivate me every time I look at them. Your jet-black hair cascades around your shoulders creating an unforgettable stream of beauty. Your half-exposed chest shines against the dark background like a crescent moon. Your beautifully accented voice tickles my ears every time I listen to you. If I were a plant, would you water me? If I were a blanket, would you lie on me? If I were a car, would you oil me? If I were a lion, would you be my lioness? We can be lovers of different races."

After reading his speech to Garcia, Alexander performed a strange dance where he was shaking his arms and legs then finished off by giving her jazz hands.

Garcia had her eyes glued to him the whole time; she was smiling intently. Alexander then spun around, finishing his dance routine. "So, what do you think?" he asked.

Garcia burst out laughing, not being able to compute what was happening. She collected herself and managed to stop laughing. "That was amazing, how did you come up with all of that?"

"I have been thinking about you a lot recently and these idioms naturally come to mind when I think of you."

"What's an idiom?" Garcia asked.

"It's a word or phrase," Alexander replied.

"I am truly blown away; I did not expect that."

"I'm glad you liked my speech."

"At first I didn't know what you were doing in your bedroom, so I kept calling your name, but you didn't respond, so I was very confused."

"Sorry about that, I was getting myself dressed for the occasion. I had to wrestle with my suit to get it on and I also had to track down my shoe polish."

"Haha, that's funny," Garcia replied.

"What did you think of my dance at the end?"

"Um, it looked kind of funny to be honest with you, you have Blu Tack and glue on the back of your suit."

"Huh, what?" Alexander took his suit off and discovered that he had forgotten to wash his suit. "Oh shit, I forgot to wash it."

"I found that creepy to begin with but then you made me laugh."

"Oh, sorry, I didn't intend to scare you, I wanted to impress you."

"Is there any reason why you wanted to impress me?" Garcia asked with playful eyes.

"Um, I don't need a reason to impress you, I can impress you whenever you want," Alexander replied, not knowing how to respond to the question.

"I mean is there something you want to ask me?"

"Oh, yes, do you want to be my girlfriend?"

"Um, let me think about it."

Alexander felt like he had his heart in his mouth, he held his head down and covered his face with his hands. He felt incredibly nervous as if he was about to win the *X Factor*. Alexander was praying that she would say yes!

"I think you are a very sweet and funny guy, but..."

"Please, please," Alexander pleaded.

"But I would be honoured to have you as my boyfriend."

"Yes!" Alexander started jumping around his living room like a kangaroo on steroids. "Yes, yes, yes! Finally, I have a girlfriend!"

"I'm excited too, Alexander, I haven't had a boyfriend before."

"I thought you would need time to think about it," Alexander said.

"What is there to think about?" Garcia replied.

"Um... Compatibility, marriage, personal hygiene, um, dating preferences, dietary requirements, family gatherings, um, daily routine. We need to decide who is a left sleeper and who is a right sleeper, also finances need to be investigated and visas and other arrangements."

"That was a rhetorical question, Alexander."

"Oh, really, my bad, OK, I probably shouldn't have tried to answer it then."

"It's fine, Alexander, those are topics that we can discuss together."

"I have another surprise for you."

"Another surprise?"

"Yes, I bought it especially for you." Alexander presented a bunch of roses, with a look of sincerity in his puppy eyes.

"Thank you so much."

"I hope you like them," Alexander replied.

"There is one small problem, I want to smell them."

"Should I bring them to Manila in my suitcase?"

"It's up to you, do you want to bring them?"

Alexander was now in confusion mode. What was he supposed to do about this situation? Alexander started stimming again, trying to find a way out of his own confusion. He stared at the ceiling and started rubbing his neck with his hands as if trying to work something out. He began walking around in circles trying to figure out an answer. Noticing that Alexander was in trouble again, Garcia tried to reassure him by telling him not to worry about it, but Alexander could do nothing but worry about it. Alexander then started writing on his wall, trying to figure out an answer whilst muttering ideas to himself. *What bag should I use? Where should I pack it? How long do roses last until they are no longer fresh?* All these questions were being written on his wall whilst Garcia watched in complete confusion. "What type of suitcase should I buy if I'm going to pack a rose?"

"Enough, enough, it's all right, I was only joking, you don't need to pack a rose, I can smell it from here, it is so aromatic.

"Ah, phew, I'm so relieved that you said that" Alexander said, trying to regain his composure. "I have prepared a romantic meal for two." He pointed his phone towards a table that had a ring of lit candles. He was also cooking chicken adobo, a traditional Filipino dish.

"I love chicken adobo, can't wait to taste it."

"I have another question for you," Alexander said with a twinkle in his eyes.

"Yes, what is it?"

"I can visit you next month, are you up for that?"

"I can take time off work, it's short notice but I am due time off."

"Sorry for the short notice."

"That's fine, Alexander, I know that you are passionate about meeting me,"

"Mahal kita," Alexander said, trying his best to impress Garcia.

"Mahal kita din," she responded, with love in her eyes.

The rest of the evening was spent with Alexander eating his adobo with one plate that was sitting there reserved for Garcia. The couple spent the evening (or Garcia's early morning), having a whale of a time.

Packing for the Philippines, April 5th, 2023

After months of meticulous planning with Garcia, Alexander had planned a three-month journey using his savings. They were going to spend the first week in Manila with her family, then two weeks in Cebu, one week in Baguio and one week in Palawan. They were going to spend the remainder of their time together in Manila. The flights were also booked, all Alexander had to do now was prepare himself for the journey ahead of him. The countdown to his new life was starting. Alexander was so hyper-focused on the trip that he hadn't even thought about what type of suitcase he would need or what he needed to pack.

Alexander returned home from a long jog. He went to open his flat door, but after a few seconds of fumbling around in his pockets, he realised that his key was missing. This fear of being locked out caused Alexander intense anxiety. He continued to search for his keys by constantly pulling at his clothes and frantically pacing around his driveway. The next ten minutes dragged by as Alexander paced around his driveway, waving his arms in frustration and stamping at the same time. The pure stress of not knowing how to handle this situation was causing immense frustration to the point where his face was starting to sweat. He held his head up high, staring up at the sky as if communicating his frustration to God. After releasing his frustration, he stood under his porch with his head down like a convict accepting their own execution. He felt something beneath his feet, what was it? It turned out that his key was under the doormat all along. Alexander had put it there for some reason and had completely forgotten about it. He picked up the key and started twisting and turning but nothing was happening.

"This is not my day," Alexander said, feeling incredibly frustrated.

He kept jangling the door clockwise instead of counterclockwise – this was the reason behind the door failing to open. But Alexander was completely mentally preoccupied again and had no room for working out the mechanics behind locks and keys. After struggling for a while, he eventually managed to get into his own flat. But something was happening, a strange feeling overwhelmed him, something had changed.

As soon as Alexander stepped foot into his flat, he recognised the dimensions as that of the Pvormlu encounter room layout. There was one thing missing – where was Pvormlu? Alexander wandered around the bare flat, staring at the high ceiling, admiring the chandelier. He noticed a mysterious white hallway, and he slowly walked down it until he saw a door at the other end. This door was painted white, the same as the walls and ceiling. Alexander slowly approached this door as if he was expecting an intruder to be there waiting for him. He carefully pressed the doorknob down as if someone was sleeping in the room. The first thing he saw was a wooden staircase. He made his way up this intriguing staircase. Another white door. Alexander cautiously opened this door.

The sight that was in front of him was very unusual. The furniture being was staring out of a sliding sash window with its back to him. Alexander noticed that his belongings were scattered around Pvormlu. These were not only his own possessions but also objects that Alexander had thought of buying but hadn't gotten round to it yet. On the green Victorian sofa, several of his books and notepads were lying around. On the bed, several bags and suitcases were piled on top of each other. Alexander stepped towards the furniture being but, as he was verging closer, he couldn't shake the feeling that the furniture being had some terrible news to tell. Alexander was halfway across the room when the furniture being turned around to face him. The clock expression was two o'clock, meaning that Alexander should be feeling jovial and excited about this new adventure of his. The lantern started shining and Alexander turned around to see what the message was.

A poster displayed a white sandy beach with palm trees dotted along it and a magnificent sunset. Above this beautiful, reflected picture read '*Beyond the horizon is something that only you can see, never give up searching for the one*'. Alexander glared at this poster, imagining himself lying on a beach with Garcia, stroking her elegant, smooth hair, whilst staring into her gorgeous hazel eyes and chatting to her about anything that could drift into their minds.

The poster faded and Alexander's attention immediately reverted to Pvormlu. The oil lamp unleashed a visual white mist, succeeded by a holographic image of Garcia Bayani. This was a life-size vision. He walked up to Garcia's hologram and gently caressed her visually stimulating arms, even though her body was frozen. Alexander wanted to believe that this was really her. "Don't worry, I will be with you soon," he said in a quiet but confident voice. Her image faded but it was still crystal-clear in Alexander's mind. Pvormlu's candle teeth retracted revealing a letter. The broomstick tongue pushed this letter forwards and Alexander caught it and opened it to try to find out what the message was.

Dear Alexander,

This experience will change your life, a chance for you to find happiness and comfort. I will be waiting for you. A chance to swim together, a chance to remember each other. We can shine together and watch time go by, whilst the candles burn into the night. We can sleep wherever we like, don't mind the bats, they won't be bothering us. Hope to see you soon.

Alexander read this letter, feeling inspired and looking forward to this new adventure of his. However, he immediately noticed that there was something strange about this letter. It seemed as if this letter was written by multiple people. He couldn't work out who would have written this perplexing letter. At first, he thought it must have been from the furniture being but then he read the part where it mentioned that someone was waiting there for him. This would appear to be Garcia Agbayani. The letter mentioned swimming together which sounded like something that he would do with Garcia. 'We can shine together and watch time go by, whilst candles burn into the night'. This sounded like something a romantic person would say, but the references to light and watching time going by, also the candles burning into the night, created a similarity that Alexander couldn't ignore. Was Pvormlu trying to send a hidden message? Did Pvormlu want to go on a date with Alexander? Although seemingly hilarious, this thought made him feel slightly awkward. The last part of the letter particularly surprised him. Why were bats mentioned? Why not mention orcas, dolphins or even monkeys? Alexander had not even thought about bats. Was the shadow figure trying to set him up on a date?

He scanned this letter up and down for a few minutes then turned his attention to all the belongings piled around Pvormlu's body. Pvormlu turned its wooden head to face Alexander. The clock eyes started spinning rapidly which signalled that he had to get a move on. Alexander decided to grab his laptop but as he did, Pvormlu's body started shaking and the laptop was fixed into place. Confused as to why the laptop wouldn't budge, Alexander looked around. He saw bags and suitcases piled upon one another on top of the bed. The undercarriage was full of electronics, all piled on top of each other, facing in all manner of directions as if someone had already been trawling through them. The sofa bed had a random collection of books scattered around. Many different board games were also scattered around, such as Monopoly, Snakes and Ladders, Scrabble, chess sets and even card games. Alexander figured out that he had to only choose the correct items, and that he needed to do everything in a particular order.

What do I need first? he thought. Then the idea that he needed a suitcase came to mind. He climbed the wooden ladder and began rummaging through the bags and suitcases. Upon further inspection, he realised that there was only one suitcase that would be suitable for him to take. Some of the suitcases were meant for children, others were broken, and some even had wheels missing. Alexander found the only suitable suitcase which was orange and very spacious. *This suitcase is perfect*, he said to himself. He carefully carried it down and placed it on the floor. He unzipped it then thought about what he needed next.

He stared at the wardrobe. *The next item on the list must be my clothes*, he thought. Alexander went to open the wardrobe, but the doors wouldn't open. *This is strange, I don't remember needing a key to open my own wardrobe, but there isn't even a lock here, so it should open naturally*. Then the realisation dawned on him that he needed more bags to fit all the belongings in. Alexander went back up the wooden ladder and continued to dig around, searching for the correct bags. He saw lots of bags with quirky badges and stickers on them, and amongst all the bags were Tesco bags. Many different variants of carrier bags and handbags were squished together. An Aldi carrier bag – no, a designer handbag (a good gift for Garcia), but still not what he needed. There were two bags left: a big backpack and a small backpack. He decided that he might need both, so he took them both down and placed them next to the large orange suitcase. Now that Alexander had worked out what bags he was going to be bringing with him, he decided that now was the time to start packing.

He started by opening the wardrobe – this time it opened. He was greeted by a crammed, mismatched wardrobe that looked as if ten completely different people had decided to hang their clothes in it. There was no order in the wardrobe, half of the clothes were women's clothes. There were so many garments that not all the shirts had hangers, some were suspended between other shirts. Many of the trousers had holes in them and were covered in paint. Alexander also found a few silly costumes like a Mickey Mouse costume. As tempting as it was to try these bizarre clothes on, Alexander desperately wanted to finish packing his suitcase.

He felt around the bottom of the wardrobe and discovered two boxes. One box contained pants, the other contained socks. All the socks were tied in pairs but half of them had holes. He quickly worked out that he would only need seven pairs of socks and seven pants. He fished out seven hole-less socks and placed them in the open compartment of the suitcase. The next job was to fish out seven pants that are wearable. He picked up the underwear and looked closely to see which ones were suitable for packing. Some of the underpants had yellow stains, others had red stains, and some had brown stains. Not wanting to dwell on what the stains were, he took seven underpants without stains and sniffed them to make sure that they were fresh. Unaware of Pvormlu's packing requirements, Alexander 'accidentally' tossed the pants in the suitcase. As one might expect, the suitcase and the underpants were not very impressed by this accidental behaviour, so they flung themselves directly at Alexander's face, so much so that it looked as if he was wearing a load of underpants as face masks. Despite this infuriating uncalled-for response, Alexander calmly placed the pants on top of each other in the same corner as the socks.

The next garments that he decided to pack were shirts. The Philippines is a hot country, so he wouldn't need any jumpers or thick shirts. He worked out that he would only need seven shirts. But of course, these shirts were hidden amongst completely inappropriate clothing. He had to wade through a sea of riffraff; amongst the clutter he found a scrunched-up suit with a button missing and a winter jacket that had a scarf tied around it. This was the most frustrating wardrobe in the world! Nothing suitable for travelling to a hot country. Lots of winter coats that had zips missing. He even found a Pikachu costume. After a few minutes of searching, Alexander was coming up with all sorts of ideas as to why there were no shirts, but one idea stood out from the rest. He started unzipping some of the coats and discovered that there were shirts folded inside of them. He managed to find seven shirts that were already folded neatly. He carefully placed all these shirts inside the suitcase. Alexander stepped back in confusion, thinking that he was missing something. *What am I supposed to wear on my legs?* he thought to himself. There appeared to be no shorts, only trousers with holes in and covered in paint. Then Alexander remembered that Pvormlu has two sides and two wardrobes. He walked to the other side of Pvormlu's furniture body. He opened the other wardrobe and discovered that it was full of hats and shorts. The seven shorts that he needed were easy to obtain, but all the hats were confusing him.

After carefully placing the shorts into his suitcase he returned to the wardrobe full of hats. He saw a sombrero and thought that it would look good on him. He scooped up the sombrero hat and placed it on his head feeling exotic. He posed and observed himself in the mirror, whilst he was admiring his exotic beauty the sombrero hat blew off and returned to the wardrobe.

What's wrong with wearing a sombrero? Alexander thought to himself. He continued searching but could only find hats with holes in. *What would I wear on my head when I'm in the Philippines?* he thought to himself. He decided that it was a cap that he should be looking for. A new idea suddenly struck him – what if the wardrobe was a computer, a computer that had frozen and needed to be switched on and off again? Alexander shut the wardrobe doors, then he reopened them. To his surprise, two baseball caps were levitating in the otherwise bare wardrobe. He caught these two caps with his hands and tried them on before placing them in the suitcase.

The only other item of clothing that he needed to pack were shoes. He drew his attention back to the first wardrobe where several pairs of shoes were lying around as if a group of 12-year-old boys had returned home and had just flicked their school shoes off. Most of the shoes were lone shoes instead of pairs. There were more shoes than a woman could count. All different sizes and shapes. Some were worn out old women's shoes, others were great big boots and even wellies (which could be useful for walks in the wet season but would look fashionably out of place if seen by Filipinos). Alexander decided that two pairs of trainers is all that he would need to pack. But amongst the heap of mismatched shoes, there were no trainers to be found. Alexander tried opening and closing the wardrobe doors, but this had no effect. Alexander had another idea. He remembered that sometimes you must keep searching through piles to find everything. He rearranged the shoes into pairs and soon discovered that there were in fact two trainers waiting at the bottom for him.

Now that the wardrobe section was complete, Alexander turned his attention to the electronics. Inside Pvormlu's undercarriage, dozens of electronics and gadgets were tossed on top of each other. All sorts of outdated gadgets were lying around – old video game consoles, laptops that wouldn't switch on, cameras that had the lens missing. Even a Henry vacuum that had the lid missing was strewn. Alexander noticed the same laptop that he had tried to pack before, he lifted it up but was curious about what condition it was in, so he unfolded it to discover that the screen was cracked. So much so that it looked as if a stroppy teenager had punched a hole in it after losing *Grand Theft Auto*. After a while of rummaging around he found the laptop, camera and electric toothbrush and all the chargers that went with those devices. *What about the alarm clock?* he thought. Alexander noticed that each time that he turned to look away, the heap would rearrange itself. He turned his back on the digital heap then started counting with his right arm ticking in a chopping motion and matching the pace with precise steps with his right foot. He did this in a circular motion until he reached the digital heap. When he did so, there was an alarm clock bleeping. He picked it up and turned the alarm off.

The next decision he had to make was where to put these items. Alexander thought that packing them next to his clothes would be too tight, so he opened the second pouch of his suitcase. He thought that there would be enough space to pack them in there. He was able to pack them in this compartment, yet Alexander thought for some reason that they didn't want to be there. As he went to take a closer look, the devices started vibrating to the point where they were restlessly moving around, almost as if they wanted to escape captivity. Alexander quickly realised that this suitcase compartment was the wrong home for his electronics. Upon this realisation, he opened the big backpack up and slotted them inside it. His electronic devices looked much more relaxed here.

The next items he needed to pack were his books and board games. He looked at the sofa. There were spare puzzle pieces everywhere, half of the boxes had lids missing, it looked as if there had been a robbery at TK Maxx. Alexander realised that he couldn't pack all of the board games, not just because the boxes had pieces missing and lids missing but also because there was limited space in his suitcase. The situation in 'Pissup Maxx' was so dire that he couldn't separate the books from the board games since the books were inside the boxes. The books had pages missing. He decided that he only wanted four board games and four books. *What do I want to play when I travel to the Philippines?* he asked himself. *What does Garcia play?* He had no idea about what would interest his new girlfriend. He decided that he definitely wanted to bring his chess sets and wasn't sure about the other board games, so he picked up four chess sets: a travel set, a glass set, a wooden set, and a paper set.

He went to pack these four sets, unaware that the requirement was only one of each game. As he was about to squeeze these sets into the limited storage space, the chess sets exploded, sending chess pieces everywhere! Pawns were sent flying everywhere, a torrential rainstorm of pawns! One pawn even managed to get into his mouth. Alexander was starting to choke, but luckily, he managed to spit it out. Knights were wreaking havoc, jumping all over the place as if on amphetamines. Bishops were being fired in all manner of direction, creating laser formations. Rooks were blasting upwards at the ceiling like a jet of water bursting from a broken water pipe, they were also blasting from one wall to the next. Queens were moving in the most unpredictable fashion, they were moving in every possible direction, creating a vortex that was spiralling out of control. Kings were also moving in the most bizarre fashion, moving one times their own body length every second, moving at a much slower pace than the other flying chess pieces. These kings seemed to be avoiding Alexander as if he was planning to check them with his body. When the kings had reached the ceiling, they tilted on their sides and dropped to the floor like a dead fly. The chess boards initially just floated around, minding their own business. This chess madness was eventually vacuumed back onto the green sofa. However, one of the chesses sets remained, and this was the small travel set. It was large enough to see the board and pieces clearly but wouldn't take up too much space. He was able to decide that the other three that he wanted were Snakes and Ladders, Jenga and Doctor Who Top Trumps.

The next stage was to pack four books that he wanted to read. He decided that four different books would be the best option. Two novels, one travel guide and one Tagalog phrase book. This list would normally be easy for him to follow but as soon as he started scavenging around, looking for these books, he stumbled upon a large chess strategy book. He picked this book up, but all the pages fell out. This was the reminder that Alexander needed not to get sidetracked. He managed to find two novels (George Orwell's *1984* and Agatha Christie's *and Then There Were None*), he also packed the travel guide and Tagalog phrasebook into his suitcase.

Next on his list were toiletries. He worked out that he needed toothpaste, sun cream, insect repellent, deodorant and shampoo. He investigated Pvormlu's wooden mouth. Instead of burning white candles, there was chaos! The mouth was like a cupboard that you would only be able to find in a manic hoarder's house. There was not an inch of free space, toiletries were spilling out, Alexander had to be careful not to cause the pile to collapse. He began fishing through the items. *Oh fuck!* Alexander yelled inside his head. The hoard of toiletries was covered in sticky leaking fluids. One of the sensations Alexander hated the most was sticky fingers. This sensation made him feel as if his fingers were on fire. He ran around the room in circles as if his fingers were literally on fire. Pvormlu had to intervene to stop Alexander from acting like a screaming little girl. Pvormlu sprayed water out of the exhaust pipes underneath the green sofa. Alexander stuck his hands out to absorb as much water as he could. Alexander was dead set against getting his hands sticky again so he devised a solution, he decided that he would use a ragged worn-out shirt from the wardrobe as a joined pair of oven gloves to protect him from the sensation from hell. Most of the liquids were leaking but Alexander was able to find all the items that he needed. These liquids had no stains on them. However, he was unaware that he needed to make sure that they had a maximum volume of 100ml.

He carried these items towards the small backpack, with the worn-out rag acting as an oven tray. Alexander picked these liquids up to carefully place them in the small bag, but as he did so, all the liquids started leaking. His hands were covered in insect spray, suncream, toothpaste and shampoo. Before reacting to the sensation of burning hands, he first sniffed his hands, and indulged in the interesting combination of fragrances, before leaping around the room like a cartoon character. Alexander waved his sticky hands at the exhaust pipes, expecting water to come out, but nothing did. "I hate using automatic taps, they never work!" Alexander yelled. He then waved his hands in front of Pvormlu's clock eyes, signalling his urgency. He tried to signal for the water to come out again and waited a few seconds. Then the water gushed from the exhaust, not only cleaning Alexander's hands but also spraying his face, so not only did Alexander have to contend with having sticky hands but he also had to contend with a wet face. Alexander stood there, trying to work out what the meaning of this was supposed to be. His clothes were now wet. He grabbed as many clothes from the wardrobe as he could and used them as paper towels. Alexander returned to the bag and discovered that it was soaking wet and stunk. He picked up the bag and emptied the leaking contents onto the wooden floor.

Alexander found the 100ml liquids, but the problem was they were stuck inside the wooden cupboard and wouldn't budge. *Why the hell aren't they moving?* He went to check the bag and thought that maybe the wet bag was the problem. *How on earth am I going to dry this bloody backpack?* he thought to himself. He then remembered that Pvormlu's exhaust could be used to dry his sticky hands. *Why not use this exhaust to clean my bag?* He waved his bag in front of the exhaust, and after a few seconds the water came pouring out. Then soap filled the bag, and finally hot air dried the bag, so it was ready to be used again. Alexander, unknowingly, took these items out (this time they were free to be moved) without realising that he needed a plastic case to put them in otherwise they might leak inside his backpack. He went to place them carefully in his small backpack, hoping that he could finally put his mind to rest, but unfortunately for him, the bastard liquids had other ideas. He zipped the bag thinking that finally his ordeal was over. But not long later he noticed a rapidly growing wet patch in the bag. *Oh no, what is it this time?* Alexander felt like he was slowly losing his mind.

He unzipped the bag, but to his absolute horror, the lids burst open and toothpaste, insect repellent, sun cream and shampoo squirted out, not only making his hands sticky but also covering his face, making him look like a victim of a high school prank. Alexander stood still for a few seconds, then let out a massive roar of frustration, before marching over to the exhaust and demanding that it should sort this mess out once and for all. Thankfully the exhaust did unleash enough water to clean his face and hands. Alexander walked off to empty his bag, but as he did so the exhaust released hot air. Feeling an intense wrath from inside himself, he tossed the items out of the bag. After a few minutes of digging around he managed to find the plastic case to put all the liquids in. *Third time lucky,* he thought to himself. There was only one problem now, Alexander was starting to shiver because he was soaking wet. He decided to dry himself from the exhaust, but to add to his frustration, the exhaust squirted soap. *Ah, there is soap in my fucking eyes!* he thought to himself. After a while of farting about with Pvormlu's exhaust, Alexander finally cleaned himself up.

The final possessions that he needed to pack were his essential items. These would go into his small bag. He opened the chest of drawers to search for these items, but unfortunately nothing was there. *Strange*, he thought. Alexander felt an itch on his legs, but before scratching it, he felt some objects in his trouser pockets and in his jacket pockets. He had a passport in his right jacket pocket, his phone in his left jacket pocket, in his right trouser pocket he had his wallet and in his left trouser pocket he had his flat keys. After feeling these items in his pockets, he felt them disappear. *Strange*, he thought to himself again. He opened the drawers to discover that they were full of possessions, most of which he swore he didn't own. The cupboards had all sorts of rubbish inside of them like receipts, loose change, bookmarks, chocolate bars, batteries, plastic wrappers and even dead flies. The number of used tissues he found was unprecedented. Alexander managed to find all the items that he needed except one crucial one. In his hands he had his phone (check), his wallet (check), his flat keys (check), his money belt (check), his gift for Garcia (check), sunglasses (check), a pen for filling out information (check), documents for his trip (check). Alexander believed that he had everything that he needed. You can probably guess which item that he had forgotten – if you can't, you probably shouldn't be travelling abroad. He had forgotten his passport. Alexander went to pack these essentials only to have them fly away and re-enter the messy chest of drawers like something from *Harry Potter*. *Uh, not again!* Alexander was growing incredibly tired of these challenges – how hard is it to pack a bloody suitcase? He kept counting on his fingers trying to work out what he was missing. *Ah, my passport, how the hell could I forget such an important item?* he thought, kicking himself in the process. After finally packing all his belongings, Pvormlu turned around and gave him a seven o'clock expression, which signified confidence.

The expression changed to eight o'clock, which showed Pvormlu's pride. Next was the four o'clock expression which signified a recognition for Alexander's hard work. Then came the two o'clock expression which represented a positive future that Alexander should be looking forward to. Pvormlu then turned to face the side sash window. The Victorian bed began shaking, which was the cue for Alexander to climb on it. Alexander climbed the wooden ladder, then perched himself at the front of the bed with his arms dangling over the frame at the front, a bit like a child wanting to get the most out of a ride. They both peered out into the sunset, admiring the natural beauty. The windows opened, letting in a breeze that lifted Alexander's stomach up and made him feel like he was on cloud nine. Alexander reached out with both his arms, stretching his body forwards, his hands were glued together, pointing forwards, reaching into the sunset. Pvormlu started slowly swaying side to side, causing the bed to tilt, making Alexander feel as if he was gliding in an aeroplane. As Pvormlu gently swayed, Alexander's arms swayed in sync to the rhythm of the wind. After five minutes of this romantic motion, Alexander decided to sit back and rest. He noticed that the suitcases and bags were still on the wooden floor. He decided that he was royalty now and therefore he shouldn't climb down and carry the cases himself. He noticed that there were two bell pulls on each of the wooden shoulders. He tapped the bells with his hands, causing a ringing sensation. Two butler apparitions immediately rushed to the suitcase and inserted it in the undercarriage. The two backpacks were handed to Alexander.

Pvormlu tilted round again, this time there was a long wooden ramp which led up to the roof. Pvormlu's body started vibrating slowly as the exhaust pipe was starting to activate. The cartwheels started slowly moving and heading towards the wooden ramp. This wooden ramp wasn't steep, but it ascended quite a distance until it reached the roof. The first thing that Alexander noticed upon reaching the roof was the mini runway which formed a square around the roof. The runway was flat, but the triangle rooftop was in the centre. Alexander could see over the rooftop – the view was spectacular! He could see the whole of Stroud, the most vivid scene he had ever witnessed. The sunset was like a fire, engulfing his entire local area in orange and pink and yellow flames. The curvature of the light bending around the rooftop creating an impenetrable wall. After half a lap of the runway, Pvormlu stopped and exited on a ledge that overlooked his local town. Alexander took his camera out then began taking photos of this awe-inspiring scenery. He took his phone out, then pointed it in a south-easterly direction towards the Philippines. He stared at Garcia's profile picture and sent her the message, 'Here I come'. Pvormlu returned to the runway and started taxiing around the roof. Lap one: a slow and gentle ride, taking in the crisp summer air. Lap two: the engine sounded, an accelerating vibration. Lap three: the engine was at full capacity, wind was racing past. Three, two, one, take-off!

Journey to the Philippines, April 20th, 2023

Alexander and Anna were sitting next to each other on a bus, heading for Heathrow Airport. "Are you ready for your new adventure?" Anna asked Alexander.

"I am raring to go," Alexander said feeling confident.

"Have you got your—" Anna asked.

"I brought my phone, camera, passport, my laptop, my pyjamas."

"It's all right, it's all right, I was just joking. I'm sure you have packed everything."

"Ah, phew, I thought you were going to ask me to check my bags, then I was going to find out that I had forgotten something.

"You don't need to worry about that since I have already double-checked everything for you."

"Wow, you did that for me?"

"Of course I was going to do that."

"Thank you for checking."

"You're welcome, that's what sisters are for."

"I wish I was coming to the Philippines," Anna said admiringly.

"Why don't you?" Alexander asked.

"I have got too much coursework, plus someone needs to look after Arthur."

"Who's Arthur?"

"Arthur is my male black cat."

"Well, OK, you have a cat to look after. So how was your gap year trip to Thailand and Cambodia?" Alexander asked.

"That was a trip that me and my college friends definitely enjoyed."

"What did you enjoy about it?"

"Apart from the exhausting 'trips', you mean?" Anna replied.

"You found the trips exhausting?" Alexander said, without being aware that she was referring to drug trips.

"I mean drug trips; me and my friends did some stupid stuff when we were travelling. We took some psychedelics."

"Woah, what happened on these 'trips?"

"You don't want to know."

"I do want to know," he said persistently. "If you must know, I met the Devil and the Grim Reaper inside a cafe, we were talking about death and funerals."

"OK, can you remember what they said?"

"Not really," Anna replied slyly.

Alexander's demeanour changed as he engaged in this conversation, he enjoyed doing impressions. "Greetings, citizen, we are here to discuss your funeral arrangements," Alexander quoted in a deep and raspy voice.

"It might have been that; I don't remember anything specific, only seeing the Devil and Grim Reaper trying to make funeral arrangements with me."

"Do you want me to make you the brew from hell," Alexander continued in his Devil voice, unaware that people could hear him.

"OK, you need to stop that, I think people are listening to us."

"No one can hear the Grim Reaper."

"Alexander!"

"OK, I'll stop doing Devil and Grim Reaper impressions," he said in his normal voice. "So did anything else happen on this three-month journey apart from drug trips?"

"Lots of parties, long hiking trips through jungles, lots of temples, swimming. Lots of monkeys too."

"Did you meditate?" he asked.

"I saw Buddhist monks but didn't feel they needed me to join them."

"I have always wanted to experience Nirvana," Alexander said.

"You can always join a Buddhist temple in the UK."

"Nah, that would be too sociable for me, I would rather get to Nirvana alone by meditating in my bedroom."

"Ah, OK, that would be a good plan for your future, meditating in your bedroom all day, waiting for Nirvana to arrive."

Alexander's phone started vibrating – it was Garcia, she wanted to watch him travelling on this bus with Anna. This was the first time that Anna and Garcia had called each other, so Alexander was feeling nervous. "Hellooo, Anna!"

"Hellooo, Garcia!"

"I have been waiting to meet you," Garcia said in a bellowing sociable voice.

"It's great to meet you too, my brother has said so many great things about you."

"He is so romantic and funny, I'm so glad that we met."

"Hellooo!" Alexander said in a booming voice, slightly annoyed that the women were taking over the conversation, however, Alexander said this in a voice that was slightly too loud, so half the bus turned to see who was making weird noises. Luckily Alexander had a window seat, so he was difficult to notice. Regardless of this, he still ducked down the moment he saw heads turning towards him. This was completely off-cue and caused Anna and Garcia to jump. There was an awkward pause for about ten seconds. It was like an awkward stand-off between Alexander, Anna and Garcia. Just before he was able to come out with something, Anna and Garcia burst out laughing. Alexander was feeling completely confused, why were they suddenly laughing?

"That was me just saying hello," Alexander said, trying to work out what was going on.

"We all know that you're here," Anna said. "We are just two women trying to get to know each other."

"Ah, I thought you wanted me to say 'hellooo'."

"You didn't need to say 'hellooo', we were eventually going to include you in our conversation."

"You scared us by saying hello far too late."

"Sorry for scaring you both."

"Well, now that we know you are here with us, are you enjoying the bus journey?" Garcia said, trying to resolve the awkward situation.

"I am enjoying the bus ride, can't wait for this bus to finally arrive at the airport, then I can't wait to get on the plane so I won't be stuck inside a busy, noisy and smelly airport, then I'm looking forward to landing in Manila where I will fix my back pain and get some much-needed rest."

"So, you are not enjoying the bus journey?" Garcia asked, confused about Alexander's rambling response.

"I am enjoying the ride, but I am feeling anxious about the journey to Manila. I just want it to be all over."

"Don't worry, Alexander, it won't be long until we meet," Garcia said.

"Yes, you're right, it won't be long. I guess 19 hours in busy terminals and crammed into an economy seat is nothing to worry about."

"Alexander, you just have to go with the flow, it will be fine, you will survive," Anna said.

"That's what I just said – I can handle 19 hours of discomfort."

"Try to enjoy the journey," Anna said.

"OK, I will try to enjoy crowded, busy airports, weird smells, a lack of sleep, back ache, an overwhelming feeling to throw up, constant fear of losing something or missing a flight and the constant dizziness of travelling."

"I packed some medicine for you if you end up feeling ill. How do you know that you will suffer all these problems? You have never been on a long flight before."

"I understand how my body works; I feel aches and sickness when I am forced out of my comfort zone."

"So, why didn't you mention this before?" Anna asked.

"I just thought that suffering on long journeys was inevitable, it happens to everyone."

"There are ways to medicate to prevent uncomfortable experiences," Anna informed Alexander.

"I usually just tough it out, I don't take much medicine for my problems."

"Medicine can be expensive," Garcia said.

"It's not that, I just can't work out where my discomforts come from and I can't predict when they are going to affect me, so I prepare myself just to survive whatever comes my way."

"The medicine is there if you need it," Anna said. "Back to Garcia," Anna said, trying to change the flow of the conversation.

"Alexander is very romantic; he bought me some roses and delivered a romantic speech."

"He bought you some roses. He hasn't even met you yet."

"I bought her some roses as a gesture to win her over, I mean, I bought myself a bunch of roses but pretended that she was in my flat with me."

Anna couldn't contain herself anymore and burst out laughing.

"What's so funny?" Alexander asked.

"Nothing, it's just... it's like Garcia was your imaginary girlfriend and you bought flowers for her as if she was with you. I like the idea, but I'm just surprised that you did such a romantic gesture, I've never heard of you doing anything romantic before."

"I wanted to make an effort for Garcia, so I decided to come up with a proposal."

"What was the speech like?"

"I performed a speech for her."

"Yes, he did, it was very surprising and touching. At first, I thought that he was trying to scare me, but then he came out with a romantic speech, comparing our love to a baby that was growing inside of him. So, he walked out of the room, closed the door, then reappeared with his arms stretched out as if he was reciting the Bible. He finished this speech by doing something like a gospel choir performance."

"Gospel choir? Alexander? I have never seen Alexander read the Bible before. What happened next?"

"He showed me a bunch of roses that he had bought. I loved seeing these roses but then I asked him if he was going to bring the roses with him."

"I didn't get the question. I thought you wanted me to bring you these roses so you could smell them."

"Wait, hang on, Alexander was considering packing roses in his suitcase?"

"I wasn't really."

Anna couldn't contain herself any longer, she burst out laughing, in a roar of laughter that gave her a laughing fit. Garcia was laughing too. The other passengers on the bus started wondering what was going on. Alexander didn't find the topic that amusing, but he forced himself to laugh, which made this situation even weirder. So now the unfortunate bus passengers had to contend with a noisy video call, explosive laughter and manic fake laughing! Anna was laughing so much that she nearly fell out of her seat. She grabbed onto Alexander's arm to stop herself from falling onto the floor and possibly resulting in them being kicked off the bus despite being in the middle of a motorway. Alexander noticed the bus driver giving them the stern eye, so he quickly ducked down to hide his appearance. After a very entertaining video call between Anna and Garcia, Alexander was curious about Anna's love life.

"How is your love life?" he asked.

Anna appeared uncomfortable with being asked this question, but she still tried to answer it. "Now that you mentioned it, I wanted to tell you that Peter and I are no longer together."

"Yes!" Alexander stood up and stretched his arms out in celebration. The entire bus turned to look at look at Alexander as, yet another unexpected show was unfolding.

Anna, not happy with this reaction, shot up immediately after Alexander and waved her arms out and shouted, "Yes!" She did this as an act of detracting attention from Alexander, the way she did this was like the way James Bond would protect an innocent bystander from a bullet.

Alexander, feeling elated by this news, hugged his sister and she hugged him back. To their surprise, instead of being kicked off the bus, they received clapping from the other passengers, even the bus driver was clapping. This unexpected reaction made Alexander duck in fear. Anna decided to pull Alexander back up so that they could both bow to the bus passengers and driver.

After a few minutes of awkward silence, Alexander revealed that he had been counting the days on his kitchen wall until Anna would break up with Peter. "I'm on day 127, so when exactly did you break up with him?"

"Something like three months ago," Anna said in a blank tone.

"Ah, so I'm still right, because it was 127 days ago since we last discussed the topic of Peter."

"Well, I haven't been counting, but yes, 127 days since we last talked about my ex. I call him Peter Pan, because he dances around like a fairy and wears green pyjamas that don't at all look good on him."

"Ah, OK, Peter Pan, I like it."

"But you have never met him before."

"I have seen all of his terrible social media posts and videos. Have you tried dating since the breakup? Maybe Captain Cook or Long John Silver, or maybe even Captain Jack Sparrow."

"That was a difficult break up, you know," Anna said, feeling annoyed.

"Sorry, I thought you were glad to break up with him."

"Yes, I was, but we were together for nearly two years. I found him annoying because he didn't do any housework, and he got annoyed with me because I spent too much time chatting to my friends. I thought we loved each other and would start a family together, he could be romantic when he wanted to be, but everything was always about money with him."

"What a loser, there is more to life than money. How did the breakup affect you?"

"I spent two weeks just shutting myself away, not wanting to talk to anyone or do anything, just the exhaustion of the whole relationship took everything out of me. Now I'm just focusing on me and Arthur the cat, and my veterinary course."

"That sounds like a great plan, a chance to focus on what really matters."

The bus arrived at Heathrow Airport. Anna decided to stay with Alexander to help him deal with his fear of large buildings. They both waited outside for 20 minutes, with Anna explaining to him that everything would be fine.

"I researched that 117,000 passengers fly through this airport every single day, that's about 5000 per hour or about 80 per minute, that equates to 17 million a year. I wrote all the statistics on the wall next to my front door."

"Don't worry about the statistics, it's a big airport, so there will be plenty of space for you.

"That's my other concern, it's 12.3 square kilometres in size, by far the largest building that I have ever been in. I will have to navigate through swarms of busy people and endless gates and zones. Supposing that someone is late for their flight, if I don't have eyes all round my head then they might crash into me and cause an injury, then I might miss the flight."

"You just have to be careful, walk slowly, look where you are going and ask the staff members if you have any questions," Anna said, trying to reassure Alexander.

The pair walked into Heathrow Airport. Alexander tried his best to focus on what was in front of him instead of being sidetracked by all the passengers and signs. Anna guided him to the security section before saying farewell.

"This is the start of your independent journey, to see what you can make of yourself, I will be waiting to find out how everything goes."

They gave each other one final hug before parting ways. Alexander was now left to his own devices. His nerves quickly settled down, he felt as though Anna was right all along, there really is nothing to worry about. However, it wasn't long until he started getting distracted by his surroundings. As soon as he noticed the flight information screens, he instantly forgot about what was going on around him. He paused to check out the screen, but as soon as he did so a family was coming the other way. They nearly walked straight into him.

"Can't you see we are coming, look where you are going. Jesus Christ."

Alexander appeared nonplussed like a deer in headlights, he quickly leapt out of the way and then fixed his eyes on the screen, scanning it multiple times before being satisfied. When Alexander finally found the boarding gate, he felt like he needed space away from the crowded areas. So, he went to the toilets and tried to have some alone time. Apart from the constant flushing and footsteps Alexander found it relaxing until he heard a knock on the toilet door.

"Is everything all right in there?"

It turned out that an observant cleaner had noticed Alexander come into the toilet and was confused as to why he was still in there. Alexander had no idea how to respond to the knocking, so he shouted, "I'm coming, I'm coming," then he darted out of the toilet without washing his hands.

As he was making an emergency escape, he heard, "Why is there writing on the wall?" Alexander had been working out how to handle the long flight, what position he should sit in and what to eat and not to eat on the flight, he didn't want to be throwing up and walking around like a cripple when he and Garcia would meet for the first time.

Alexander headed back to the departure lounge feeling slightly displeased that he didn't have enough alone time to figure things out. Alexander felt tired from all the walking around, he still had a lot weighing on his mind, he felt that his time was running out. In less than one hour he would board the plane. He subconsciously started whispering to himself and talking to himself using his hands. The chaotic environment plus the unpredictability was causing him to start stimming. When Alexander was in a state of perpetual confusion, he needed to form a square shape in his mind. The way he would do this was by walking around the square perimeter of a room, covering all four walls. He would normally be able to suppress this urge when he was in public, but the stressful situation made him lose control over his urges. He started frantically pacing around the walls, his hands pointing out as if he was scanning the walls, he kept motioning himself along the walls, discussing ideas on how to handle the long flight and on how to present himself to Garcia. During lap two of Alexander's stimming, the airport staff started finding his behaviour slightly suspicious. After completing his second square lap, two airport staff asked him if he was all right.

"Yes, I'm fine, it's my first time flying in a busy airport, I'm just working everything out in my head."

"That's good that you are all right but what's the problem with sitting down?"

"There are quite a lot of people there and I am feeling restless."

When boarding finally came, Alexander's hands were shaking with adrenaline, he had never experienced anything like this before. As he was standing, his right hand was constantly moving in chopping motions. As the queueing continued, he felt the need to count how many people there were, so that he could prepare himself for the experience that awaited him. He managed to count 20 people that were in front of him. Luckily for Alexander, he was situated near a toilet.

This was a moment for him to celebrate, finally he could put his mind and body to rest. Alexander parked his exhausted bum on the economy seat, then let out a huge yawn of relief, however this feeling of relief was short lived. To his utter horror, he was sandwiched between two people that he certainly didn't want to share the flight with, let's call them Mr Tall and Mr Large. A whole host of misters were going to be stuck on the flight with him. On his left side sat a 250-pound man, and on his right sat a 6-foot-5 hairy Londoner, with a bald head and a great big bushy beard. Alexander had a very reproachful feeling about the seating arrangements, he felt like he should have researched how to book seats that weren't situated next to large people. Alexander kept thinking to himself, *how am I going to impress Garcia when I look like a squashed sandwich?*

The dry air was suffocating his senses, the constant rustling and rummaging around made him feel extremely irritated, he felt like an elephant was sitting on his chest and all he wanted to do was knock it off. His eyes kept twitching, the constant fidgeting and lack of personal space was making him feel incredibly uncomfortable. There was a slight relief when the plane took off, but shortly after the discomfort continued. Sitting in front of Alexander was a leaner, this constriction of space made him feel even more claustrophobic. To make matters even worse, the leaner was now snoring so loudly that he could barely hear the plane engine – this guy's snoring had become an extra engine. The realisation that Mr Large, Mr Tall and Mr Snore were on board was sounding alarm bells in his mind, an emergency alarm had gone off in his head yet there was nowhere to run to. But wait... there appeared to be loud crying in the background, the tedious wailing of a baby. Not only was Alexander stuck on board with Mr Large, Mr Tall and Mr Snore, he was now stuck with Mr Cry-baby as well.

Alexander tried his best to ignore what was happening around him. He tried listening to music, watching a film, hc also tried falling asleep, but the constant sensory discomfort made any distractions futile. Long legs, huge arms, encroaching on his personal space, he felt like Poland in 1939, being squashed by two much larger forces. There was a lingering smell that Alexander had been noticing for a while, it was a combination of sweat and cabbages, but the stench really got to him when he heard subtle farts wafting in from the same source. The last thing Alexander needed was a gas leak, now that he is 35,000 feet in the air. Feeling overwhelmed from the sensory discomfort, he began lifting his head back and forth.

The fifth mister, Mr Fart (or Mr Odour) was endlessly fidgeting around, readjusting his seat. Mr Large was either snoring or rumbling around, every time a meal would appear before him, he would devour it in an instant, which confused Alexander as he was slowly nibbling away at the food, trying to regain his appetite. Mr Tall kept stretching his arms and legs out, seemingly oblivious to Alexander's discomfort. Mr Cry-baby wasn't helping matters – it appeared that Alexander wasn't the only one in constant discomfort.

After four hours of hell, he finally succumbed to his surroundings and drifted off, only to be woken up by the roaring toilets every few minutes. After only being able to sleep for one hour, he heard a persistent hushed voice as someone was trying to whisper something to him. "Stop sleeping on me, get off, use a pillow." It so happened that Alexander's head had slid off the economy seat and had landed on the right shoulder of Mr Large. Upon realising his mistake, Alexander's head shot up as if the headmaster had caught him sleeping in class. He quickly looked around, whilst thinking about how to respond to this.

"If your shoulders weren't so large then I wouldn't have to sleep on them."

Mr Large didn't like this response, so he threatened to tell the stewardess that Alexander was behaving disorderly. Alexander retaliated to this by threatening to tell a stewardess that Mr Large was behaving in a disruptive manner. In the end they both agreed to a truce because neither of them wanted to get into trouble. Mr Snore was busy buzzing away like a lawnmower that had been left running. Although the mowing was mostly consistent, there were short intervals where he would wake up and start sneezing or coughing then continue mowing into the night.

Feeling tense and nervous, Alexander took out his notepad and started writing. He came up with ideas on how to greet Garcia.

As soon as I see Garcia Agbayani I must run to her with open arms and squeeze the life out of her. Maybe I should take out my gift then slowly walk towards her as if I'm carrying a birthday cake. Maybe I should skip towards her whilst clicking my fingers, she might find that amusing. Even better, I could kiss her hand then bow to her as if she were the queen of the Philippines. I have another idea: I will propose to her straight away. Which one should I choose? Option one looks good, but I want to surprise her. Option two sounds romantic but what if I drop the gift – then it's all over. Option three sounds very sexy but it doesn't suit my personality since I'm an introvert. Option four sounds very sincere and respectful yet it might be interpreted as creepy since she will not expect me to treat her like royalty. Option five shows that I'm committed, but I think that it might be a bit too soon.

These ideas were scrambling Alexander's exhausted brain, his mind was switching on and off like a broken lightbulb. Alexander was struggling to decide what he should write, he had an overwhelming urge just to nod off, yet he couldn't get the suspenseful feeling of how he was going to meet Garcia out of his head. Alexander was able to eventually narrow down the list to two options. This was a decision that Alexander had to make quickly as time was running out. Should he run towards Garcia then squeeze the life out of her as she was his long-lost sister, or should he slowly and dramatically carry his gift towards her?

This overwhelming decision was creating an atmosphere of stimming in his head. His motor reflexes were starting to give way under the constant sensory and psychological pressure. His middle finger was ticking between the first two options, as if it had a mind of its own. Meanwhile his left hand was rapidly crawling on the left side of the page like a drunk spider on steroids. The incessant rattling from these movements was disturbing the sleep of Mr Tall who didn't appear pleased at the sight of Alexander stimming. Alexander took a brief pause from stimming and stared at the ceiling of the fuselage. The whole time he was doing this, he was completely oblivious to Mr Tall giving him annoyed looks. During this time, Alexander was actively imagining all the different scenarios that could arise from him either running to hug Garcia or slowly walking towards Garcia with the gift in his hands. Alexander made his mind up!

He would run towards Garcia, give her a great big hug, then he would slowly take the gift out of his bag, like a magician taking a rabbit out of a hat, and finally he would grab her hand and kiss it. Alexander rushed to write this down, but he knocked the notepad on a very grumpy Mr Tall's feet. Mr Tall had the same facial expression that an angry maths teacher would have. He stared directly at Alexander, then directly at the fallen notebook, then back at Alexander's sheepishly blank face, then back at the notepad. Alexander slowly inched his hand forward, attempting to gesture something. He leaned his head forward, scared shitless of the situation that he had gotten himself into.

"Can I… Can I please have the notebook back?" he pleaded in a whimpering voice.

Mr Tall responded just by glaring at him. *Maybe Mr Tall doesn't speak English*, he thought.

Just as Alexander was about to turn his head away in defeat, Mr Tall said in a groggy, raspy voice, "First you disturb my sleep now you want me to give you your bloody notepad back."

"That would be great, please."

"No."

"What?" Alexander said in a confused voice.

"If you want it back you will have to pick it up from my feet."

Alexander felt a sudden rush of adrenaline from this reaction. He had absolutely no idea how to respond to this, so he turned away for ten seconds whilst staring at the ceiling in utter disbelief. "I'm not going to bend down to get it, I can't, I'm squished because of you and that other prick on the other side of me."

"Well, tough, you are not getting it back then."

"I will inform the stewardess of your misconduct." This brave response from Alexander made all the difference.

"Fine, but next time I will tear your bloody notepad."

Alexander carefully took his notepad back, thinking that he had a lucky escape. Aware that Mr Tall was still watching him, Alexander pretended to be sleeping. He lifted his right hand but kept his fingers open, so that he could see through them. He kept peeking through them, trying to make sure that Mr Tall was asleep. After three minutes of doing this, Mr Tall eventually fell asleep. Alexander used this opportunity to finish his 'greeting Garcia' plan.

After seven-and-a-half hours of torture, the plane finally landed in Doha airport in Qatar. The relief that Alexander was feeling was indescribable. He had never been so happy to get out of somewhere in his life. He now had a three-hour rest before catching his connecting flight to Manila airport.

The connecting flight was a breeze compared to the first flight. Alexander had three seats to himself, and he took full advantage of this by lying down. This time he was able to fall asleep in peace. Everything was fine and dandy until he was served yet another meal of aeroplane food. Alexander thought 'why not' as he forced another meal down his reluctant throat. However, this was one meal too many, as Alexander would soon find out. The hours quickly went by, but Alexander felt suffocated inside. His insides felt like a balloon that was about to pop. He had had this feeling many times before, he knew that there was a high probability that he might throw up. But Alexander's stomach was like an active volcano, you never knew exactly when it would erupt but you knew that it would erupt. Even though he could detect tremors from within his gut, he hoped that he could withstand the force with the help of self-discipline.

Alexander was busy revising his notes on how to greet Garcia when the overwhelming urges continued. The horrifying reality started setting in, Alexander knew that there was now a very real possibility that he was going to throw up. The vision of himself covered in sick, whilst already having the appearance of a worn-out mouldy sandwich, was raising alarm bells. Alexander needed to do something fast to suppress his rising bodily fluids. *How would someone make peace with their body?* he thought to himself. Then the idea came to him – people who meditate can calm their bodies down. This was the solution Alexander believed he needed to solve all his problems. *Why didn't I think of this before?* he thought to himself. He folded his legs into a yoga position, tucked his index fingers into his thumbs whilst leaving his remaining fingers suspended in the air, he then shut his eyes, hoping that this would cure his stomach problems. This method appeared to be working, Alexander was feeling more relaxed. A few passengers and crew members noticed this unusual behaviour but chose not to disturb him.

What Alexander didn't realise is that this relaxing of muscles would only temporarily suppress the urge to vomit, the long-term relaxation of muscles would cause his bodily fluids to be suddenly released, resulting in an uncontrollable urge to throw up everywhere. This meditation session of his was going well until he started coughing. Alexander suppressed any urge to leave his meditation position. Ten, the wave was coming.

Nine, eight, seven, six, five, four. His body was shaking uncontrollably. Three, two, one... An eruption of aeroplane food burst out of his meditated body, a fountain of puke spilled out all over the aeroplane seat, covering his notepad and ruining his smart black trousers that he had packed especially for her. Alexander was either unaware or choosing to ignore the massive eruption that had just taken place. It took a stewardess to tap on his shoulder for him to realise what had just happened. At first, Alexander slowly opened his eyes, not expecting anything to happen, but when he noticed the mess that he had created, he let out a yell that attracted the attention of all the nearby passengers. Alexander suddenly stood up and stared at the bodily fluids that he had unleashed.

"Are you OK, are you OK?" The staff were trying to calm him down, but Alexander's state of shock made it impossible to rationalise with him.

His eyes were darting around, like flies trying to escape a superheated windowless room. His trembling hands were flapping around in utter shock and frustration, he picked up his notepad that was soaking wet and stared at the smeared writing, trying to salvage his masterplan with his frenzied eyes. Whilst he was freaking out in silence, the staff were gathering paper towels and medicine. When the crew members came back to Alexander's aid, he was still staring at his notepad with a blank expression. The crew members were wiping Alexander's trousers and offering him medicine. He finally put the notepad down, then he snapped back to reality. The reality of the situation shocked him, he was now aware that the crew members were being super friendly towards him, and he felt a huge wave of embarrassment.

His cheeks went bright red, and his head slowly turned towards the staff members. “I’m so sorry, I’m so sorry, how do I make it up to you?”

“Don’t worry, you have just thrown up, there is nothing to worry about, we can clean it up for you.”

Alexander then took out his wallet, then took his debit card out and started waving it saying, “I can pay for any damages.”

“Don’t worry, you don’t have to pay, maybe it’s the aeroplane food that caused this reaction from you.”

“How do I make a good first impression on Garcia now that I am covered in sick?”

“There are toilets that you can use when we land in the airport.”

Alexander felt much better now that he had released his demons all over the plane seat. He continued doing his meditation in the hopes that he would be as cool as a cucumber when the time came for him to meet Garcia. The plane was coming into landing, the rush of adrenaline woke Alexander up, now it was time for him to start the next phase in his life.

Meeting Garcia in-person, April 21st, 2023

After arriving at Manila airport, Alexander felt as though he had just been experimented on by a mad scientist. He had no idea where he was going, what he was doing. After finally making it through customs, he decided that the best option was for him to clean himself up. Alexander's weary overstretched eyes were so gluey that he was worried that they might stick to his sloping dark eyelids. He entered the restroom, feeling incredibly light, almost as if he were in space. He had to keep stomping his feet on the ground just to stop himself from drifting off. *I need to wake myself up, to create a good impression of myself.* Alexander devised a plan to wash his face with soap and tap water, then he would stand in the cubicle and practise his body language and speech. This routine involved rubbing his face with water, then adding soap to his face. After adding soap, he would press his face under the dryer, using the heat to wake himself up. After this 'waking up' process he would stand in the cubicle for a few minutes rehearsing his 'grand entrance'. This routine was going well until fellow restroom users started noticing this unusual behaviour.

"Why are you rubbing your face with soap?"

"Why are you drying your face instead of your hands?"

Alexander thought long and hard about how to respond to these questions, then came out with, "I'm busy, I don't have time to talk."

Garcia sent Alexander a message confirming that she had arrived. The news naturally made Alexander want to race towards her like a bullet, but he realised that he still didn't feel awake, so he told her that he was still in customs.

After spending 20 minutes in the restroom, a cleaner knocked on the door. "Is everything all right in there?"

"Just a minute," Alexander replied.

Garcia had brought along her brother, sister, father and aunt, but Alexander wasn't aware of this, he had only planned to greet Garcia. Alexander was now heading towards Garcia, walking in long strides of confidence, his head tilted back, using his shoulders to pull himself forwards and with a smile as wide as his face. Alexander did not want to mess this up. He exited the airport without remembering her instruction on where to meet.

"Hey, Alexander, over here."

Alexander jumped to face her, tilting his entire body at a 180-degree angle. Garcia and her family were calling him over, roaring with passion and excitement. Alexander stared at Garcia and her family with an eager expression on his face as if there was a pit between them both and he had to jump over the pit to reach his princess. *Mental notes: run over to Garcia and squeeze her with all you might, then slowly reveal your gift to her.*

Alexander raced towards her like a rabbit on cocaine, leaping with long cartoonish strides whilst also having a face that was so worn-out, it looked as if it was going to fall off. He was flapping his arms and hands almost as if he thought that he could fly, he was so distracted that he left his suitcase behind. Three, two, one, impact. Alexander wrapped his long arms around Garcia's short figure, whilst Garcia was holding onto his skinny waist for dear life. He had so much passion that he was unable to stand still; this resulted in the pair of them spinning around like an out-of-control pendulum. Were they dancing together, were they wrestling each other? One was not to know, but one could only imagine the joy that they were both feeling. Alexander opened his bag, then waved his right arm to symbolise anticipation. He slowly took out his gift and presented it to Garcia.

"Wow, I love it," Garcia said.

Alexander then took Garcia's arm and kissed the back of her hand whilst giving her a sincere bow. At this point, he still hadn't said a word to Garcia or her family, he was behaving like a romantic mime from Paris. Garcia and her family were thoroughly enjoying this experience. He then dropped to his knees and said, "I'm so glad to finally meet, will you consider marrying me in the future, I know that we haven't known each other long but what awaits us should surely be worth fighting for."

"Wow a proposal," Tita Genie exclaimed.

"I told you he is romantic," Garcia responded. "Of course, I will consider marrying you in the future, Filipinas love marriage."

"Here is your suitcase," Garcia's brother, Adam, and her younger sister, Angelica, said together.

"I'm so glad that someone wants to marry my daughter," Papa Michael said.

"Michael!" Tita Genie said in an austere tone.

"Sorry, I was just joking, na."

"What was the journey like?" brother Adam asked.

"It was... uh, interesting," Alexander responded. "I travelled with my sister, Anna, on the bus, I then flew to Qatar, had a short gap, then I arrived in Manila seven hours later."

"So, what is the thing you like the most about my sister?" Angelica said.

"There are many things that I love about Garcia."

"Like what?" Papa Michael interjected. "Her stunning eyes, her flashy booty?"

"Michael, I warned you already, na, don't make jokes like that." Tita Genie had had enough of Papa Michael's jokes. She whacked him on the head.

"I'm sorry again, I was probably a bit over-excited ano."

"Aren't we all a bit over-excited?" Angelica said.

"Can we let Alexander answer the question?" Adam interjected.

"I think the thing I like the most about her would be her intense hazel eyes, I could look at them all day," Alexander said in a poetic tone.

"I could look at them all day too," Papa Michael said in a cheeky tone.

"How many times I warn you, naman."

"It's true, everyone likes her eyes."

"That's a lovely thing to say," Tita Genie complimented.

"So, what do you want to do now, Alexander? Sleep, sleep or sleep?" Papa Michael said.

"Maybe sleep," Alexander replied. "I think we have forgotten something," Alexander said.

"Mag-selfie?" Garcia asked.

"I don't think it's that, I think that we have all forgotten to do something."

"Have we forgotten to eat?" Angelica asked.

"I think we haven't introduced each other yet."

"Oh yeah, no handshakes, or 'nice to meet you'," Michael said.

They all stared at each other awkwardly then stuck all their hands out at the same time. Alexander had no idea whose hand he should shake first, so he stuck both his hands out simultaneously and shook whoever's hand that he could get to the quickest. Before the group had the chance to get in the van to give Alexander a chance to rest, Tita Genie whipped out a box of fries and chicken and fish balls for everyone to snack on. Alexander felt like he couldn't accept these because of his executive dysfunction from the flight. But he didn't want to come across as impolite, so he accepted the food. One handful fries, another handful chicken, another handful fish balls. Even though Alexander enjoyed eating finger food, he hated sticky fingers. The combination of the intense heat from the sun and the greasy food made his hands feel as they were being cooked. Alexander's hands were shaking, he formed a cup shape with his hands with all his fingers pointing upwards. He formed this cup so he could monitor the condition of his sticky hands. Alexander could have just gone back into the airport to wash his hands, but he was afraid that the cleaner would be watching him if he entered again. He had his back to the family and every few seconds he would lick his fingers like a cat discreetly licking their paws. Despite his best efforts to obscure his sticky hand cup, Tita Genie noticed.

"You have sticky hands, ha," she said.

Alexander quickly broke up his sticky hand cup and turned around and mentioned that his fingers were a bit sticky.

"Here, I have wipes, ano." The very resourceful Tita Genie whipped out a packet of wipes and wiped Alexander's hands and fingers for him.

"Thank you, Tita Genie."

"It's selfie time," Angelica announced.

The family quickly sprang into action, Angelica was the lead photographer. The group all squeezed together and smiled like a pack of hyenas eyeing their next meal. "Smile!" Even just keeping his eyes open was hard enough, never mind posing for a photo. Alexander looked back on the photo that had just been taken, regardless of all the comments saying that he looks handsome, he thought that it looked as if a family of actors had dragged a homeless foreigner off the streets and made him join their photography session.

Phew, I'm glad that's over, he thought to himself.

The journey to Garcia's apartment was very enjoyable for Alexander as he was finally able to sit next to Garcia. Throughout the whole ride his eyes were almost glued to her, he couldn't stop obsessing about her pulsating cheeks that stretched every time she said something, her large hazel eyes that kept twitching every time that she was thinking something. Throughout the whole journey, Garcia had her warm petite hand on top of Alexander's. There were two thoughts lingering on his mind: the first kiss and bloody sleep. Alexander knew that he could have killed two birds with one stone right then and there, but the overwhelming adrenaline of the situation was forcing his eyes open and causing his heart to race whilst his body was frozen in place, just admiring Garcia's stunning beauty and personality.

Garcia was mostly nattering away in Tagalog to her family with the occasional question directed at Alexander.

Alexander could understand some of what she was saying but was far more interested in getting to know her body (if you know what I mean).

By the time they arrived at Garcia's apartment Alexander felt like he was the beast from *Beauty and the Beast*. He felt so worn out and dishevelled, yet he couldn't take his eyes off Garcia for a second, meanwhile Garcia was flourishing in her natural beauty. She wore a light pink t-shirt with blue jeans, she also had a necklace on. The necklace had '*love*' written on it. Just when Alexander thought that he could finally get some rest, an older woman came racing towards him. Alexander was standing inches away from the door, he could have just walked into her apartment to avoid having to deal with this woman.

"Hello, hello, nice to meet you, Alexander, I'm Tita Mae, Tita Genie's sister."

"Uh, hello," Alexander responded, not knowing what to say to her.

"How was your trip to the Philippines?" she asked.

Not again, Alexander thought to himself. In hindsight he should have written the answers to all these questions in his notepad (in the hope that his notepad wouldn't get covered in sick). "The journey was very smooth, I took off fine, I landed fine, nothing to worry about there."

"Ah, OK, would you like to come into my apartment to have some tea?"

Certainly not, I want to go straight to bed, he thought to himself. "Yes, I could."

They made their way into Tita Mae's apartment. Alexander had never seen so many Bibles and wooden crosses, he thought that she had invited him in for the Last Supper. They all sat around the kitchen table.

By 'they' we are referring to Alexander, Garcia, Tita Genie, Papa Michael, brother Adam, sister Angelica, Tita Mae and her husband, Tito Chris, and her teenage daughter, Hanna, and her teenage son, Marcus. If you count the total number of people, that's 10 people sitting around one table. That's not including the people who were sitting on her sofa. A few kids, some neighbours, family friends? Alexander had no idea who they were, so he called them the sofa crew. The sofa crew were mumbling amongst themselves and seemed to be disconnected from the group that Alexander was sitting with yet appeared perfectly at home.

"How did you two meet?" Tita Mae asked.

Not now, not again, I thought I had already told everyone this, he thought to himself. "We met online, we dated... we texted each other." Garcia quickly jumped in and gave a lengthy explanation, to which Alexander just nodded in agreement.

Papa Michael formed a grin on his face. "You are just like me when I was your age, Alexander."

"Uh... OK." Alexander had no idea what to make of this comment.

"Young, handsome and determined,"

"Uh, thanks, po."

"I reckon you have a lot of things to show Garcia."

"Stop it, Michael, you can leave the table if you say those things."

"I mean he can show her things that he has done."

"Hanna and Marcus, do you want to get things for us to eat?" Tita Mae commanded her kids to get snacks that they could all eat.

A great big bowl of pandan jelly arrived followed by a bowl of halo-halo (a Filipino dessert that is flavoured ice cream with bits of jelly and ice), followed by a plate full of spring rolls, followed by large bowl of sinigang (a sour soup with pieces of meat on the bone and Asian vegetables). Alexander had the appetite of a field mouse, yet he felt compelled to eat everything that was put before him, maybe this was the Last Supper after all. Alexander's tactic was to choose very small amounts of each option so that he could give the illusion that he was enjoying himself. Papa Michael picked up his bowl of sinigang and slurped it all down, swallowing all the vegetables and chicken. The sound he made resembled a half-full bath when you pull the plug. Alexander had never seen someone so enthusiastic to eat anything before. The sofa crew seemed oblivious to all the food, maybe they had already eaten, Alexander thought.

Alexander scanned the surroundings, looking for an excuse to escape. The rest of the conversation went by with the group members all simultaneously chatting to each other like a group of bees buzzing around each other whilst Alexander was silently observing all the ornaments in the room. He did try to keep up with the conversation, but the fast pace meant that he could only manage a few words in edgeways. Alexander turned to look over his shoulders to see what the sofa crew were up to, but they had mysteriously vanished. *Maybe they are a family of magicians,* he thought to himself.

Don't get Alexander wrong, he did enjoy the food and Filipino hospitality, but he just didn't have the strength to manage it all. After a long session of back and forth chitter-chatter and a large serving of Filipino compliments, Alexander was finally able to make a break for it. *Phew, that's a relief, I knew I would somehow survive,* he thought to himself.

Alexander found himself in the same position as before, inches away from making it to safety yet his presence was captured by yet another character, the neighbour, Manuel. Neighbour Manuel, a bouncy Filipino man of around 50, who was always patrolling the streets looking for favours that he could do for the other residents in return for a small amount of money. This was a proud Filipino man who would help those who had nothing. Even though he was someone who the Filipino community love (probably because he was noisy and liked chatting to everyone in sight), Alexander felt his blood boil when this extrovert had the nerve to pester him when he felt so exhausted that he wanted to drop to the ground.

What do you want? is what Alexander wanted to say. Instead, Alexander said, "Hi, nice to meet you as well, I had a good trip." Whilst he was putting his mask on and faking an interest to be sociable, he noticed that his suitcase was missing. (The truth was that kuya Adam and sister Angelica had taken it to where Alexander was going to be sleeping but no one had told him this. This was creating a feeling of dread within him; he was now in panic mode. Neighbour Manuel invited Alexander and the extended clan with him into his apartment. Now, Manuel was known as a pleaser but also a nonstop talker, sitting down with him meant that your ears better be ready for battle that lies ahead of them. Manuel was a great person to have a quick chinwag with but not the person you want narrating a story.

He poured everyone a tea, then he began his tales. There were five tales that he wanted to share; the first one was about that one time when he won 3000 pesos from the casino. The second story was about how he got dumped by his first girlfriend (no surprise there). The third story was about that one time when he fell off his motorbike. The fourth story was about that time when he took the wrong jeepney. The fifth story was about his job as a parcel boy.

Alexander felt relieved that he didn't have to explain his journey to yet another stranger or must explain how he and Garcia became boyfriend and girlfriend. Manuel felt the need to make everything about himself, he elaborated on every single small detail.

Why are people like this, why do they have to repeat the same old stories repeatedly as if they are new? Alexander thought to himself. He had always struggled with conversation because he could ever think of anything interesting to talk about, but conversation is all an act. It's about making a boring person appear exciting, it's about making a poor person sound rich, it's about making a nervous person appear confident. All of this was something that Alexander would never buy into. Why should he pretend to care about something that didn't matter to him? All these thoughts were suddenly bubbling away in his mind. *Am I always going to be like this, when am I going to learn to become an actor?*

Whilst Alexander was feeling sorry for himself, Manuel was droning on and on almost as if he was forgetting that he had already mentioned this thing six times already. (I won't mention what exactly all these things that were mentioned were because I want you to continue reading and not fall asleep, but these were useless facts that are probably better unheard). It was becoming increasingly difficult for Alexander to keep his eyes open; his eyelids were slowly closing. He felt as if he was stuck on a mountain ledge, trying incredibly hard to stay awake and not succumb to hypothermia. He kept discretely punching his legs so that stimulation would make it challenging for him to fall asleep. He also kept scratching his neck to stop himself from yawning. Alexander was sitting on the sofa along with the first group (the people that Alexander met at the airport), the second group (the people that Alexander met in Mandaluyong) were sitting in chairs spaced out in a circular shape. Manuel was sitting in a chair facing Garcia's family. Alexander was at the end of the sofa, so Manuel wasn't looking directly at him.

As the minutes wore on, it got to the stage where Alexander had no choice but to succumb to the avalanche of boredom. His eyes fell shut. At first, nobody noticed since Manuel was somehow able to captivate everyone's attention by telling his fascinating stories. Within 20 seconds of falling asleep, he began meditating. Alexander probably began mediating because he was dreaming of being at one with himself, not at ten with this group of people that he didn't even know he was going to meet. This meditation shocked everyone as no one knew that Alexander was a Buddhist. As Manuel finally stopped talking about himself, the group started whispering, debating about what to do. Garcia proposed letting him sleep there until he woke up. Angelica proposed that they could guide him out whilst he was sleeping. Then Papa Michael proposed that they could pour cold water on him to wake him up. This suggestion did not go down well with Tita Genie who had already put Michael on his last warning. She ushered him out of the apartment.

Whilst the Agbayani family and Manuel were faffing around, trying to work out what to do with the sleeping monk, Alexander, snoring could be heard. It appeared that Alexander was so tired that he began snoring.

"We are going to be here for a while," Tito Marcus said.

"Thanks for your help," Tita Mae said sarcastically.

Garcia Agbayani whispered in Alexander's ear, "When you are done meditating, we can sleep together."

This revelation went down well with Alexander so much so that he stopped snoring.

Neighbour Manuel was starting to grow impatient. "I'm busy, I don't have time for this".

He ordered the Agbayani family to wake him up. Big mistake – you never wake up a sleeping monk. The family started tapping on his shoulders and pulling his blue jacket. When Alexander awoke, the reality completely overwhelmed him, he toppled over onto the floor landing on his arms and knees.

"Look what you have done, Manuel!" Tita Genie shouted at Manuel.

"Look what I have done?"

"Alexander is your guest."

"You are the one who invited him in and bored him to sleep," Tita Genie snapped back.

Alexander got up off the ground, feeling delirious. He quickly ran outside.

"Are you OK, Alexander?" The entire Agbayani family were surrounding him like a team of paramedics.

"Do you need a plaster?" Tito Marcus suggested.

"Of course he doesn't need a plaster," she replied.

"I'm fine, I'm fine, I remember where I am, and I can even count my fingers," Alexander reassured the Agbayani family. "I think I need to sleep."

"We can sleep together," Garcia said in a flattering tone.

"That would be great," Alexander replied, feeling like he was on cloud nine.

The new romantic couple laid down next to each other.

"Before I go to sleep, I have to do one thing," Alexander said.

"What might that one thing be?" Garcia asked.

"First kiss."

Garcia caught Alexander by surprise by giving him a passionate kiss. She grabbed Alexander's shoulders with both her hands, in a grip which exceeded her usual body strength. Her legs were firmly wrapped around Alexander's waist as if Alexander were a tree and she were a koala. Alexander was blown away from the amount of affection that Garcia was showing him, he had never had this much pleasure before.

"Pick me up," Garcia commanded Alexander.

Alexander lifted her up, feeling like Hercules. He carried her up the stairs and into her bedroom. What Alexander noticed when he entered her room blew him away. The room was filled with balloons, and all the balloons had messages written on them: 'Welcome to the Philippines', 'Nice to meet you, Alexander', 'Hello, Garcia's future husband to be, Mahal Kita'. The walls were covered in posters welcoming Alexander.

"Wow, you all did this for me?" Alexander said in a surprised voice.

"Yes we were all very excited to meet you."

Alexander was admiring the festivity of the room when two little rascals popped out from each side of the bed, blowing blowouts. The shock of this made Alexander drop Garcia onto the bed. "Oh shit, I'm so sorry."

"It's fine, Alexander, it's not your fault. Emila, Josef, don't jump out at us like that. Sorry, these are my cousins." These two ten-year-olds were Tita Genie's grandchildren, can you keep up with all this?

All this excitement was fuelling Alexander to become a romantic beast, with Garcia clinging onto Alexander with all her might. Garcia went to take a selfie of this romantic moment, then Alexander came up with the idea to make the most artistic and interesting photo of them both. "Why just take a selfie of both of us, when we can add the bedroom to our romantic creation?"

Garcia appeared to be confused about this. Alexander lifted the thin white bed cover and tied it around them both, this bed cover became a cloak that covered the pair of them in a mystical veil. Alexander collected all the balloons and tied them to their arms.

"Wow, this is incredible, I have never done this before," Garcia said feeling thrilled.

"Me neither," Alexander added.

He then picked up two pillows and positioned them between the wall and their necks, creating a fixed position where they could admire each other. Alexander's final romantic touch was to pick up Garcia's lipstick and to write a message on each other's faces.

Alexander wrote:
Pure joy
Passion
Devotion
Love story
New family
Memories

Garcia wrote:
Future mum
New life
Marriage
Guapo
Intelligent
Romantic

The couple were leaning next to the wall, facing each other and staring intently into each other's eyes. They both turned to face the window which overlooked the streets of Mandaluyong, not much of an impressive sight but in their eyes, this could be somewhere in Paris. Garcia took so many selfies of them both that it was a surprise that her battery wasn't drained. They both then placed their pillows back on the bed and stood in front of the window.

Garcia opened the window. "This is now time for us to fly, we can go anywhere, our souls are free for us to do whatever we want."

"Do you, Garcia Agbayani, wish to drift off with me into the world of opportunities?"

"I do," she responded. "Do you, Alexander Sommervale, agree to stand by me no matter what?"

"I do. Do you, Garcia Agbayani, agree to putting up with all my strange habits?"

"I do. Do you, Alexander Sommervale, agree to tolerate my Filipinoisms?"

'Filipinoisms?"

"You know what I mean."

"Yes, I do, of course. May we kiss each other?" Alexander announced. The pair had the most mushy and exotic kiss you could ever have.

Their dream together was just starting. After smooching, squeezing and caressing each other, they both took off their love gear and settled down for bed. Alexander crashed out due to sheer exhaustion and began meditating in his sleep again. Garcia watched Alexander meditating and decided to join him. The journey to Nirvana was certainly their next destination.

Experience in Cebu

Alexander and Garcia decide to write 3 postcards detailing their experiences in Cebu, Baguio and Palawan. They decided that Alexander would write about their experiences in Cebu, Garcia would share her experience in Baguio, and they would write about their experiences in Palawan using both of their perspectives.

We are having the time of our lives, exploring exotic places that we have never been to before, squeezing into jeepneys, or what I refer to as 'sardine wagons'. Garcia loves them because they are cheap and reliable, but I hate them because I have no space to breathe. Garcia has been an amazing tour guide. Garcia's gift to me contained two silver necklaces with our names engraved, one that read 'Garcia' and the other 'Alexander'. We decided to be quirky and wear the other person's necklace. Kawasan Falls – a place that we will never forget, motivating each other to participate in canyoneering, swimming with each other with the passion of two love dolphins. Olango Island – a hidden gem, a mysterious island that we both indulged in. Sitting in the Bahay Kubo huts, observing the endless waves, being at one with the world. We both enjoyed our experience at Shalala beach. I was floating on my back, forming a human raft- I would let Garcia lie on top of me, with our cheeks resting together. I was the canoe; her arms were the paddles.

Temple of Leah – the wonderful Taj Mahal of Cebu. We were admiring the architecture of this magnificent shrine. We were discussing the importance of our own lives, how to remember the past, how we should live in the present and how to prepare for the future. The past is always worth remembering, the present is always worth preserving and the future is always worth waiting for. Taoist Temple – I was reading a book about Taoism to try to understand what this temple was all about. This temple was finished in 1972, and it represents the religious commitment that the Filipino Chinese community had and still has to this day. After doing my research I discovered that there are three main principles in Taoism that this temple represents. Piety – wanting to belong to something that is bigger than yourself. Prosperous life – admiring a world full of opportunities, never missing a golden opportunity. Humility – the ability to be humble and accept the reality of the world. Hilltops – we had the most amazing view from here, we felt the wind breezing over us. We grabbed each other tightly and kissed passionately whilst feeling that we owned the world. Ocean Park – I really enjoyed this because I love animals.

Garcia described the marine world as a world that is parallel to our world, yet the ocean holds secrets which could explain life forms on other planets. I was surprised to learn that Garcia was filming me everywhere I went like a cunning detective or insistent journalist. I had yet another idea, I wanted to create a video where we were mimicking the movements of these creatures. Garcia would point to a fish, and I would show her the gesture that we should perform. We both observed the eagle ray, then we slowly flapped our arms in the air whilst aimlessly wandering around the room. The Caribbean reef shark caught our attention, so we would bend down then stick our arms on our back with our hands facing upwards mimicking the dorsal fin, we would prowl around the room in circles acting like predators surrounding their prey. Next came the giant grouper. We both held our mouths open in a grumpy expression, then aimlessly wandered back and forth. We also decided that the Burmese python would be a great creature to act out. We put our arms by our sides, and we slithered around the walls. By this time many people were watching us, but no one wanted to intervene, since they were all recording us, making us feel like celebrities. For the Burmese python, we laid on our fronts with our hands pressed together, we slowly slid towards each other, then we touched each other's fingers. Despite my quirky and unusual behaviour, Garcia was able to enjoy being with me on this exotic adventure.

Experience in Baguio

Garcia wrote this letter reflecting on her experience in Baguio.

Baguio is the highest city in the Philippines. I was watching Alexander trying to make sense of the paintings and sculptures by writing his interpretations in his notepad, I was filming him writing suggestions in his notepad. I wanted him to pose at every piece of artwork. Alexander is always trying to understand things, he wants to write the world down on a piece of paper. *We both had an amazing experience in Baguio, a town that is unlike any other Filipino town. The highest, the coldest, the least polluted, founded by the Americans in 1900, this town offers an experience that you will find nowhere else in the Philippines. We admired together the awe-inspiring view of the hills, the steep undulating valleys which are a pain in the ass to walk up but a pleasure to look down on. We never missed a sunset kiss. The Bencab Museum – artwork from the Igorot people, showcasing wooden sculptures, meanwhile I want to record the entire world on my Samsung. Our experience in Burnham Park was one of great surprise and great pleasure. We both swanned off together across the Burnham Lake, pedalling away as if we were playing* Mario Kart. *The swan pedalo was the most romantic boat journey we have ever had. We both enjoy our experiences in different ways, Alexander internalises everything whilst I visualise everything. I will admit that I have a bit of a smartphone addiction, but Alexander has a notepad addiction problem. I guess we both need therapists.*

Experience in Palawan

Alexander wrote this letter talking about both their experiences.

This island blew us both away, islands of paradise plus a feeling of soulful rejuvenation. The Puerto Princesa Subterranean National Park gave us an experience that we will never forget. We felt like we were in an Indiana Jones *movie, we had no idea where we were heading but we knew that venturing into the unknown was better than waiting to be caught. We encountered plenty of surprises in this mysterious cave, statues built by the Spanish explorers, and unique geological formations. We both really enjoyed this experience together, although there was a degree of frustration stemming from our differences that was slightly detectable at the time.*

Coron was the most naturally stunning place that we have ever been to. Kayangan Lake, Twin Lagoon, Barracuda Lake, we both absorbed as much pleasure as we possibly could have. The feeling of holding someone you love whilst basking in the open tropical sun is golden. Considering all the sunlight that I have absorbed, you might think that I should have turned into one of the Simpsons *characters by now. I may still be an incongruous tourist but I certainly felt like Homer Simpson in the morning, I felt like Bart Simpson when*

I was with Garcia in the water, I felt like Lisa Simson when I was strolling around with my notepad, evaluating the world around me, I felt like Marge Simpson when I was in bed with Garcia, I felt like Ned Flanders whenever Garcia would take to a Filipino restaurant and I even felt like Chief Wiggum when I had to prepare myself for the day. All these are awe-inspiring places that everyone should visit, if they could visit, which implies that eight billion people should travel to one small island, possibly by boat or plane, in which case we should contact Noah to see if his ark is available. On the topic of religion, Palawan must have been the first place that God had in mind when he announced, 'Let there be light'.

Alberto Encounters

After six weeks of having adventures that would never be forgotten, Alexander and Garcia decided to spend the rest of their time in Mandaluyong where Alexander could get to know the Agbayani family. This was a chance for him to develop his personal routine. After a couple of weeks, Garcia's apartment had become his second home. To manage his new life, he set up a weekly schedule that allowed him to socialise as well as experience Manila and get all his daily tasks done.

Monday	*Spend time with the Agbayani family*
Tuesday	*Spend time with Garcia's cousins*
Wednesday	*Meet Garcia's friends*
	Visit Mall of Asia
Thursday	*Get all the house jobs done*
	Video call my family members
Friday	*Go to the market to buy groceries*
	Watch a band
Saturday	*Travel around Manila*
	Watch my favourite films with Garcia
Sunday	*Go to church*

Alexander was feeling incredibly proud of himself that he was able to establish a new routine. He and Garcia were the perfect match, she provided him with a sense of security that made him feel safe. Apart from the constant interruptions from neighbour Manuel, who felt the need to offer his services four times a week. Garcia would shield him from the overenthusiastic local Filipinos who might make Alexander feel too weary of his surroundings. But when Alexander did venture out alone, he made sure to move briskly and subtly like a leopard, so that he could avoid being detected by what he called the 'foreign cash poachers' or by what normal people would refer to as street sellers. Alexander would only enter stores and markets that were nearby to him, he would avoid the local public transport and taxis. The main transport that Alexander couldn't stand was the 'sardine wagons' or what Filipino people refer to as 'jeepneys'. Every uncomfortable sensation imaginable all rolled into one – having no personal space, having no air con, no way of stopping it other than shouting 'para', which Alexander did not want to shout. He also didn't have a comfortable seat, so he had to constantly budge up and sit between strangers. Garcia kept telling him that it was good transport because it was cheap and there were plenty of them. Alexander kept protesting using this transport, saying these sardine wagons were tree killers and should be obsolete.

The next challenge Alexander had to keep on top of was the money-spending. This paper nightmare was rustling away in his mind. Alexander's pockets were normally full to the brim of tissues, half-used tissues and some used tissues as well as wet wipes and various other bits and bobs that he couldn't remember putting there. His solution was to wear a money belt. This solution worked well for a while until the humid air caused him to develop a fever. In Alexander's mind, the dry season was when his nose stopped running and the wet season was when snot was constantly streaming out of his nose. This balance between tissues, wet wipes and cash was proving a problem, he only had small pockets and his demand was ever-increasing. The scorching heat was causing Alexander's skin to sweat and for his lips to crack; this required constant wet wipe use. All the unusual smells and dust caused a mild fever, this required extensive tissue consumption. The demand for cash was also a problem since Alexander found it difficult keeping hold of things. This money belt was supposed to be his solution, a way of managing all his clutter – in fact this money belt became the biggest problem. The whole reason for him wearing one was to protect himself from pickpockets, but when he purchased this belt, he hadn't considered his fidgety and picky nature. This belt became a distraction for his restless sweaty fingers, his fingers were drawn to this belt like a swarm of flies drawn to a pile of excrement left out in the hot sun.

Due to Alexander's unusual obsession with objects and recording things, he had to take out his money to count how much he had left every time he entered a shop and every time that he had completed a purchase. Not only did he need to constantly count his money, but he also needed to record everything in his notepad. This created a chaotic juggling game between his cash, phone, notepad, tissues, wet wipes and keys. Alexander had a backpack that he would bring with him, but this would only add to the confusion. Alexander needed a routine for all his possessions, yet this routine could be disrupted at any moment. There were many occasions where he would find his money belt full of used tissues and wet wipes and his pockets full of cash. Taking care of his phone and keys was a challenge; Garcia noticed him moving his belongings around a lot so she would often confiscate them and put these objects in her small handbag. This of course rattled his cage a bit, but he knew that his belongings were in safer hands with her.

A further challenge for Alexander was his attire. The usual tourist attire would be shorts and a white shirt and sandals, but this was too revealing for his taste. You see, Alexander was quite a skinny guy, he could also be a bit oafish when it came to his appearance. He wanted to make himself appear bigger, so he would often wear more clothes than what he needed to wear. When he was with Garcia, he felt like he could copy the usual tourist dress code but when he was by himself, he felt as though he needed extra protection. When Garcia wasn't looking, he would slip on his heavy gear. A jacket over his shirt, heavy boots so that the creepy crawlies wouldn't bite his toes. He also needed an umbrella for protection against the sun and unpredictable torrential rain, this umbrella could also be used as a weapon if Alexander felt like he was being targeted. This was as well as his notepad, which he used to record everything. All this safety gear might appear practical in Alexander's mind but what he wasn't aware of was how much he actually stood out.

Another thing he had to keep up with was the phone messages, his family were constantly asking him questions about his experience. Alexander naturally wanted to keep things to himself and not overshare, but his family, on the other hand, wanted to know exactly what he was up to.

Dad: 'Hello, Alexander, how is your time in the Philippines? Have you remembered to extend your visa, compliment Garcia, withdraw cash and pay your bills?

I'm sure you are having a great time, son, wish I could be there with you. Have you remembered the budgeting strategy that I taught you? Try not to waste your money, and don't let people rip you off.'

Anna: 'Hello, Alexander, just checking to see if everything is going well. We all miss you, and hope that you are enjoying yourself.'

William: 'Hey, Alexander, I bet that you wished you were in Thailand, there are better beaches, more attractions, exotic jungles and cheaper prices. In case you haven't lost your phone again I would like to call you and catch up on what you are doing in the Philippines.'

Samantha: 'How are you doing, Alexander? Your dad keeps talking about you, he wants to know what you are up to. Your dad tells me that you have been having a wonderful time. He also wants to remind you to wear condoms, just saying. Make sure you take care of yourself.'

Martha: 'Hello, how are you, Alexander? Hope that you are enjoying the Philippines, I wish that I could return to my home country. If you want to meet more people, I can get you in touch with all my contacts.'

These messages were typical of weekly communication between Alexander and his family. The overwhelming multitude of phone calls and text messages would often take up an entire day, where he would do nothing but try to respond to all the messages. Despite being a very reserved and reclusive person, Alexander had the passion to want to experience things and meet new people.

Alexander felt as if there was someone following him around every time that he went somewhere with Garcia. It seemed like paranoia at first, but a certain pair of eyes became a bit too familiar to him for his liking.

It was another hot day in Mandaluyong. Alexander was feeling thirsty, so he decided to buy some water at the local Alfamart. So, he slung on his money belt, grabbed his keys and headed out. Everything appeared normal; however, he could sense that something was amiss. The feeling of being watched. Alexander chose to ignore this feeling as he always felt like he was being watched. If Alexander had more spatial or social awareness, he would have noticed the mysterious character that had been following him. His purpose of the journey was to purchase an eight-litre water bottle, yet again Alexander had failed to do the forward planning, which would make this shopping trip much more manageable. Leaving the Alfamart, Alexander had to carry his umbrella, notepad and eight-litre water bottle, but help was waiting just outside of the shop.

"Do you need a hand?" A Filipino man, around 30, with a beer belly, wearing a blue button-up shirt with smart black trousers. He was also wearing a baseball cap. This man's attire was arguably even stranger than Alexander's.

"Uh... yes, no, actually yes, I could do with a hand." Alexander forced these stumbling words out of his mouth.

He seemed to just be loitering around and happened to notice Alexander struggling with his errands or was it not a coincidence that this supposed Good Samaritan was standing in the right place at the right time? He introduced himself as Alberto. He offered to carry the water bottle for Alexander. Naturally, Alexander did not want to accept this offer as he was afraid of being scammed. Due to the pressure of being approached by a stranger, he unwillingly accepted. The two had a chance to get to know each other (or a chance to get to know each other's masks). Alberto claimed that he was a local businessman who worked in finance, he claimed to have a six-figure salary. But the truth of the matter was that he was a former drug dealer who had recently been released from prison. The smart clothes that he was wearing were borrowed from his friends and family, this guy had never even worked in finance! But how was Alexander to know this? Alexander might have been thinking that helping someone who was struggling to carry their shopping would be a very gentlemanly thing to do, like when you offer to carry shopping bags for an elderly woman, but Alexander was no elderly woman and this was the middle of Manila that you're talking about, a city full of all sorts of people with all sorts of intentions.

The next mistake he made was by taking this stranger to Garcia's apartment, he also made the mistake of revealing personal information about himself such as his real full name and he also mentioned his routine. He gave this supposed 'Alberto' all the ammo he needed to take full advantage of him. Alberto offered to take the water inside Garcia's apartment, Alexander wanted to refuse but the heat and social pressure was getting to him, so he relented and opened the front door for Alberto. This, of course, didn't go down well with Garcia, who had no idea who Alberto was. Alexander tried to sneak Alberto into the apartment, so he could get this extremely awkward encounter over and done with, but he ended up being caught out by Garcia. He pretended that Alberto was a delivery boy to avoid being lectured about the 'dos and don'ts' of the Philippines.

The next mistake Alexander made was showing his money belt to Alberto and asking him how much. "Uh… how much?" Alexander awkwardly asked.

"One thousand only," Alberto came up with spontaneously, almost like a magician pulling a rabbit out of a hat.

One thousand pesos is equivalent to 20 US dollars, this of course was way too much for the meticulously budgeting Alexander to hand out. The sheer panic and anxiety of this awkward social situation meant that Alexander was willing to do anything just to escape. He handed the money without making any eye contact and quickly said, "Salamat po."

Alberto's reaction was far more expressive. "Thank you, sir, thank you, sir, thank you so much." Alexander stood by the doorway with his head down, just wanting Alberto to piss off. "I can help you anytime you want, do you want to give me your number?" Alexander did certainly not want to hand his number to some stranger who had taken 1000 pesos from him. Alexander felt like he had no choice but to give his number. Alberto gave Alexander a big pat on the back, which made him freeze like a statue. "Bye, Alexander, bye, Garcia."

"Uh, bye, Alberto."

This encounter with Alberto brought Alexander much anxiety, he felt like he was being watched 24/7. He spent the rest of the day wondering what he should have done differently, the anticipation of where and when Alberto was going to strike next was killing him. Two days had passed, and Alexander heard nothing from him, but this was just the eye of the hurricane. Alexander received a text message inviting him to a club at six in the morning, this of course raised alarm bells, so Alexander decided not to respond to it. The lingering fear was causing Alexander to pretend that he was feeling sick, so that he would not have to witness Alberto's next surprise. After a week of avoiding going out by himself, he decided that he had had enough of hiding away. *It can't hurt just to buy some stuff from Alfamart*, he thought to himself.

He plucked up the courage to enter Alfamart, thinking that he was just being paranoid. As he was making his way to the shop, he noticed someone dressed in a clown costume. *Not now*, he thought to himself, *all I want to do is buy some stuff from Alfamart, how difficult can it bloody be?* It turned out that Alberto had been planning a surprise for Alexander. What exactly was the purpose of this, to scare Alexander, to make Alexander laugh? Now Alexander had to worry about a crackhead clown on the loose.

Alexander thought about heading back but he didn't want Alberto to think of him as a pussy, so he decided to enter the shop when the clown wasn't looking. Of course, Alexander was carrying his notepad with him as well as his umbrella and was wearing his blue jacket. He was standing a few feet away from the clown, hovering around whilst reading his notes. Alexander's plan was to wait for the clown to disappear so that he could finish his shopping trip in peace. Instead of disappearing, the clown started talking to Alexander.

"Hey, Alexander, do you like my costume?"

The realisation that this was Alberto's voice sent shockwaves throughout Alexander's body, causing him to drop his notepad on the ground. Alberto offered to pick it up, but Alexander quickly snatched it up.

"Nice to see you, Alexander, I have been to a party today, that's why I am dressed as a clown."

"Uh… yeah, cool," Alexander responded.

"Do you want me to help you with your shopping?"

"No, I'm fine," Alexander responded coldly.

He unfolded his umbrella (this was happening during the rainy season, so Alexander never knew when it was going to rain so he would walk around with his umbrella fully extended even when it was sunny).

"Have a wonderful shopping trip," Alberto said in a loud and bubbly voice.

"Yes, I will," Alexander quickly replied, trying to end the awkward encounter as quickly as possible.

He had only entered the shop to buy a bottle of coke and some tissues, but the lingering presence of this clown was making him feel excruciatingly uncomfortable. After five minutes, Alberto was still hovering around chatting to random strangers. To pass the time, Alexander read the product information for random objects to pretend that he was busy. After every biscuit packet, drink or other item that he would read the back of, Alexander would take a glance to see if the clown was still outside. After 15 minutes of this, Alexander's patience was starting to wear thin. *I hate clowns, why do there have to be clown sightings in the Philippines?* After the purchase was complete, Alexander slowly tiptoed behind the clown in an attempt to leave undetected.

He managed to leave the shop without Alberto noticing him, but a few metres later he hears, "Hey, Alexander, do you want me to carry anything for you?"

Alexander stood still, wanting to ignore Alberto, but he quickly turned round and shook his head with his arms flapping around, making himself appear like a distressed chicken.

Alexander spent the rest of the day trembling; he kept wondering what Alberto was planning to do next. He went to bed with his pillow on top of his head, trying to calm himself down.

"Are you OK, Alexander?"

"Uh, yes, no, I think I have the flu again.

"Ah OK, rest na Alexander."

Alexander took some sleep for a few hours. After this sleep he woke up and spent the evening with Garcia feeling very shaky. Alexander did not want to mention his latest clown sighting, so he started waffling on about the planets in the solar system instead.

After spending the evening together, they both headed to bed. Alexander tried to sleep but the terrifying thoughts of Alberto breaking into the apartment dressed as a killer clown, holding a long knife, kept spinning round and round in his graphic mind. This was a night in the rainy season, the torrential downpour coupled with the constant thunder and lightning strikes was creating an atmosphere of internal dread. Alexander decided to sit down on the sofa and stare at the wall clock to see what time it was.

It was 12:25 in the morning. Alexander paced back and forth for five minutes, reflecting on the day's events. The hands on the wall clock suddenly pointed towards the window, a warning from Pvormlu. Alexander immediately turned his head and noticed a figure that was lingering around his street. This figure appeared to be walking back and forth holding an umbrella – walking in the same manner that Alexander would be when he needed to process his thoughts. Alexander pressed his face against the window in the same manner which a child would when spying on a neighbour. Upon closer inspection, he realised that it was Alberto!

Alexander's instincts told him to check the locks on the front door and make sure that the windows were shut, he then bolted up the stairs and into the bedroom like a bat out of hell. The fear was so great that Alexander cautiously but also forcefully removed the thin duvet from Garcia with the tenacity of a professional bank robber. He hid under the bed, hoping that he would find solace under it. What a night this was going to be!

Garcia woke the next morning, wondering where on earth her duvet was. "Alexander!" she called out.

"Uh, yes, I'm here."

"Why are you under my bed?"

"I uh… I think that I might have fallen off the bed, I think I had a dream where I was wrestling Cockroach Man. I was so repulsed by Cockroach Man that I hid under the bed to avoid him," Alexander said, whilst coming up with the worst story that Garcia had ever heard.

"Who won?" she asked.

"Who won what?" Alexander replied, not really thinking about the story that he just fabricated.

"The wrestling match between you and the Cockroach Man."

"Uh… I can't really remember that well, I believe that I pulled its head off but then I hid under the bed, in case Cockroach Man came back for revenge. You know cockroaches can survive without a head. As you might already know, Garcia, I can't stand cockroaches and spiders, if a spider or cockroach is in the room, then I'm out of the room."

"So it isn't that you are scared of something or someone in the real world?"

"Well, OK, fine, I lied about Cockroach Man. You know that guy who delivered the eight-litre water bottle?"

"Yes, what about him?"

"He is not a delivery boy, his name is Alberto, I met him in the street."

"So, do you know him?"

"Uh... I don't, I do, I don't really know him, I think he is stalking me."

"Why you think that?" Garcia replied, sounding confused.

"Every time I go to the Alfamart he is there as if he knows what I'm doing every minute of the day."

"Maybe he works there?"

"I don't think so, I think that he is trying to scam me." A quivering Alexander took out his notepad and showed Garcia all the detailed notes on his interactions with Alberto.

"Why have you written this down?"

"I didn't think that people would take me seriously."

"Why do you think that he is trying to scam you?"

"Can I write my calculations on the wall?" Alexander asked gingerly.

"Certainly not," Garcia quickly replied.

"I think he is trying to scam me because I wear this jacket, I think that the colour blue attracts attention because it represents the sea, he might think that I am rich because I walk around with an umbrella like Mary Poppins. Seeing as I'm English, he might think that

I come from the upper social class. I also think that my notepad makes me look like I'm from the middle class, he might think that I'm some businessman who has lots of money."

"No, that wasn't the question."

"Uh… what, I thought you asked me 'why do you think he is trying to scam you'."

"I meant what has he done to make you think that he is stalking you or trying to steal from you?"

"Oh, thanks for the clarification." Garcia rolled her eyes. "Apart from bumping into him every time I buy something at the Alfamart, he wears strange clothes. Now I know that I wear strange clothes as well, but his attire is even stranger than mine."

"How can his attire be stranger than yours?" Garcia replied flippantly.

"Well, you see, not only does he wear smart clothes when he is shopping at Alfamart but he also wore a clown costume the last time that I went shopping at Alfamart." Garcia started laughing. "Why are you laughing, I'm terrified out of my mind thinking that I'm going to be murdered in my sleep by a Filipino killer clown who wants to rob me, and you are laughing!"

"Maybe he is just having a bit of fun and messing around."

"Messing around?"

"Yes probably," Garcia replied. "You still haven't told me why you were hiding under the bed like a scared child."

"I saw him walking around last night, he knows where we live."

"Oh my God, do you think that he is watching us?" Garcia asked, panicking.

"I'm afraid so."

"What should we do about Alberto?" Garcia asked.

"I have been brainstorming this in my notepad for a while," Alexander replied.

"Let's see these ideas."

"Plan A: we wear disguises so that Alberto won't notice us."

"Hmm, how do you say it in British English – rubbish." Garcia did not like this idea.

"OK, that was just one option. Plan B: we dress up as killer clowns and follow Alberto around to give him a taste of his own medicine."

"I'm not dressing as a killer clown," Garcia replied.

"You haven't heard Plan C."

"What's plan C?"

"We will report him to the police."

"I thought I told you that was the only option, why is that Option C?" Garcia asked. "I don't think that the police will do anything, it seems like a last resort here."

"So how are we going to stop him terrorising us?" she asked.

"I think we can set up a security camera to record what he does."

"That sounds like a good idea but how are we going to stop him following you around?"

"I suggest that we confront him to see what he is up to. You, me, Tita Genie and even Papa Michael, give him a taste of his own medicine."

"That sounds like a great idea," Alexander replied.

The pair set their plan in motion. It was evident that Alberto would only make an appearance when it was just Alexander. The plan was for Alexander to walk towards the Alfamart alone, wait for Alberto to make an appearance, then the three Filipinos would charge towards him like a pack of angry wolves, forcing him to confess to stalking Alexander. They waited three days for Alexander to build the confidence to confront his Filipino demon.

It was a Monday morning around 10am. Alexander had finished having breakfast with Garcia's family, it was now time to confront Alberto! Alexander decided that he would wear typical foreigner clothes this time (which included a white shirt, shorts and sandals). The fear of being kidnapped by Alberto was causing Alexander's hands to shake, the other fear that Alexander had was being bitten by an insect, rat or dog. To combat this fear, Alexander would take one long step at a time, look both ways as if he were crossing a road, then proceed forwards for a few steps, then stop and check both ways for any surprise visitors. He walked further along the street until Alfamart came into view. As expected, Alberto made an appearance. This time his attire had changed completely; it was as if Alexander was hallucinating. Alberto was dressed and behaving like Alexander. Alexander had his official confirmation right then and there that Alberto was officially a madman and needed to be sectioned. He was wearing the same blue jacket as Alexander, very similar brown boots, a black umbrella, and he was even carrying a notepad! What the hell was going on? It was like some kind of alternate reality deja vu experience for Alexander, he just stared in utter disbelief.

Not far behind him were Garcia, Tita Genie and Papa Michael. They were yet to discover the surprise of the century. Alexander froze in complete shock, not knowing whether this was some sort of hallucination, or was Alberto some sort of Filipino spy sent to find out information about Alexander?

"Nice to see you again, Alexander, look what I'm wearing, nice jacket, useful umbrella, I love these brown boots, and I have written everything about you in my notepad."

Alexander, still completely dumbfounded, just stared, motionless, at Alberto. Luckily, the three Filipino heroes jumped in to save the day. However, the shocking realisation hit them just as hard as it hit Alexander. The three of them froze, unable to process what was going on.

"Nice to meet you again, Garcia, nice to meet you, Tita Genie, nice to meet you, Papa Michael."

This psychotic Alberto stuck his hand out, trying to shake their hands but no one was able to respond to this surreal experience. The skies were turning grey again, it appeared that the rain might be coming earlier than expected. Alexander glanced up at the sky as if looking for answers from God. This reaction was synchronised by Garcia, Tita Genie and Papa Michael; they all stared at the grey sky as if waiting for God's response. Alexander then made eye contact with Alberto (something he rarely did). He pulled a wrathful facial expression and, for the first time ever, Alexander was standing his ground. "I don't know what you think you are playing at, mate, this is Alexander Sommervale who you are messing with."

This unusual confrontation was followed by thunder, which elevated his presence making it appear that he was talking using the voice of God.

This speech of immense bravery was followed by, "I don't know what you think you are playing at, mate, this is Garcia Agbayani who you are messing with."

"I don't know what you think you are playing at, mate, this is Tita Genie who you are messing with."

"I don't know what you think you are playing at, mate, this is Pappa Michael who you are messing with."

These thunderous echoing phrases sent Alberto into a state of shock, now he was frozen solid!

"We know who you are already, na," Garcia said, taking advantage of Alberto's silence. "Come here again, papatayin kita (I will kill you)."

"I never forget a face, that's why I have 2000 friends on Facebook," Papa Michael said with a serious expression on his face.

"You have got me all wrong, naman, I like Alexander."

"As in like-like Alexander?" Tita Genie asked.

"Yes I do like Alexander very much. I have been trying to impress him, make him laugh. I want to prove that I am better for him than Garcia."

Pappa Michael burst out laughing.

"Why you are laughing, na?" Tita Genie asked Pappa Michael.

"I'm laughing because I know that there is no competition for Garcia," Papa Michael responded.

Alberto pulled out a letter and showed it to Alexander. It was a love letter.

I am writing to confess my feelings of love towards you. Ever since you moved to Mandaluyong, I have longed to stroke your hair and hold you tight. Every time I see you, my heart dances with joy. There is not a moment that I don't think of you.

I know that I have entered your life unexpectedly, but I am here to stay forever and ever. When I gaze up at the stars, I always think of you, you are my star.

Don't worry about Garcia, I can explain to her, I bet she doesn't make adobo like I can. I know we are forbidden to love but I can make us real.

Here is my address: 37 Claridel street, Mandaluyong, Manila.

Shh, keep us a secret, don't go telling anyone.

Charot na

"So, what do you think of my love letter, Mr Alexander?"

"Do you have a bucket anywhere?" Alexander flippantly replied.

"Why aren't you interested?" Alberto wailed like a spoiled child.

"Well, I appreciate the gesture and love letter, but as you can see, I'm not single and I'm not attracted to guys, so..."

"We are forbidden love; can't you see that?"

"Yes, we are forbidden love, so we shouldn't be together."

"Please, Alexander, we could be so happy together."

"What planet are you on, Alberto?"

"Why won't you give us a chance?"

"Reason one: I don't know who the bloody hell you are. Reason two: I'm not single. Reason three: I'm heterosexual. Reason four: your stunts made me lose sleep. Reason five: you scare the hell out of me. I appreciate this love letter, but I am not on the market."

Alberto's demeanour changed from romantic begging to confrontation. "You white snob, you are full of yourself, think you are special because you have money?"

"I think that we done," Alexander replied to this outburst.

"You will never be done with me, mark my words."

"If you come near me again, we will report you to the police," Alexander stressed with complete conviction.

"You will report me to the police? What a joke, all the police care about is money, they won't listen to you even if you have money," Alberto said mockingly.

"I know what will get rid of you," Papa Michael announced.

"Ano?" Alberto asked.

"I will report you to all of your friends and family members."

"You can't do that."

"Oh yes I can, I have all your Facebook information right here." Papa Michael showed Alberto all the information that he had gathered about him. "I will also unfriend you from Facebook, I'm willing to go down from 2000 followers to 1999 followers."

"Fine, you have won, but I will be back." Alberto walked away like a stroppy teenager.

"You added Alberto on Facebook?" Garcia asked.

"Long story."

Alexander shook Papa Michael's hand. "I owe you a drink," Alexander said confidently.

"You owe me a drink and a friend request; you will be my 2000th Facebook friend."

"That's a deal," Alexander exclaimed.

The four walked back to Garcia's apartment, only to be disturbed yet again by Neighbour Manuel. "Ah, hello, Alexander, I can fix your gate for 30,000 pesos only."

"Fix what?" Alexander asked, confused.

"Fix everything."

"I think we'll pass," Alexander replied.

"What about fixing your front door locks?"

"What about fixing the front door locks?" Alexander replied flippantly.

"I can fix your front door locks for 10,000 pesos only."

"I'll think we'll pass on that as well," Alexander replied.

The First Farewell, July 19th, 2023

After three months together, it was time for Alexander to return to England as he needed to make plans for his future. The pair promised each other that they would message each other every day. They decided to write each other a farewell letter.

To my beloved Garcia,

As a timorous lonely pigeon from England, I have flown over six thousand miles to meet you, my beautiful perfect swan from Manila. I am so grateful for you for allowing me to spread my wings. We will always be soaring high above what anyone might see of us. What a pleasure it has been to dance with you, my flamboyant flamingo. What a pleasure it has been to sing with you, my musical songbird. My cheeky parrot, who always reminds me how silly I sound. My woodpecker who never lets me forget the things I need to do. My hummingbird, who always lifts my mood. My loyal dove who is always open and honest with me about everything. My wise owl who always knows what's best for me. We can remain as eagles forever, too fast and agile for anyone to stop us. Ravens by sunrise, seagulls by sunset.

For as far as my arms may stretch, I will reach for you. For as fast as my legs may move, I will run to you. What a wonderful experience we have shared together, thank you for being my first true soulmate.

Mahal kita.
Alexander Sommervale

Dear Alexander, my precious asawa,

I have enjoyed having you in my life, very much. From the very beginning, you have shown me a side of yourself that you have never shown anyone before. At first, I couldn't understand you, but now I have grown closer to you than I could have ever imagined. You have taught me what it is to be romantic, what it means to love someone who is so different from myself. You are my missing piece; you make me complete. For a thousand years you will always be the one.

Thank you so much for taking me on this wonderful adventure.

Mahal Kita.
Garcia Agbayani

Whilst Alexander was writing this euphony, he imagined different birds representing their combined spirits. This feeling of escapism inspired Alexander to consider making serious decisions and life plans that would enable him to be the bird that he wanted to be. Whilst writing these romantic ideas, Alexander gazed up at the sky and started listening to 'A Summer Place 'by Percy Faith. He only listened to the orchestra performance, and this song stayed in his head for a while and made him feel more at ease with his departure.

These letters exchanged hands with the swiftness of a butterfly. Butterflies were fluttering around in their stomachs. The last moments of this epic adventure were spent by Alexander and Garcia silently staring at each other, trying to hold back their tears. Alexander decided to show Garcia a dance routine that he had envisioned in his head. He called this the 'Clock Dance'. This routine was a way in which Alexander could show his appreciation for everything that the furniture being had done for him.

Garcia had no idea what this dance routine was about, but she was looking forward to it greatly. The left arms would be held out at a 45-degree angle, with the left hand stuck out in chopping position, whilst the right arm would move in a clockwise motion. One person would be leading the clock dance, they would be moving in the clockwise direction whilst their partner would mirror them, moving their right arm in a counterclockwise direction. The dance routine consisted of three clock hand orbits. The first orbit would reflect Pvormlu's clock expressions, the second orbit would increase the speed of the rotation by only stopping at every quarter turn and the third orbit would encompass a full cycle in one fluid motion. At the one o'clock position, the couple would give each other a faint smile, at two o'clock, the couple would widen their smile, showing their joyous connection. At the three o'clock position, they would give each other concerned looks. At the four o'clock position, they would place their foreheads together whilst concentrating hard on the ground. At the five o'clock position, they would rest their heads on their partner's shoulder. At the six o'clock position, they would stare at their shoes in disappointment. At the seven o'clock position, they would establish a connection as if a great idea had suddenly come to them both, they would both raise an eyebrow to create this effect. At the eight o'clock position, they would give each other a proud look, they would both wink at each other. At nine o'clock they would stare at each other with intense eye contact. At the ten o'clock position, they would look up at each other as if there was a loud noise. At 11 o'clock, their heads would be turning side to side as if they were trying to find out where they were. At the 12 o'clock position, they would both look up at the stars with their arms raised high in the air.

During the second clock orbit, the speed would increase, as would their determination to connect with each other. The rotation would stop at three o'clock, six o'clock and nine o'clock. The third orbit would be the fastest and most passionate, one quick powerful fluid movement. After the first dance routine was completed, their roles would swap as the follower became the leader. Alexander wanted to thank Pvormlu for inspiring him to take on this journey. He decided to send a symbolic message to Pvormlu. They were gracing each other's presence. They went round again, this time they started picking up the pace, cathartic giggles were bubbling away. The final arm clock orbit went by with maximum strength and determination – not only was this a sign of admiration and gratitude for Pvormlu, but it was a sign that time was going to fly by as fast as they wanted it to.

New Life Plan, August 21st, 2023

After weeks of grieving Garcia's absence, Alexander realised that he needed to come up with a plan of where he should go with his life. Alexander had three A-levels: English literature, English language and German. The prospect of attending a university was too daunting for him so he decided not to apply. Instead, Alexander chose to look for jobs, but due to his social inadequacy and lack of perseverance, he was unable to start anything. Alexander's depression made it difficult for him to find motivation in day-to-day life, even wriggling himself out of bed was a mighty challenge most days. All he could manage was ten hours a week volunteering at the local community centre and library. His social life at this time was non-existent, only seeing distant contacts once every two weeks, if not that only once a month. He also lacked the confidence to socialise at bars and nightclubs, so he would only mingle with women remotely. This cycle of unemployment and social isolation dragged on until his mum was unfortunately diagnosed with cancer. This period of his life caused him to retreat into himself even further than he had ever done before. Alexander wanted to be there for his mum in the most supportive way possible but all the commotion from the extended family and treatment options were stressing him out to the point where he struggled to visit her as often as he should have. Alexander also had difficulty with expressing emotions, he didn't know how to show that he cared, he always felt like just being there wasn't enough, but with Tony and Anna working tirelessly to provide all the treatment and moral support, Alexander could only linger in the background, making futile attempts to be useful.

Over the three-month period, during Rose Sommervale's horrific decline, Alexander felt powerless. He wanted to help his dying mother, but he had no idea what his role was. He purchased a load of medical books based on cancer research and spent hours reading them and writing notes on the walls of his bedroom, almost as if he was trying to solve a complicated maths problem.

The next few years after this ordeal went by with the Sommervale family trying to reconnect but things were never the same. Rose Sommervale was the glue that held the family together. She was the cement of the household. It was like the family were living in a house which was built by builders carelessly piling bricks on top of each other without cement, a house that could collapse at any moment. Alexander felt proud of himself for managing to work at The First Inn, he felt even more proud of himself for being able to meet Garcia and showing how much she meant to him.

The next mountain to climb was the career mountain. Anna and William had already started their journey, now it was time for Alexander to join them. Alexander set about coming up with a plan of what he should do next with his life.

New Life Plan

Apply for a literature and modern language course at different universities.
Remotivate myself to find a job that I enjoy doing.
Work out how to use public transport effectively.
Learn new life skills that will help me progress.

This new life plan of his would require an immense effort as Alexander would have to learn how to become a completely different person. Alexander felt that he was up to the challenge. It was just a matter of discussing his plans with his family.

After weeks of informative discussions with his family, Alexander decided that he was ready to apply for different universities.

"You can join me at Oxford University, there are plenty of courses for you there," Anna said, showing her full support.

"I don't know if there are any spaces left at my university," William replied with a smug look on his face.

"I didn't attend university until I was 25," Tony said, reassuring Alexander that he was making the right decision.

"I think that I could study a foreign language to become a translator or maybe a proofreader."

"You should study to become a mind-reader, that will be more interesting than correcting full stops and capital letters," William remarked.

"Correcting full stops and capital letters is more entertaining than reading your mind," Alexander responded.

"Nice one," Anna praised Alexander.

"Are you familiar with how to use public transport? I've got a travel card that you can borrow," Tony offered.

"I have learnt how to use different types of public transport," Alexander replied.

"If not, I have a mate of a mate of a mate who can give you a lift," said William.

"I don't think you have that many mates," Alexander replied.

"I will be able to give you a lift in my BMW once I'm a successful international lawyer."

"That's if you are able to pay off all your debts," Alexander replied.

"The only person I'm indebted to is God himself."

"When was the last time that you went to church?" Alexander asked.

"Five years ago, but I know that God is always with me, what else would explain my marathon results and my perfect grades?"

"That's five years without visiting a church!" Anna said.

"I know that God is always with me, so I have no need to go to a church."

"I go to church every week," Anna replied.

This plan appeared to be the best option for Alexander as he needed a career path, something that would give him financial success as well as a meaningful life. Alexander had dreams of writing a panegyric, then reading it in front of a crowd of active listeners. Even though Alexander struggled with social confidence, he had so much inner charisma built up inside of him like dynamite waiting to explode. Even though his views and opinions about university were that they were crowded, a building built like a maze, exams that were designed to make you fail, teachers who had no patience for slackers, sleepless nights, and having to share a dorm with a potential villain, he knew that it was now or never.

Ninth Encounter, September 25th, 2023

Alexander was deeply missing Garcia. He spent his days applying for jobs and flicking through his photo album, wishing that he was still in the Philippines. Alexander was sitting at his kitchen table, twiddling his necklace that Garcia gave to him. The necklace gave Alexander a very redolent feeling. Despite all the video chats that they had participated in and all the messages that he had received from her, the hole in his heart wasn't getting any smaller. He picked up a photo taken of them both which showed their favourite romantic pose (the lipstick and balloon selfie). He placed it next to the photo of his younger self kneeling in front of the clock snowman. Seeing this photo made him feel complete. On the left side he wrote 'maganda', on the right side he wrote 'perfect', on the top he wrote 'angel', at the bottom he wrote 'asawa'. This was written in the colour yellow. Alexander's feeling of hope was now greater than ever before.

He turned to face his bedroom window and spent a long five minutes gazing up the blue sky. He noticed that the furniture being was staring out of the window alongside him. Alexander wanted to be free again, he wanted to explore more of the world instead of having to start a new life in the UK. Alexander turned around and discovered the same wooden ramp that he had seen before. Pvormlu also turned around to face the wooden ramp, revealing the green sofa, which was shifting left and right, signalling to Alexander for him to take a ride. He sat down, and used the cushions to strap himself in. Pvormlu started taxiing up the ramp, the roof runway came into view.

Lap one: a slow and cautious cycle. Lap two: the speed increased to a moderate speed; Alexander started to feel the gravity changing from beneath him. Lap three: Pvormlu accelerated, Alexander felt like he was on a rollercoaster. Up the ramp and off into the quaint wilderness, a quintessential journey that made Alexander feel like he was a member of the royal family. This extravagant journey reminded him of the wonderful beauty that existed in his local area. The furniture being went across the iconic Cotswolds in a zigzag motion, creating a very dynamic ride. The furniture being gave Alexander an aerial tour of Cheltenham, Cirencester and Stroud. As Alexander witnessed the various species of birds flying past, he remembered the 'Summer's Place' theme tune. Alexander saw himself as a free-spirited bird that could conquer anything.

Awkward Encounter with Sophie and Sophia, December 15th, 2023

Alexander was shopping in Sainsbury's, walking around with his shopping notepad which he used as a shopping list. He was walking past the hot drinks aisle when he spotted two identical old women arguing over tea.

"We should get PG Tips."

"No that's too expensive, we need Tetley's."

"Tetley's is weak, we need Earl Grey. Put the Tetley's down."

"No, I'm not putting the Tetley's down, you put the Early Grey back."

Alexander recognised their faces as Sophie and Sophia, he quickly looked away, hoping that they had not noticed his presence. Alexander hated unexpected encounters with people who he hadn't seen in years, it felt like he was being haunted by ghosts. Alexander increased his pace. *Butter – check, eggs – check, bacon – check, chocolate – check, coke – check, doughnuts – not yet, apples – not yet, milk – check, tea – check. Oh shit, I need to get the tea when the coast is clear. If I walk slowly, it will increase the chances of Sophie and Sophia leaving but if I walk quickly, it will increase my chances of making it out of here before they leave.*

I think that they might be here all day, knowing them, so I should make a run for it. Alexander quickly ticked off his checklist. *Just tea to go.*

Alexander was hoping that Sophie and Sophia would have resolved their differences and would have decided which tea to buy, but, to his horror, they were still arguing. Alexander leaned against the aisle, taking occasional peaks to see if Sophie and Sophia were still there. He felt like James Bond waiting for the mafia bosses to leave the premises of their secret project so he could gain intelligence on the activity. He picked up his phone to pretend that he was busy doing something. Emails, flicking up and flicking down, taking a peek – they were still there. WhatsApp messages, flicking up and flicking down, they were still there. Notifications, flicking up and flicking down, it looked like they might be leaving. *Yes!* Luckily, they had agreed to buy PG Tips, Tetley's and Earl Grey, two each to be specific, like the hoarders they were. They exited on the opposite end of the aisle. Alexander used this opportunity to sneak in and retrieve the PG Tips. "Butter –check, eggs – check, bacon – check, chocolate – check, coke – check doughnuts – check, apples – check, milk – check, tea – check, that's checkmate, I have got everything that I need," Alexander whispered to himself.

He saw Sophie and Sophia heading away from the checkout tills, so he quickly headed to the self-checkout. *Oh shit, there's a queue, still I don't think that they will be heading this way anytime soon,* he thought to himself. As the queue shortened, Alexander felt like he was going to make it out of there without being caught. Of course, that was just his belief, in reality the slow tortoises had become the hares. They were now in a rush to finish their shopping, Agent Sommervale was completely oblivious that villains, Sophie and Sophia, were right behind him. *Mission complete*, Alexander thought to himself.

Three, two, one. "Alexander! Hello, Alexander, over here!"

This unexpected call-out sent a rush of adrenaline through Alexander's body. *Oh shit*, he thought to himself, *I have been compromised, what should I do? Judy Dench isn't here so I have to come up with something myself.* Alexander knew that the voice was coming from behind him, but he pretended to look elsewhere as if he couldn't work out the source of the noise. Alexander flicked his head in different directions – up and down, side to side, as if he was doing neck stretching exercises. *They won't be able to identify me just by the back of my head, maybe it's another Alexander who they are calling*. Alexander kept this up for seven seconds until the attention was becoming too much for him.

"Hello, Alexander, behind you."

Alexander was the only one who was looking in the opposite direction of the noise. He decided to slowly turn around and face the music. Sophie and Sophia were frantically calling his name and waving at him. Alexander decided to give them a wave back, whilst feeling the presence of fellow shoppers and staff all glaring at the situation in complete confusion. Alexander didn't normally have a problem with interacting with people but unexpected interactions at awkward times made Alexander feel as if human interaction was impossible.

"Hello, Sophia and Sophie, no – Sophia and Sophia, I meant Sophie and Sophia."

"How are you doing, Alexander? Long time, no see."

"Uh… yes, I'm just waiting in a queue right now. No time, long see." Alexander attempted a quick joke but the puzzled looks on everyone's faces told him that the joke didn't go down too well.

"OK, Alexander, see you again soon."

"See you, Sophie and Sophia."

Alexander was so relieved when the awkward encounter was over. He was not expecting to ever see those two again. He enjoyed his experience volunteering but did not want to get sucked back into the chaotic world of Sophie and Sophia.

Adventure at Blaise with Martha, April 16th, 2024

Alexander was frequently video calling Garcia; they made a lot of promises together. Alexander took a multitude of selfies to meet the needs of Garcia, whilst Garcia learnt how to play chess to meet the needs of Alexander. He was offered a place at Oxford studying literature and foreign languages, and Garcia was so pleased for him. She told him that college was a great experience for her as it taught her everything that she needed to know. However, Alexander was only 50 per cent pleased because he saw a very steep mountain ahead of him and he wasn't sure that he could climb it. Everyone was trying to convince him that he would enjoy it and strive in the academic environment because Alexander was very studious. The social and organisational aspects worried him the most.

Martha offered to drive Alexander from Stroud to Blaise Estate, a journey that she had never been on before but was confident that she could easily make. Some people might think that it wouldn't be a good idea for Alexander to be spending time alone with Martha because she was a Filipina, but Martha had become friends with Garcia as they both came from Manila. In fact, Martha had trained Alexander on how to date a Filipina.

The journey from Stroud to Blaise went well apart from Martha missing a turn and ending up touring around Avonmouth, which Alexander missed because he was sleeping. Once they arrived, Martha immediately sprang into action, deciding what to bring out of her cluttered boot. Spring rolls, a picnic blanket, a selfie stick, some leftover chicken soup, two pairs of sunglasses even though the weather was cloudy, an umbrella, a notepad for Alexander and whatever else they could salvage. After ten minutes of negotiating what to do with their supplies, Martha decided to carry her selfie stick and handbag whilst Alexander carried the picnic backpack and his notepad for historic landmarks. Alexander was wearing sunglasses that Martha had bought for him even though he already had two pairs of sunglasses. Before entering the estate, they agreed to have a picnic. During this time, Martha was video-calling Garcia with her selfie stick waving in the air. Alexander tried his best to act romantic but Martha and Garcia's natural Filipino connection took over, making Alexander appear like a conversational beggar.

"Can I have permission to speak?" Alexander raised his hand in the air.

"Of course you can," Garcia permitted Alexander to speak.

"Uh, I forgot what I was going to say."

"Are you enjoying the trip, Alexander?" Garcia asked.

"Yes, we are having a picnic. Uh… the mansion was built 1796-98 by John Harford, uh, the Harford family resided there for over 100 years, uh, the castle was built in 1766. Um, the area is 650 acres." Alexander slowly read all this information out from his notepad, unaware that Martha and Garcia had already moved on to talking about wedding gossip.

"Alexander is going to university. Wow, how smart he is," Martha said.

"Yes, I know, very smart, he will do very well," Garcia added.

"Thanks, Martha and Garcia," Alexander said.

Alexander and Martha decided to walk into the Blaise estate with Garcia tagging along via Martha's phone screen. As soon as they entered the estate, Alexander felt a familiar presence. Long shadowy table legs were dangling down at the corners of the room. Shadowy curtains were opening and closing over the paintings. He knew this was Pvormlu sending him another message, it appeared that there was going to be much more to this trip than Alexander had expected. They entered the room that contained Victorian ornaments, and it wasn't long until he noticed the Victorian lights. These lights appeared to be glowing for Alexander. He felt like he could see what was happening inside the lights. He felt a warm glow in his heart, which was telling him that he would soon reach someone very important to him.

"Wow, those are British lights?" Martha asked.

"Yes, from the Victorian era, that one is the Victorian streetlight, that one is the desk lamp, that one is the oil lamp."

"Wow, you know the names of all the lights."

"Yes, I am very familiar with Victorian lights, before the use of electricity, lamplighters would use a pole to ignite the flames then return to put them out."

"In some cities in Europe they still have lamplighters to attract tourists, in cities like Wroclaw, Brest and Zagreb."

Martha and Garcia were busy conversing about Batchmates and high school reunions, whilst Alexander was activating his cognitive Encyclopaedia.

Alexander and Martha were now heading down the trail that led to Blaise Castle, they agreed that Blaise Castle would be their next destination. Alexander used Google Maps and his compass to navigate the way whilst Martha kept stopping people and asking for directions. Alexander was unaware that Martha had gone a separate direction, he carried on, determined to find the castle, feeling like a knight in shining armour. The castle came into view. *Wow, this looks interesting,* he thought to himself. *Wait, where is Martha? Maybe she is searching for wildlife.* Two swarms of eight-winged bats came diving in, forming two walls that were surrounding Alexander and the castle. The shadow figure appeared on top of the castle.

"Greetings, Alexander, you have explored the Philippines, you have become quite the traveller. The world is very much your oyster, but you have yet to conquer the battle of your nerves."

"Whatever you have prepared for me, I am ready for, bring it on," Alexander said, more willing than ever to conquer the bats.

"I am glad to hear your enthusiasm, let the battle commence."

The shadow figure poised the stick in a position that made it seem that it was going to throw a spear at him. The bats formed individual lines appearing like rays of bat sunshine. The shadow figure thrusted the stick forwards in a stabbing motion, the bats were darting towards Alexander like meteorites with wings. Alexander has no idea how to respond so he stuck his arms out with wide open hands, he created a wall which the bats couldn't cross, the bats surrounded this impenetrable wall. "Shoo!" Alexander yelled. The bats retreated to their original position. The shadow figure bashed the wooden stick against its shadow head, and the bats swarmed around Alexander, pulling at his clothes and flapping their wings in his face. Alexander remembered that it was best to stay still when bees were attacking you, he tried this tactic, but the bats persisted to attack him. He then remembered that the shadow figure bashed the stick against his head to activate the assault. Alexander slapped his head with his hands. This reaction made the bats disperse like a flock of scared pigeons.

The shadow figure then waved the wooden stick around in a circular motion, the entire unit of bats formed one long curly line. They charged directly towards him. Alexander tried to sidestep this attack, but bats were locked on to their target. Surprisingly, the bats did not aim for his body but went straight under his legs then looped over his head and back under his legs. This unusual formation freaked him out. *A bat wheel? What the fuck?* He tried running around in different directions to exhaust the bats, but the bats didn't seem dizzy at all. Alexander tried jumping in the air, but this only increased the bat wheel from hell. *If I lie down, they will just get bored of me,* he thought to himself. Alexander lay down, but he could feel the weight of the bat wheel on his spine. Alexander stood back up, just to find out that the bloody bats were back at it. An idea dawned on him. *I need to clamp the bat wheel.* Alexander closed his legs – the bats slowed down but then decided to form a loop around his waist instead. He opened his legs which caused the bats to loop between them again. *Maybe I should clamp my arms as well as my legs*. Alexander clamped his legs and arms at the same time, turning his body into a pencil, the bats froze in place. Both Alexander and the bats were frozen – no one could move.

Two minutes went by, and Alexander was shaking with stiffness, he felt as if his limbs were going to crack. The squished bats trying their best to break free. *Unclamp the wheel*, he said to himself. Alexander released his limbs, creating a strong ripping motion. The eight-winged demon bats were sent packing! Instead of retreating, they were sent flying back as if being grabbed behind by an invisible force.

"Well done, Alexander," the shadow figure commended him. "You are now teaching me new tricks, it won't be long until you are the one pointing the stick and I am trying to control the bats."

"Haha, I love exotic animals, and I like waving sticks around," Alexander replied, having no idea what to say.

"This is your castle now, Alexander, you will always be the king of your own destiny."

Martha made a belated appearance. "I was wondering where you were," Alexander said, confused about where Martha had been.

"I met another Filipina called Christine, she has three kids and works as a nurse at Southmead Hospital."

"Cool," Alexander responded.

Alexander and Martha took selfies with the castle in the background.

"So, I was wondering…"

"Yes, Alexander?"

"Do you like Batman?"

"Yes, I do, what's this about?"

"Well, it just so happens that I have been seeing a lot of bats lately, I was thinking that maybe Batman might be around somewhere."

"Seeing a lot of bats? Where?"

"Just everywhere, I have been seeing lots of shadows too."

"Oh, OK," Martha replied, having no idea what Alexander was on about.

Martha showed the castle to Garcia. "Wow, that looks epic, I want to visit that."

"I would love to show this castle to you," Alexander replied.

Alexander decided that they should head back up the trail and sing the 'Grand Old Duke of York' nursery rhyme. Martha was carrying a selfie stick in her right hand and holding Alexander's hand with her left hand. Alexander told Garcia to join in.

Oh, the grand old Duke of York
He had ten thousand men
He marched them up to the top of the hill
And he marched them down again.

Tenth Encounter, 15th July 2024

The Sommervales were sitting around their living room table, discussing this pub crawl event around Bristol that had piqued Tony's interest.

"Who wants to go to this pub crawl event in Bristol city centre?" he asked. At first nobody raised their hand. "Uh, OK, so the first round will be on me." William raised his hand with enthusiasm. "This will be a memorable event, only three pubs, a chance for us to spend some quality time together." Anna raised her hand followed by Alexander who hated drinking events.

The first pub was The Prince of Wales, located in Bishopston. Tony bought them a round of beers which resulted in a lengthy conversation about politics and sport, which made Alexander want to fall asleep. They all had a small meal each. After two beers, Tony was giving a multitude of stories about what he did during his younger days. Anna was buzzing around other drunk women, talking about celebrity gossip and boyfriends. William was flirting with all the women he could find, claiming that he was a top-performing university scholar. Meanwhile, Alexander was left alone with his dad telling him no end of stories, with him responding in one-word replies.

The second pub was the Duke of York, followed by the Clubhaus, harbourside. By the time they had finished the pub crawl, it was like they were a completely new family. Tony was cheering at nothing and burping every few minutes. Anna was singing a collection of songs that had just entered her head and dancing in an uncoordinated fashion. William was leaping around the place like a hyperactive rabbit. Alexander was observing his surroundings with a grin on his face. They were walking along the harbour looking like a family of animated characters. Alexander thought that this trip was worthwhile after all. They started off at Castle Park. Alexander kept looking over the harbour as if he was waiting for something to happen, whilst the other family members could barely keep their eyes open.

Over the other side of the harbour, Alexander could see the furniture being staring at him with intent. The clock facial expression was two o'clock. Alexander was glad that Pvormlu approved of him going on pub crawls, something which Alexander would normally say no to because of all the noise and chaos and unpredictable behaviour from drunk people. Pvormlu activated the beam from the Victorian streetlight, Alexander closed his eyes and soaked in the spiritual power. He could see himself dressed in a suit looking smart, he also noticed that he was holding someone's hand – the size and colour of the hand gave it away as Garcia's. He noticed that she was wearing a white dress – a wedding dress, perhaps. Alexander imagined the two of them walking in along the Bristol Harbour holding hands.

They were walking near the Queen Square. His drunk family were babbling away, talking about anything that happened to enter their heads, whilst Alexander was fixated on the harbour, waiting for Pvormlu to reappear. The time was now 9pm. Alexander was drunk with internal pleasure, seemingly not reacting to the alcohol the same way his family were. Pvormlu came into view again, this time the oil lamp was releasing a bright mist. Alexander was curious to know what was going to appear in this mist. He saw his five-year-old self holding a Winnie the Pooh teddy bear in one hand and a *Mr Men* book in the other. This vision of his former self was waving at him with the objects in his hands, Alexander decided to wave back.

"Who are you waving to?" Anna asked in a slurred voice.

"He is waving to his secret girlfriend," William replied in an impertinent tone.

"Shut up, William," Alexander replied, "I'm waving to my reflection."

"I think we will all be waving to our reflections soon," Tony laughed.

The vision evolved into his former 12-year-old self. This time he was holding a Nintendo in one hand and his phone in the other. Alexander waved back once more, feeling a strong wave of nostalgia. *How blissfully unaware I was back then,* he thought to himself. The vision evolved once more into his former 15-year-old self. This time he was holding a revision book in one hand and his phone in the other (a recipe for disaster, I know). The two waved at each other as if they were close friends. The final vision was of his former 21-year-old self. This made Alexander face open with sorrow as he saw the troubled facial expression on his face. The apparition was holding the final photo of his mother in one hand and his notepad in the other. The vision was giving a very sombre wave. Alexander didn't feel as if he wanted to wave back at such a sad version of himself.

Alexander then glanced back at Pvormlu as if asking it for advice. Pvomlu maintained the two o'clock facial expression and nodded slightly as if telling Alexander to go through with the wave. The idea then came to him – he needed to change the facial expression of his former self. Alexander pulled a fake smile that became genuine once his apparition smiled back at him. Alexander was then able to say farewell to his grieving self.

The family then proceeded to wander around the Wapping Wharf. Pvormlu re-emerged, this time the lantern was shining. A projection appeared on the side of a tall building. This image showed Alexander trying to climb into a window whilst Garcia was inside. But this was of Alexander trying to get into a building because he had lost his keys as opposed to trying to escape being caught during an affair.

The next destination that they ended up in was Redcliffe. Behind them was St Mary Redcliffe church. The furniture leaned its wooden head forward. The chandelier shone brightly into the water, casting a shadow of Alexander and what appeared to be little shadow birds. These shadow birds were racing ahead of him, he saw his shadow chasing after the birds, disappearing down the harbour. He saw his shadow chasing his dreams, struggling to keep up with the fast-paced shadow birds. A few seconds later he saw his shadow heading back towards him, still trying to keep up with the shadow birds. *It seems that my shadow is just going with the flow and the current is too fast for him,* Alexander thought to himself. Just when it appeared the shadow had lost the race, the shadow took a completely unexpected turn – up the side of a building! The shadow birds were now trying to keep up with Alexander's ambitious plans. Alexander realised that sometimes black and white ambitions were always going to be too fast for him but, if he wanted to travel far in his life he would need to keep turning until he would find the right path for himself.

The family had now managed to end up near the Temple Meads train station. The desk lamp lit up. The desk lamp drifted up into the twilight sky, forming a new moon. Alexander was staring in awe, his eyes darting around wildly with his hands twitching.

"Are you seeing something, Alexander?" his dad asked him.

"I am just observing the moon," he replied.

"Oh, you are observing the moon, you look like a cat chasing a ball."

"In my drunk state the moon appears like an astrological ball that needs to be captured."

"Good luck with that," Tony replied.

On the glass appeared a reflection of his former self and his younger mother. The first reflection displayed his five-year-old self. He appeared to be chasing his mum who was holding a teddy bear. The reflection went round and round the desk lamp in a similar fashion to *Tom and Jerry*. The next reflection showed Alexander's 12-year-old self, with his Nintendo in his hand with his mum chasing him, trying to grab it off him. Alexander found this show hilarious, he couldn't stop laughing. The reflection of his 15-year-old self-showed Alexander chasing his mum with a textbook in his hand as if he wanted his mother to tell him all the answers. The final reflection showed Alexander walking away from his mother, shaking his head in denial, whilst his mum was trying to tap him on his shoulder, persuading him to turn around. Alexander held his hands together in a praying position, hoping for his former self to face the music and accept the reality before him. Eventually his former self turned around and his mother held his hands; they both looked at each other with a very deep and meaningful expression.

The Sommervale family took one last look over the harbour.

"I wonder how many people have drowned in this very spot," William asked.

"Uh, why would you ask that?" Anna replied.

"Were you thinking of jumping in?" a drunken Tony asked.

"I'm just curious because I plan to become a successful criminal lawyer. I might one day investigate a murder in this harbour."

"Good luck with that," Tony responded.

Alexander could see Pvormlu staring back at him, the candle flames were changing colour. Alexander knew that he was about to witness a great display. The candle flames were rising and swarming around like flies or fairies. The flames turned blue, a large blue flame emerged, it appeared to form the base of this ethereal display. The flames turned green; two fiery walls were trying to encroach on the space of the thriving yellow flames. The blue fire base was holding the green toxic flames back. The candle flames turned purple, purple hearts rose up and were devoured by the bustling yellow flames. Alexander was mesmerised by the spectacular beauty. He interpreted the blue flame base as the opportunities that would shape his life.

The yellow flames were people who would be in his life. The green walls were harmful influences that could cause harm and destruction if he wandered too close to the edge. The purple hearts represented feelings of passion. Alexander wanted to thrive in this world and not let the notorious green wall get too close to him. *If I can rise up above the blue flame base, I should be able to join the thriving fairy candle flames. The green flame wall will not destroy me.*

The four returned home.

"Same again next week?" Tony asked. No one replied. "Just joking, but we can meet again and share our memories of your mum."

"I can definitely make time," Anna replied.

"Me too, I have a photographic memory," William replied.

"Sure, I love memory games too," Alexander replied.

An opportunity to reconnect and share their fond memories, the Sommervale family were looking forward to this family time.

Memories of Rose Sommervale, August 3rd, 2024

After having a wonderful roast chicken, which they all cooked together, Tony had bought a stash of cider that they could drink whilst reflecting on their lives with Rose Sommervale.

"Let's start off with Alexander."

"My favourite memory was when we played chess at the seaside resort in Plymouth. I was confident that I would beat her again, my queen was wiping all her pieces off the board, it was only a matter of time, I thought. But then a shocking turn of events – she noticed a checking move with her queen which resulted in a checkmate."

"Wow, I remember this, I spotted it a mile off, but I was going to say anything," William replied.

"Shut up, William, how many times have I beaten you at chess?"

"Not many times, how many times did I beat you at tennis and badminton?"

"That's all right, enough," Tony interjected.

"I knew that I should have done something about that knight," Alexander said regretfully.

"What about you, William?"

"Well, my favourite memory was when she bought me that *Call of Duty* game, that was the best game ever!"

"So, your favourite memory was when Mum bought you some silly video game," Anna said.

"It's not a silly video game if I'm the top of my class at it."

"You must have better memories than that," Tony said.

"OK, that was just a wind-up, I do have much more meaningful memories."

"Like the time she bought you that *Halo* game?" Alexander interrupted.

"No, my most memorable moment was when I aced that science test."

"Here we go," Alexander said.

"I don't mean to brag about the result on the science test."

"That makes a change," Alexander said.

"I did study very hard for that test. I showed her the result, and she gave me a massive hug and told me that I would make it someday. I just wish that she was here to congratulate all of us on our progress."

"That's right, well done, William, I'm sure she would be giving you all a big hug if she was still here."

"What about your memories, Anna?"

"I bet it is going to be something to do with animals," William said.

"Yes, all right, William, just let Anna have her turn," Tony interjected.

"OK, William, you're right."

"I knew it," William replied.

"I think this happened when I was around seven. I had the flu; I was lying on the sofa feeling awful. I remember mum picking me up and tucking me into bed. She made sure that my Hello Kitty pyjamas matched the Hello Kitty bed set."

"I thought you said, this has something to do with animals?"

"Well, it was a Hello Kitty duvet set and Fluffels jumped on the bed and sat next to me."

"That sounds like a great memory," Tony complimented her.

"That's what was so great about her, she would always help you when you were ill or struggling," Anna said. "Even if she was drowning in paperwork and having to do a full house clean at the same time, she would still prioritise other people's needs over her own. I remember that she used to stay up until midnight to make sure that we all had everything sorted, she wouldn't rest until we had completed our homework," Anna added, feeling reminiscent.

"Yeah, I remember, I used to hate homework, I would always leave it to the last minute."

"She always told you to clean your trainers and finish your homework, but you refused, saying that there is a time and a place for everything, but now is not the time or place," Anna replied.

"I used to do everything in God's time, which just so happened to be the night before."

"You are full of such rubbish," Alexander added.

"I think we all know whose turn it is," Tony said.

"Go on, Dad, what have you got in store for us?" Anna said.

"This will be a long one, I'm not sure if I have told you this before. I will tell you all the story of our wedding."

"Haven't you told us this before?" Alexander asked.

"I have told you the story but not in much detail. I have asked people for more clarification so that I can give all the details. It was in the summer. My cousin, Derick, was my driver and best man. He was terrible with directions; I have no idea why I let him drive me. As you know, he drove me to the wrong church."

"What a moron, I could drive backwards to any location without even needing a map," William added.

"Well, you weren't driving in the '80s, William," Tony said.

"What has the time period got to do with anything?"

"For starters, cars were unreliable and there was no satnav to follow, you had to use some old map," Tony replied.

"So, how did you not notice that Derick was driving you to the wrong church?" Anna asked.

"I was busy trying to get all the paperwork sorted, making sure that we had all the correct legal documents."

"Why couldn't you get the documents sorted after the wedding?" William asked.

"Because I like to have everything organised and ready, I get stressed out when things aren't sorted correctly."

"How long did it take you to notice?" Alexander asked.

"I noticed as soon as he pulled up at the wrong church. He got muddled up between his wedding church and our wedding church."

"How on earth can you get those things muddled up, are you sure that he didn't do it on purpose?" William asked.

"Why would he do it on purpose?" Tony asked.

"As a prank, maybe. I know that I might be able to pull off a prank like that, to see how observant my passengers were," William replied.

"I wasn't paying attention to where he was driving me because I needed to sort things out, he told me that he had been to this church before, obviously he didn't know what the hell he was doing."

"What happened when you realised that he had driven you to the wrong church?"

Alexander asked.

"I was initially super pissed that he had pretended that he knew where he was driving, I could have missed my own wedding because of him. At first, he had the bleeding audacity to claim that I must be mistaken, but then I showed him, the paperwork proving that this was the right church. Guess what he said next?

"Maybe you have the wrong paperwork," Anna suggested.

"He claimed that I had made a mistake by telling him to go to the wrong church, when I never even mentioned the church that he took me to. As you remember, we had a big argument, which resulted in me driving to the church."

"So, it was his car that you drove?" Anna asked.

"Yes, it was, a Ford Escort, to be specific, a car that he had customised himself. He would only drive the car slowly because he didn't want to damage it on the bumpy roads in Herefordshire. I, on the other hand, am used to fixing unreliable cars, so I didn't have a problem with speeding to get to my destination."

"So, how did you convince him to let you drive his car?" Anna asked.

"At first, he was very reluctant, he said that he would drive me to the correct church, but I wasn't in the mood for messing around, so I told him that I would get out if he didn't let me drive his car. He argued that if

I damaged his car then I owed him the repair costs, but then I told him that if there were any wedding cancellations then he should pay for my wedding. He finally agreed to let me drive since he didn't want to risk making me miss my wedding."

"So, how did you drive, like Vin Diesel and the Rock?" William asked.

"Who are they?" Tony replied.

"He is the *Fast and Furious* actor."

"I have never heard of that."

"Never mind, it's about government agents who drive around like lunatics in order to defeat super villains."

"Do I look like a government agent?"

"Definitely not," they all replied.

"Do I drive like a lunatic?"

"That's debatable," William replied.

"I do not drive like a lunatic, I just don't like driving like a fairy."

"I'm sure that's what the drivers on *Fast and Furious* tell each other," William said.

"OK, I give up," said Tony.

"What was the journey like?" Anna asked.

"As you know, I didn't have time for cruising along, so I cut any unnecessary time out."

"So, you were speeding," Alexander asked.

"I wouldn't call it speeding, there were no cameras and road police, so I think I would prefer to describe it as defensive driving."

"So, how did your cousin, Derick, react to your driving?" Anna asked.

"He wasn't too impressed, as I recall. I remember him holding his head down the whole time, not wanting to witness the damage and destruction that he thought I was going to cause."

"Did you cause any damage?" Alexander asked.

"Of course not, those bumps and scrapes were already there." The family laughed together. "Derick told me to never drive him anywhere again, which was fine by me as I hate nothing more than backseat drivers, or front seat driver's since he was sitting right next to me."

"How late were you?" Anna asked.

"Well, 30 minutes late, to be exact."

"How did you avoid missing the wedding?" Alexander asked.

"The pastor arrived one hour late because he had a meeting at a different church."

"Just a quick question, was this a knock-off wedding?" William asked.

"You think we got married on the cheap?"

"You did mention before that your parents paid for most of the wedding. I have never seen your parents buy anything expensive, it is usually second-hand or from some lousy antique store," William said.

"A second-hand wedding!" Anna started laughing.

"Look, this was no second-hand wedding, we just went with whatever was on offer," Tony persisted.

"Sorry for asking, but how on earth could a pastor be one hour late, are you sure that he was a real pastor?" William asked.

"I didn't question it, this was the '80s you are talking about, and in the bloody sticks, no smartphone notifications to tell you that you are late, hardly anyone had a mobile phone as they had just been invented. You had to use a phonebook if you wanted to find anyone's contact details, everything back then was manual and unreliable. We didn't think much of people being late back then since people had more patience and understanding."

"But people had watches and clocks," William replied.

"We were all annoyed at first and wondering if we had all gone to the wrong church, but your mother told me to wait and be patient."

"What was the response, when you and Derick arrived 30 minutes late?" Anna asked.

"Me and Derick planned to tell them that there was a breakdown, and we needed to fix it with our bare hands."

"Wasn't there an AA service?" William asked.

"Yes, there was, but we lived out in the sticks, we needed to be self-sufficient, we couldn't afford to pay a mechanic to fix our cars, we needed to become our own mechanics."

"That makes sense," Anna replied.

"Did they believe your story?" Alexander asked.

"They had to, so yes," Tony replied. "When the pastor finally arrived, the wedding went smoothly, the speeches that I edited sounded up to scratch."

"You edited the speeches yourself?" Alexander asked.

"Of course, someone needed to, it was my wedding after all."

"Uh, all right," Anna replied.

"The speeches went well; we were just about to finalise after saying 'I do' half a dozen times when my mother felt the urge to interrupt the pastor in the most insulting way possible."

"Oh yeah, I remember, she kept shouting 'objection' instead of waiting for the wedding to be finalised."

The Sommervale family kept laughing uncontrollably. "Oh my God, I still can't believe that Grandma Margeret would interrupt a pastor by shouting 'objection' not once, not twice, but three bloody times instead of waiting five seconds. What an absolute lunatic," William replied.

"Well, we know where you got your lunatic genes from," Anna said.

"Shut up, Anna, she was the one with the lunatic genes not me. I inherited most of my genes from your grandad, that's why I am smart, hard-working and handsome, people always used to say."

"Wait, that makes absolutely no sense, biology states that you inherit 50 percent of your genes from your mum and 50 percent from your old man," William replied.

"But genes aren't the same as characteristics – you don't inherit all of your personality traits." Anna argued.

"But you do copy your parents' attitudes and behaviour to a certain degree, similarities do exist."

"What were the things that were so important she had to almost cancel a wedding over?" Anna asked.

"The first thing was 'we haven't shown the photos of him as a boy'."

"Why on earth would she want photos of you as a boy just before you are about to get married?" William asked.

"She brought a collection of photos of me as a boy and was going to show them to all the guests that we invited, but not only did she forget that she had brought these photos with her, but she also thought that someone else was going to show the photos to the guests."

"What! How can people be this oblivious?" William replied.

"This was the 1980s and people didn't have Google Calendar and computers," Alexander said.

"You know your Grandma Margaret; she had a bubbly personality, but she was incredibly forgetful and impulsive. The second thing that she blurted out right at the last second was 'church donations."

"Church donations!" William responded. "Why on earth would she shout an objection over that?"

"Maybe because she believed that church donations would bring good fortune," Tony replied. The Sommervale family burst out laughing once again. "The next thing she shouted an objection over was one last photo that she wanted to take, just before we got married."

"Did she get what she wanted?" Anna asked.

"Yes, she did, it turned out that she had the childhood photos stuffed in her old handbag, the pastor allowed her to share all these photos, which annoyed the living shit out of me. She also handed her spare change to the pastor, and she had to take a load of photos just before we were about to get married."

"How did the pastor react to Grandma Margaret testing his patience?" Alexander asked.

"He got super pissed off as you would imagine. He threatened to cancel the wedding if she shouted another objection."

"The pastor must have thought that Grandma Margaret had Tourette's," William said.

"That's not the excuse that we came up with, but I did apologise for her outbursts."

"Why did she need to shout 'objection'?" Alexander asked.

"Probably because she was panicking – definitely not something that I inherited –but I think that she has a last-second memory, so she won't remember something until it's almost too late," Tony replied.

The Sommervale family thoroughly enjoyed their time together, they all felt like this was an opportunity for all of them to move on with their lives, without feeling empty about the past. They all had a big group hug.

The Final Encounter with Pvormlu, 8th August 2024

A day many ago, a sight to behold, a masterpiece never to be forgotten.

Alexander was pacing back and forth around his bedroom, chanting these phrases repeatedly. Alexander really wanted to have another encounter with the furniture being. The time was now 12:30 and he closed his eyes, then covered these shut eyes with his hands, forming a blindfold. His body was erupting with adrenaline – the same feeling that a child has just before they open their birthday present. He could sense the presence of the furniture being. One, two, three, he removed his blindfold hands and discovered that the furniture being was right in front of him, the clock eyes staring directly into his soul. The swirling vortex grew deeper and deeper. Alexander could sense that Pvormlu had a lot in store for him.

Alexander noticed something different about the clock eyes. The glass lid was not there, leaving the clock eyes completely exposed. The swirling vortex was creating a strong breeze which was pulling Alexander closer to the clock eyes. Alexander could feel the preternatural electromagnetism pulling his hands closer to the clock hands. He reached towards these exposed hands. Pvormlu leaned its head so that the wooden clocks were within reach of Alexander's curious hands.

The time on the clocks was 12.:30. Alexander was struggling to stay on his feet as the current pulled him forwards. The minute hand turned to 12, changing the clock time to 12 o'clock. Alexander decided to go with the current instead of resisting. He grabbed the hour clock hands with both of his hands, making sure to grip them with full force. He was gripping them as if holding on for dear life. He could feel the current changing direction, from clockwise to counterclockwise. The force was pushing him away from the direction that he needed to go. The heat from the candle flames was providing him with strength and energy. Alexander yanked the clock hands with all his might as if he had been forced to enter an arm-wrestling competition. The hour hands were bending counterclockwise halfway between the 12 and 11 position. Alexander managed to shift the hands back to the 12 o'clock position, and he now needed to reach one o'clock. On the count of three, Alexander prepared himself to reach this number. One, two, three – he shifted his full body weight to the right and managed to wrestle the clock hands until they reached the one o'clock position.

Cracks started forming down the sides of the walls. This initially worried Alexander as he feared that the room might cave in, but as he knew that this position had a jovial connection, he did not fear a collapse. A bright yellow light seeped in. Alexander could feel the sunlight seeping in, tickling his senses. Alexander realised that these wall cracks represented facial expressions. These cracks were moving in a rippling motion, constantly changing expression, trying to distort his sense of reality. Through the sash bay windows (behind Pvormlu), Alexander could see the weather changing just as unpredictably as the cracks in the walls. One second it was sunny, blink, the next it was stormy, blink, the next second it was snowing. Alexander turned his attention to the clock, not letting the mysterious outer world distract him from his main goal.

He tugged the clock hands to the two o'clock position. A skylight appeared above him, this window was letting in sunlight, which made Alexander feel as if he was on a beach in the Philippines. Alexander felt the urge to feel the sunlight with his bare hands, this urge was nibbling away at him like a heat rash, but Alexander refused to let go of the clock hands. A shower of sunlight was photosynthesising Alexander's spiritual core, he kept reminding himself that the clock faces were the only things that he should be paying attention to. After a while, the sunlight turned harsh. Alexander could feel sweat pouring down his back. The clock hands were heating up, causing Alexander's hands to form blisters. The heat from the candle flames were adding to Alexander's torment. *I can't cope with this heat much more*, Alexander said to himself. The signal finally came to him, he yanked the clock hands as hard as he possibly could as if he was trying to get a lawnmower to start up, he was hoping that he wouldn't accidentally pull the hands right off the clock.

Eventually he reached the three o'clock position. Alexander glanced to the side of Pvormlu to view the bay sash window. He had a wider view than ever before; it was as if he was looking out of the window of a skyscraper. He could see the whole of Stroud in a spectacular panoramic view. The more he looked, the more the view started to change as if he was moving.

Alexander felt like he was in a helicopter looking down on his local area. The journey was progressing through Gloucestershire and into Wiltshire, he was brushing past the towns and cities as if they were waves. As someone with symptoms of agoraphobia, Alexander wouldn't normally be able to make long journeys by himself in the fear that something might go wrong, and he wouldn't know how to get help. This experience of casually drifting through the countryside made Alexander feel as if life was a breeze. Oxford came into view and Alexander could see the university. Shivers were sent down his spine. *How hard is a degree, how am I going to manage?* he asked himself. Whilst he was pondering his future, he looked at the clocks and realised that the next number was four. This represented hard work and dedication. Alexander yanked at the clock hands as hard as he could, but to no avail. "Is there a malfunction somewhere?" Alexander said. He decided to stop and wait for a few seconds. The second time round, the hands were almost touching four o'clock. Alexander thought that he was going to make it, but the hand got stuck halfway between three o'clock and four o'clock. *One more try,* Alexander said to himself. Alexander closed his eyes and froze his mind, he let his body shift the clock hands to the four o'clock position.

Alexander was now staring at the ground in front of him, his legs were bent, he was in a squatting position with his arms bent tightly. He felt as if every muscle in his body was working to its full capacity, including his brain. Pvormlu was deliberately lowering its head so that Alexander would have to squat down to be in-line with the clock hands. Alexander felt the wooden floor starting to move forwards, as if he was standing on a treadmill. As well as having to hold the clock hands in place so that they didn't spring back to the 12 o'clock position, he now had to keep his feet moving. Strange objects started appearing on the wooden floor. Bricks, shoes, a radio and even a football. These objects were approaching his feet from behind as additional obstacles that had to be cleared. A conveyor belt of madness, trying to trip him up. More and more objects were arriving behind him, he needed to jump to clear the increasing numbers of rubbish that were coming up from behind. *Where is all this stuff coming from? I feel like I'm on bloody* Mario kart. A sea of marbles was emerging behind him, banana peel and whatever you could shake a stick at. As he was pulling the clock hands towards the five o'clock position, he felt the urge to pull back to the four o'clock position. A feeling of shame and disappointment was filling his veins, he wasn't prepared to dig down into his insecurities. This hesitation caused the clock hands to take control. The clock hands were resisting Alexander's grip. Three o'clock, two o'clock, now one o'clock. If Alexander couldn't dig deep into his anxiety, then the clocks might trap him in a cycle of counterclockwise depression!

The best way to climb down a steep wall is to not look down and breathe carefully. Alexander closed his eyes and sank his body weight; the clock's hands began slowly dropping again. He opened his eyes and was relieved to find that he had reached the five o'clock position. He felt his body weight drop like a sack of potatoes. *I don't want to force the clock hands down too hard; I might damage my wrist. Sometimes the only way up is to go down first, so what if the only way down is up this time*, Alexander thought to himself. *I must alleviate myself from all this heavy baggage that I'm carrying*. Alexander drifted off to sleep whilst still holding on to the clock hands; this was a risky move as he might unconsciously let go of the clock hands, but Alexander knew that this was the only way. The feeling of zero gravity entered his body caused him to become airborne, his legs were waving about in the air, there was nothing going through his mind or body, he could have heard his own heartbeat if he was listening. As Alexander started to regain consciousness, he realised that his fingers were slipping, he had to find a way down! The clock hands were making their way back to the 4 o'clock position. *How on earth am I supposed to get back down?* Then the thought came to him – *go the same way down as you came up*. Alexander closed his eyes and went to sleep once more. He could feel the gravity changing around his centre. He was slowly starting to drop, when he felt his feet touch the ground. He slowly opened his eyes to discover that he had reached the six o'clock position.

Alexander found himself staring at his black shoes. He had the body language of a convicted felon who was waiting to be hanged. He felt a huge amount of guilt, the feeling that he had failed as a son, the feeling that he had failed as a human being. He couldn't shake off this feeling. Alexander senses a darkness brewing. Underneath him a dark swirling void appeared – a tornado of regret. The suction force was dragging Alexander down. When he first reached the six o'clock position, the six numeral was waist level, now the numerals were way above him. The dark swirling void was now chest level, Alexander was waving around like a flag in a storm, struggling to maintain any kind of composure. Alexander refused to look down the whole time. Alexander could hear the demon bats chanting beneath him. "Carry on hanging around this vortex, weirdo, you will never complete your turn. Mind the gap, you already have one foot in the grave. How are you going to get your way out of this?" The high-pitched cackling was messing with Alexander's senses, he desperately wanted to put his hands over his ears. The bats' shrieking sounded like a loudspeaker was being blasted in his ear, it felt as if his ears were going to explode.

The next horrifying phrases were of manager Chloe, this time she was reading aloud the insulting letter that Alexander had the utter displeasure of having to read. "My targets. Listen to what people tell me, I must take only 30 minutes for my break, I must smile when guests are talking to me, I must say hello to guests and my coworkers." The horrible intonation of Chloe's gruff and patronising voice was driving Alexander insane, he wanted to shut her up but he had to keep holding on to the clock hands.

That horrible bitch, why does she always find a way to get to me?

The next menacing voice to grace Alexander's ears was head chef, Gary's. "You are just wasting time. You need to be moving faster. Tidy up after yourself. Why have you dumped these onions here?" Alexander's ears were bleeding with rage, he wanted to strangle Gary the same way that Homer Simpson would strangle Bart.

By now, Alexander had become accustomed to the infuriating racket, but his ears were ringing, which was causing him to become dizzy and lose concentration.

Alexander was unaware that his fingers were slipping again. He needed a voice to wake him up. "Forget life and life will forget you. Seek nothing and nothing will become of you. In the everpresent pitfall of doom, you only need to find the way up." This deep bellowing voice instantly woke Alexander up.

"Who on earth is that?" Alexander said. It sounded like an old man with a loud voice. Maybe it was the voice of Pvormlu, or maybe even the voice of Alexander as an old man. Alexander felt the signal telling him to swing like a wild monkey, when he could, but Alexander didn't have the physical motivation to swing like a monkey when he could barely hold on to the clock hands. He remembered that the seven o'clock position represented hope. *Maybe I should try smiling,* Alexander thought. Alexander forced a smile, hoping that this would give him the physical energy to reach the next position. The longer he held this forced smile, the more he felt like smiling naturally. He felt the overwhelming tension disappear, and he gathered his strength then shifted the clock hands to the seven o'clock position.

The swirling vortex faded away. Alexander let out a massive sigh of relief. Alexander could feel a light breeze drifting in and out of the room. The windows opened and the light breeze transformed into a gale. Memorable photos and certificates were blown in, but instead of landing on the floor, these objects were being blown around in a spin cycle around Alexander and the furniture being. The clock eyes were slightly above Alexander's face, his arms were stretching out as far as possible, his hands were almost glued to the clock hands. As the photos and certificates breezed past his face, Alexander cocked his head up instantaneously like a cat when its owner prepared its next meal. As the breeze grew stronger and more and more taunting documents were blowing around in circles – photos of a future Alexander and Garcia on their wedding day, symbolic letters, even photos of their potential future family – Alexander was feeling incredibly restless. It was like tying a starving person up and waving food around them, the urge to look at these mysterious documents and photos was killing him. The pretentious paper fortunes were trying to mislead Alexander; he needed to be obsessed with reality, not with a propagandist perception of his future. Alexander looked down and avoided showing any attention to these misleading letters. Maybe these photos were visions of the future, but Alexander needed to separate reality from desire. Alexander started shaking his head in disbelief, trying his best to convince Pvormlu that he was not falling for desire. The mighty gust ceased. The photos and letters stopped moving and dropped to the ground with the white backs facing upwards, making it appear like a blanket of snow. Without looking at the clocks, Alexander pulled the clock hands to the eight o'clock position.

Fog was obscuring the view out of the windows. Alexander was curious to know what was on the other side. After one minute of this nauseating fog, Alexander felt incredibly confused. After two minutes, he felt like falling asleep. After three minutes, Alexander was tapping his feet on the floor, desperately waiting for something to happen. *Is this some form of white torture?* he thought to himself. Despite Alexander's boredom from the lack of action, he continued to pull towards the nine o'clock position. He had no idea what fog had to do with pride. *What on earth is the point of this exercise?* he thought to himself. After four minutes, Alexander realised that nothing was going to happen, but he wasn't willing to give up. The frustration of not knowing what to do and not knowing what was going on drove him insane. *There has got to be something that I'm missing. Maybe the fog represents a thought that hasn't yet been deciphered.* Alexander experimented by pulling a variety of facial expressions, but this made no difference. He started saying random phrases but didn't see anything resulting from this. Alexander also tried falling asleep, but nothing changed as he was sleeping. *I can't let go, that would be quitting, maybe I am heading in the wrong direction, maybe the answer lies in the counterclockwise direction. I don't want the clocks to win, but I can't keep heading in this direction, it's a total dead end.* Alexander pulled the clock hands simultaneously in the opposite direction. The journey back up the clock was far easier than down and within a few seconds he had reached the original 12 o'clock position. He heard a knocking on the window behind him. "Who the hell is there?" he said. The fog faded revealing Garcia Agbayani. She was smiling in a very cutesy fashion. She was waving her hands, trying to trick Alexander into waving back at her. Alexander realised that this was a nihilism fog, a blinding fog that made people think that there was no purpose to anything, if you looked back far enough in time, you would find a purpose for everything. Garcia started writing on the window with her fingers.

Alexander, I am proud to be your girlfriend.

Alexander felt the overwhelming urge to let go of the clock hands and run towards Garcia. He gave her a regretful smile then continued focusing on the clock hands. Another knock, this time the window behind Pvormlu. Alexander could see that it was Anna Sommervale. She wrote, *I am proud to have you as a brother*. Alexander smiled back at her. Three knocks came from behind him and Alexander turned to see who it was. William Sommervale. "Oh great, what does this cretin want?" William continued banging on the window. "What now?" Alexander grunted. "What is he going to write?"

William had a smirk on his face. "He is going to draw a penis, isn't he." William wrote, *I am proud to have you as my brother, Buttwipe*. "I am proud to have you as my brother, too, knobhead," Alexander said.

A knock from the window in front of Alexander. It was his dad, Tony Sommervale. He had an annoyed look on his face, he was gesturing as if to say, 'let me in'. "How on earth does he expect me to let him in?" He wrote, *let me in, Alexander, I am proud to have you as a son*. Alexander quickly looked away in shock, he had never heard his dad say anything like that before.

He heard another knock from behind him and turned around to discover that it was his mother, Rose Somervale. Alexander kept turning his head back to the clocks, feeling incredibly anxious about seeing his mother's face so close. She was waving, the same way that she would wave every time that Alexander would leave the house when he went on a school trip. Alexander was struggling to know how to respond to this, he kept pulling all sorts of faces, an attempt to smile, an attempt to laugh, an attempt to put on a straight face. She wrote, *I will always be proud to have as my first-born, Alexander*. Alexander nodded sheepishly then turned back, having no idea how to process what he just saw.

After a few deep breaths, he shifted the clock hands to the nine o'clock position. The lighting was changing, flickering light bulbs, the distinction between day and night blurred. Alexander's senses were being tormented. A scorching release of hot air from the Sahara followed by a cold blast of Arctic air. Sweating, followed by shivering, Alexander felt as if his body was being experimented on. A loud roar, silence. A loud scream of a little girl, silence. A boom from an explosion, silence. A smash from a plate that landed on the floor. Alexander's head was shaking uncontrollably as he was trying to ignore the spontaneous chaos that was all around him. A red dot appeared and bounced from the floor to the wall, to the other wall. *What am I, a cat?* Alexander thought to himself. *Do I really have to stare at this red dot when all this sensory crap is going on all around me?* Alexander knew that to pass the test he needed to maintain all his focus on this annoying red dot. The red dot slowly drifted along the floor around his feet. The temperature became cold, causing Alexander to shiver. The dot started picking up pace along the wooden floor, the strong Arctic winds causing Alexander to dance side to side to keep himself warm. The red dot jumped to the ceiling, the temperature increased, Alexander felt comfortable for a few seconds until he realised that his entire body was soaking wet, and he stunk. The red dot was now running along the bottom of the walls. Alexander could hear a deep groaning, but when the red dot went up the wall this noise became a high-pitched scream. The red dot traversed the walls in a fluctuating motion, creating a cacophony of deep and high-pitched noises. This was coupled with the flickering of lights which made Alexander's eyes sore, he felt the need to blink every second just to readjust his eyes to the chaos. After several minutes of sensory torture, the red dot landed on the ten o'clock position. Alexander was massively relieved; he lifted the clock hands until they reached the ten o'clock position.

Alexander could feel the ground shaking from beneath him. "Uh oh, this isn't going to be good," he said. The tremors increased until the walls started shaking. Alexander would not consider the Cotswolds to be an earthquake zone, but the undeniable vibrations made it appear so. These tremors made Alexander feel incredibly dizzy. A large crack tore through the wooden floor, right in the middle of Alexander's legs and Povrmlu's wooden table legs. The gap widened creating a terrifying pit. "Do not look down, do not look down," Alexander kept telling himself. Alexander could hear the swishing and swooshing of waves. "You know what comes after an earthquake," Alexander said apprehensively. Pipes rattled, constantly thumping and thudding. Alexander looked to his left and saw two large white Victorian doors, about two metres behind him he noticed that they appeared to be moving inwards as if something was trying to get in. After three vigorous battering attempts, the doors flung open as if being kicked open by a SWAT team, releasing a surge of water. The entire room became a swimming pool! The water kept flooding in until it was waist high. A strong current emerged, lifting Alexander off his feet. By the temperature of the water, Alexander knew that this was a flood from a UK river, his legs were shaking from the cold. He used his legs to keep his head above water. The crack beneath him was draining a lot of water. Alexander had to continue gripping the clock hands as hard as he could to avoid being sucked in. But there was more to worry about.

Alexander could smell smoke. He felt a source of intense heat coming from above him. Large cracks were appearing in the ceiling, and the realisation that the roof was going to collapse terrified Alexander. *Am I going to die?* he thought to himself. *No, I won't die, I trust Pvormlu.* As the cracks grew larger, Alexander could see smoke. He managed to pull himself to one side of the wooden head. The roof collapsed on both sides of the furniture being as the rubble was diverted. The burning rubble was cooled by the flood. Smoke was filling the room, fire was burning all along both walls, the fear of choking to death was on the horizon. Alexander felt tremors coming from the crack beneath him. Alexander started nervously kicking the water like a dog. Unbeknownst to Alexander, he was building up pressure that would lead to a gush of water that would extinguish the fire and clear the flood at the same time. Alexander looked down to see that bubbles were being released, meaning that a huge amount of pressure was heading his way. Alexander took cover by pulling himself to one side of the wooden head as a jet of water shot up like an Icelandic geyser. The entire roof area was covered in foam. Alexander held tightly to the clock hands so that he wouldn't be dragged upwards. After all the water had been vaporised, the crack disappeared, followed by the roof which regenerated itself. Alexander shifted the clock hands to the 11 o'clock position.

Alexander was looking forward to this number as it signified the feeling of surprises. It didn't seem that anything was happening, so he shut his eyes and waited for 30 seconds but still nothing happened. Alexander realised that surprises weren't always waiting to happen, sometimes you had to make them happen. He noticed all the bells and decided to find a way to ring them to attract attention. He headbutted the house bell and saw paranormal flickers of light. This gave him the indication that he was making the right decision. He tapped the bottom desk bell with his head, then the next two up. The top desk bell seemed too high for him. *How am I supposed to hit this bell?* he thought to himself. Alexander decided that he would use the clock hands as a gymnastics bar to launch himself in the air. He made a few practice jumps to prepare himself. He then made a dramatic leap, narrowly avoiding hitting his head on the streetlight. Alexander then tapped the other two desk bells. He could feel the entire room moving from side to side as if he was operating a crane. There were two bells remaining that he needed to ring. The servants' bells. The only problem was that these were about a metre above his range.

If Pvormlu carries me with its wooden head close enough for me to be able to headbutt the bells... but wait, my neck won't stretch that far. Oh no, that's a crazy idea, I can't possibly do that. Alexander had a wild idea in his head. *If I use the clock hands to catapult my feet, I will be able to reach the bells. But how can I kick Pvormlu's bells? That must be out of the question, I can't possibly damage Pvormlu's sacred body parts. But I don't see how else I can reach those bells. I wish I could phone a friend but I'm kind of stuck here at the moment.* The servants' bells began moving side to side but without ringing. Alexander saw that as a taunt. *I will have to kick those bells now;*

I'll aim for the bell on the right side. Alexander did not see himself as an Olympic gymnast, but he hoped that Pvormlu's clock hands would help turn him into one. One, two, three, he launched himself to the side of the clocks like a kung-fu master. His head was now above the clock's eyes, and he flicked his right foot, causing the bell to ring. The ceiling responded to this by raising itself slightly then dropping back down like a lid that wants to be taken off. Alexander swung his body around the other side and kicked the other servants' bell. Both bells were ringing, and the roof slid down the right side of the building like an ornamental jar being opened. Alexander now had the full view of the sky. The two white walls began flapping like wings from a dragon.

"Wow, these walls are actually wings and not solid walls," Alexander said with surprise. Holographic diagrams of various indecipherable coordinates and unknown maps were being projected through the window in front of Alexander. The window behind him projected holographic images of memories. Alexander could only describe this room as some sort of extraterrestrial time machine, a new version of reality that only Pvormlu could understand.

Alexander had no idea whether the Victorian room was stationary or travelling through the air. The floor was raised at an angle, the same angle that a plane is at when ascending after take-off. He felt a rush of air as he could see a cloud that was becoming larger and larger, eventually covering the entire room in a blanket of mist. "I can't see anything," Alexander said. "How am I supposed to get out of this?" The realisation struck him that he needed to find a way of controlling the flight. He could sense that the room was continuing to ascend, making the room cold. Alexander could not see anything at all.

"How on earth am I supposed to be a pilot when I can't even drive a car?" Alexander knew that he could only move the clock hands in a counterclockwise direction. He pulled the clock hands down to the seven o'clock position, and the sudden shift in gravity made Alexander feel as if he was riding on a rollercoaster. The clear sky came into view again. Alexander shifted the clock hands to the nine o'clock position to stabilise. The more he travelled through the sky of this mysterious reality, the idea came to him that this must be some form of a mid-reality – a junction between normal reality and alternative realities. A bit like a computer, the physical computer was in the same reality that he was in, but all the different signals from other realities would create a whole new reality depending on where the signals originated from. Of course, this was only a theory, but it would explain the transformation of his flat into this mysterious Victorian building and how the shadow bats and shadow figure kept appearing.

He knew that Pvormlu was powered by paranormal energy and electricity and was materialised in the afterlife. He had this idea that the furniture being was some form of a paranormal computer, which could connect to spiritual and symbolic forces using its clock eyes. Alexander wanted to connect to experience a form of reality that was compatible with his mentality and inner self. Pvormlu wanted to connect to a human being to whom it shared an intellectual partnership with. A journey for Alexander, and also a journey for Pvormlu. After a few minutes of cruising, Alexander could see a flock of seagulls heading in his direction. "Oh, seagulls, now I understand what pilots have to put up with." Alexander had no idea how to avoid them, so he lifted the clock hands to the ten o'clock position. The seagulls split off in two different directions, meaning that Alexander had just done a pointless manoeuvre. Alexander shifted the clock hands back to the nine o'clock position. He could sense a change in weather, the sky was turning grey, a rumbling sound could be heard. Alexander had been navigating by observing the sky above him, he had no idea how to avoid a thunderstorm. It started raining. Alexander's clothes were soaking wet, he desperately needed to find a way out of this storm. "Oh my God, I have absolutely no idea what to do, I might get electrocuted." Alexander began panicking, he started anxiously stamping his feet and pulling the clock hands as close to his chest as he could. His eyes were shut, his face was shaking uncontrollably. When Alexander opened his eyes, expecting to be electrocuted, he was surprised to discover that it was snowing.

The overwhelming urge to pick up the snow and throw snowballs was suppressed by Alexander stamping his feet on the floor. A white blanket covered the room and Alexander fell asleep again. When he woke up he discovered that the sky was clear again. A hot air balloon came into view, it was on the same path. He quickly shifted the clock to the three o'clock position, causing it to turn in the opposite direction, avoiding the hot air balloon. Next, he saw a swarm of drones surrounding the front of this room. "I have to make a U-turn," Alexander said.

He shifted the clock hands back to the 12 o'clock position, causing a sharp turn that made the room spin around, the drones were unable to keep up and decided to head back down. Alexander was now aware that he was heading backwards. He decided to continue heading in this direction for the sake of exploring this reality. Alexander took occasional glances behind him to see if anything was coming his way. To this surprise, a missile was heading in his direction. Alexander kept turning the clock hands to different positions, but the missile was locked onto the 'flying Victorian room, time travellers machine thingy'. Alexander knew that he couldn't run, so he decided to do another U-turn and face this missile. He started at the original counterclockwise position and managed to complete a full clockwise cycle. The missile was heading straight for him – boom!

Alexander lifted his head to check that he was still alive. He could see stars, moons, planets; it was as if he was looking through a telescope, there were details that he had never noticed before. "Am I heaven?" Alexander looked down to discover that he was still holding on to the clock hands.

Alexander felt as if he and the furniture being were married – literally one item. The numerals on the clocks were spinning around and Alexander had no idea what this meant but he was still fascinated by it. The hypnotic voids were spinning at the same pace. Alexander wanted to get absorbed by these divine clock eyes. He pressed his forehead against the left clock eye, 365 opportunities all spinning around in his mind, 52 friendly people waiting to chat to him about anything, 12 chances to make things right, four people hugging him at once, one person to live. Now, for the right clock eyes – 60 flies buzzing around his body, 60 ants crawling all over the wall, disturbing his reading and writing session, 24 snails heading for the finish line, knowing that they would eventually make it. Alexander felt that he was ready to remove his hands. *They are completely black; it's going to take hours to get this off.* Just then, a butler spirit handed him a packet of wet wipes. "Yes, thank you," Alexander said.

As Alexander was wiping off the stains from his hands, he could feel the candle flames increase in temperature. The eternal flames of hope, never dying out. Alexander stood back for health and safety reasons. He finished wiping his hands then put the wipes back in his pocket. Pvormlu created a firework display from the candle flames. Flames were shooting up then bursting into colourful displays which complimented the starry sky. The heat from these flames was hitting him like a warm fire on a cold winter's day. The candle flames turned blue; a thousand raging fire droplets rose up then started to rain on Alexander. The buzzing, tingling sensation when the flares touched his body made him feel like he was a magician of hope. The candle flares turned green; a thick fiery cloud filled the room. This cloud represented Alexander's fears of the real world. Alexander watched with pleasure as it drifted off into space then exploded, creating a supernova of relief. The candle flames turned purple. The purple flames began swarming around Alexander like sorcerous flies. Purple wisps of amour floating around him. A vivid storm of burning confetti blowing in a million different directions.

After the display was over Alexander turned to face the streetlight. The flame inside the streetlight was flashing. *I wonder why it's flashing.* Alexander thought to himself. He decided to investigate by opening the streetlight. The light bulb darted straight out like a fairy that had been freed. Alexander stood stil,l wondering what the lightbulb was escaping from. The room darkened as Pvormlu's lights dimmed. The fairy light bulb fluttered around the left wall, revealing a few sentences which had been written on the wall. Alexander quickly realised that these were questions from an anonymous person.

How are you doing, Alexander?
Where do you think I am now?
Where is my Mother's Day card?

After reading the last message he knew that this was from his mum. Just seeing these questions brought tears to his weary eyes. He had been hoping to have one last chat with her for the past five years and now was his chance to reconnect. Alexander was about to answer aloud when the fluttering lightbulb moved to the right wall revealing three more questions.

What were the first words you said when I was born?
What do you think of Garcia Agbayani?
Do you think I will be able to get a degree from Oxford University?

To Alexander's surprise, these were more questions that he had really wanted to ask his mum. Alexander was confused, he didn't know if these were rhetorical questions or questions that needed an answer. Alexander found himself looking at both walls with a feeling of deep-rooted curiosity. The fluttering lightbulb moved back over to the left wall and revealed answers from his own questions.

> *Wow my first baby, welcome to the world, Alexander.*
> *I think that she might very well be the one for you, if you do get married, please save a seat for me.*
> *I'm sure you will make it; you just have to believe in yourself.*

These answers made Alexander's head explode with emotion, he covered his face with his two hands, his face feeling like a beetroot, liquid pouring out of every part of his body, his face feeling like it was going to melt into a river of tears. He had never heard such beautiful answers to questions that he had always wanted to ask. Reading these messages gave Alexander a sense of comfort he never imagined that he would be capable of acquiring. Alexander walked back to the right wall to see what answers he had given his mum.

> *I am trying my best to manage things for my future, I think that I am doing OK.*
> *I think that I'm supposed to say that you are looking down on me from heaven, but knowing you, I think you might be under my bed waiting to jump out at me.*
> *I can write you a Mother's Day card if you want, I have pens and pieces of paper and plenty of time, I can also get it stamped.*

Seeing the answers made Alexander burst out laughing. *Am I the only person in the world who would come up with these answers?* he thought to himself. As Alexander was reflecting on how different he was to other people, the roof slid back on. Pvormu's chandelier started glowing brightly. Alexander recognised the silhouette as himself and the other as his mother. He was standing still, looking lost. The silhouette of his mother drifted towards him. Alexander saw himself shaking his arms representing his fear of social interaction. She took Alexander's shaking hands and guided him around the walls of the room like something out of *Peter Pan*. They were both floating harmoniously. The shadows drifted out of the front window; Alexander wondered where she was taking him.

The lantern began glowing, it projected the final image of Rose Sommervale, who was standing in the photo studio, waving with a smile on her face. Alexander liked to think that she was waving hello as a pose to waving goodbye. Alexander was observing this photo like a child in an aquarium observing manta rays floating above them. Above the photo of her was a caption that read *'Until we meet again'*.

This evoked a feeling of dread within Alexander, he wanted to tear up the photo postcard. "Why 'until we meet again', I am here now." This photo postcard started fading. "You can't fade away, I'm still here. You can't leave me, please don't go." Alexander stared at the ceiling in utter disbelief, he jumped and waved his arms, trying to signal the attention of anyone who would listen to him. The desk lamp started glowing like a moon. Even though the last photo of his mother had faded away completely. Alexander refused to look down. So, the desk lamp levitated to the same spot that Alexander was fixated on. He could see his initials, AS, written on the desk lamp. And his mother's initials, RS, were on the right of his own initials. *I wonder what is supposed to be the meaning behind this,* Alexander thought to himself. The white curtains opened, and a letter drifted to Alexander's hands.

Dear Alexander,

Lonely hearts drift through empty fields
Drifts past abandoned towns
Drifts over forgotten memories
Until the one who reminisces
Lays a hand to catch the lonely heart.
I have always been there for you, Alexander, never missing a second, I would never leave you, we can stay at nine forever.

Alexander could not remove his eyes from this letter. Reading this gave him an incredible sense of deja vu, he felt as if he had written a letter very similar to this before. He felt like he was the spitting image of his mother. Alexander had developed a hatred for the number ten after she had passed away, he only wanted to count to the number nine and hoped that ninth moment lasted forever. Alexander knew what he needed to do. "One, two, three, four, five, six, seven, eight, nine." Alexander stood still, scratching his head. "I can't do this; I can't say this number."

"Ten," said a familiar female voice.

Alexander turned around to discover that a holographic version of his mother was standing there, looking as young as ever. Alexander could feel her body heat. She was wearing a pink shirt. She had a smile on her face. Alexander had no idea how to react when he saw her, he looked as if he had seen a ghost. She ran up to him and gave him a massive hug. *This feels like her, this must be her*, Alexander thought to himself.

"Hello, Alexander, it's me, your mum." Alexander had no idea how to respond to this, he had not written down a script in his notepad for what body language, facial expressions and phrases he should use for a social situation where you are reunited with the ghost of your mother. Alexander hugged her back. "Care for a cup of tea?" she asked.

"A cup of tea, yes, OK. Let's ring the servants' bell." Alexander and his mother grabbed the pendulum connected to the servants' bells and pulled, creating a very harmonic sound, an orchestra of church bells. The back window opened, and a swarm of bats came flying out. "Oh, not again, I'm tired of doing exhausting trials." Alexander was completely surprised to see that they were carrying candles. Other bats congregated around the chest coffee table and carried it, then carefully placed it, unfolding the table legs. More bats used their wings to carry the small Victorian chairs from the undercarriage. Alexander and Rose sat down. Two more bats carried cups of tea for them to drink. Alexander was about to launch himself into possibly the most difficult conversation of his life when he heard a familiar voice.

"This is one last conversation that you will forever remember." The shadow figure was holding a long candle stick.

"Nice to see you again, shadow figure," Alexander said.

"Nice to meet you, shadow figure," Rose said.

"Nice to meet you. I can see many similarities between you and your son."

"Such as?" Alexander asked curiously.

"Where do I start? Your eyes match, you both have the same voice frequency, you both have the same interests, I could go on."

"Well, thank you, shadow figure," Rose said.

"Uh... yeah, thank you, shadow figure," Alexander added.

"You have come so far, Alexander, you should be proud of yourself."

"This speech is great, but I don't have the energy for another trial."

"This is not a trial; we are here to wish you luck as you further your life's journey."

"Oh OK, that makes a change," Alexander said, relieved.

The shadow figure waved the candlestick in a circular motion, and bats flap around the coffee table, holding candles, creating what seemed like some sort of vigil. "Let your innermost feelings surround you, for you know not of what they might entail. Never shy away from making peace with your demons, as love and hate are two sides of the same coin."

Rose started clapping.

"Mum!" Alexander squealed.

"That was a fantastic motivational speech. I have always been a fan of bats and shadow figures, we both used to watch a lot of Batman."

"Yeah, Batman is cool," the shadow figure replied. The shadow figure raised the large candlestick, then tilted its shadow arm back as if playing javelin, then launched the stick forward but without throwing it. The bats immediately sprang into action, launching themselves at their feet. They both flinched as if expecting to be bitten. These bats were forming a warm and compassionate ankle brace with their wings huddled together. "You have earnt the respect of the bats, you will no longer fear the relentless flapping and cackling. Don't let your fears control you, tell your fears what their limits are."

"Are you taking notice of what the shadow figure is saying, Alexander?"

"Of course I'm listening, it's not the first time that shadow figure has told me something."

The bats retreated once more. The shadow figure blew out the candle flame then carefully placed the large candle stick on the floor. The demon bats dropped to the floor as if praying or playing dead – one of the two.

"When was the last time you went to church, Alexander?" Rose asked him.

"Maybe two years ago," Alexander replied.

"You should go to church more often."

"Yeah, yeah, I think I'm close enough to God, thank you very much."

"The bats are praying for your souls, may all your worries rest in peace," the shadow figure said.

"I think we should pray, too," Rose suggested. Alexander and Rose shut their eyes and joined in with the praying. "Alexander, you have your whole life ahead of you, never give up climbing, never give up swimming and never give up flying."

"I will leave you two to have one final chat, I wish you both the best."

"Oh, you are leaving now?" Alexander said, feeling worried.

"Alexander meant to say thank you very much for your time, shadow figure."

"Did I really mean to say that, Mum?"

"Yes, you did mean to say it, Alexander."

"Yes, I apparently did mean to say whatever my mum just said, but seriously, thank you, shadow figure, for everything you have done for me and thank you too, Pvomlu." Pvormlu nodded in approval.

"Thank you for helping my son, shadow figure."

"It has been a pleasure," the shadow figure replied. "We will now leave you both in peace, farewell."

It was time for Alexander and Rose to have one final conversation. "What do you like the most about your girlfriend Garcia?"

"That is a very difficult question, because I like everything about her, she is kind, funny and beautiful."

"How do you say those words in Filipino?"

"What the whole bloody sentence?" Alexander asked.

"No, you doughnut, those adjectives at the end."

"You should have said adjectives instead of words."

"You know what I mean, Alexander, just get on with it."

"Kind is mabait, funny is nakatutuwa, beautiful is Maganda."

Rose repeated those words. "That sounds like a nice traditional language."

"A lot of tongue twisters," Alexander added. "We have had many great adventures together; I miss being with her very much."

"Do you miss her as much as you miss me?"

"Come on, Mum, what sort of question is that?"

"Just asking."

"I would have to go with missing you more since you are here."

"How did you leave things with her, what was your goodbye like?"

"We both wrote each other letters and created a dance routine."

"Wow, you wrote each other letters and came up with a dance as well!"

"I was meaning to ask if you had used the correct body language, facial expressions and phraseology when saying goodbye to her, I didn't expect you to be such a Romeo."

"Can I read your letter first?"

A pen and piece of paper were sent to Alexander from the chest of drawers.

To my beloved Garcia,

As a timorous lonely pigeon from England, I have flown over six thousand miles to meet you, my beautiful perfect swan from Manila. I am so grateful for you allowing me to spread my wings. We will always be soaring high above what anyone might see of us. What a pleasure it has been to dance with you, my flamboyant flamingo. What a pleasure it has been to sing with you, my musical songbird. My cheeky parrot, who always reminds me how silly I sound. My woodpecker who never lets me forget what the things are that I need to do. My hummingbird who always lifts my mood. My loyal dove who is always open and honest with me about everything. My wise owl who always knows what's best for me. We can remain as eagles forever, too fast and agile for anyone to stop us. Ravens by sunrise, seagulls by sunset.

For as far as my arms may stretch, I will reach for you.

"Wow, that is such romantic, fantastic imagery," his mother replied. "I personally would have changed pigeon to eagle, because I raised you to be an eagle not a pigeon."

"Yes, all right, Mum, I mean that I have started off as a pigeon."

"I would also change swan to angel because she is smarter than a swan."

"OK, now you are just winding me up, Mum."

"Seriously, I do like your poem, you should pursue writing as your future. I want to see what this new dance is."

"I call it the clock dance. First, we need to stand facing each other, let's stand in front of Pvormlu. One person will lead by turning in the clockwise direction, and the other will follow by turning in the counterclockwise direction."

"I will follow you, I will go counterclockwise," Rose said.

"The right arm represents the clock hand that is moving, the left arm is motionless, bent at a 45-degree angle." Alexander demonstrated how to stand. He could feel his mother's warm glowing hands. Despite her only appearing as a 3D hologram, he could also smell her tea breath.

"Wow, I am impressed that you are able to come up with such a dance routine, I have never even seen you dance before."

"Well, I'm full of surprises," Alexander replied. "Garcia taught me how to dance and sing, well, I can dance a bit, but I can't really sing at all."

"Garcia sounds like a wonderful woman."

"Yes, she is," Alexander agreed. "I would describe the clock dance as half-dance and half-symbolic ritual. We start off at the 12 o'clock position then turn to one o'clock. We will give each other a faint smile; our right hands will be gripping tightly throughout the three clock cycles. We now turn to the two o'clock position, we widen our smiles. Three o'clock, we stare at each other with a worried facial expression. At four o'clock, we rest our heads together, this is a time for us to focus and think clearly together. At five o'clock, we rested our heads on each other's shoulders to cope with our shame. At six o'clock our heads are down, our feet are together, we are staring at our feet in disappointment. At seven o'clock, we look at each other as if a great idea has struck our minds. At eight o'clock, we stare at each other with both eyebrows raised, and we are proud of ourselves. At nine o'clock, we are focusing on something important, intense eye contact is required. At ten o'clock we are both shocked, we are looking left and right as if we have heard a loud noise. At 11 o'clock we are surprised, we are looking upwards over each other's heads as if we have spotted something. At 12 o'clock we reach as high as we can, feet together like at six o'clock. We are looking up at the stars as if we are trying to reach them together. On the second rotation, we stop at three o'clock, six o'clock and nine o'clock before completing the cycle. On the third rotation we do the entire clock cycle in one fluid movement."

Whilst Alexander was showing his mum the dance routine, the clock eyes from Pvormlu were copying the motion. "I really enjoyed doing that with you, Alexander, you should become a dance instructor."

"A writer or dance instructor?" Alexander asked.

"I would have to go with a writer over a dance instructor because I have seen you write loads of things in your notepads and on the walls."

"I remember that you used to say that I should become a monk," Alexander said.

"That was because you would rarely go out and you spent all your time studying things that you didn't need to study. A writer and a monk are very similar, I think, so you should choose to become a writer."

"Ah, OK, a writer sounds like the best option for me."

Alexander and Rose sat back down. "I heard that the four of you were having a conversation about me around the table."

"Yes, we were, who told you that?"

"A secret."

"We wanted to keep your memory alive."

"Did you all take it in turns to share your favourite moments with me?"

"Yes, we did."

"Can I hear them?" she asked.

"Of course. My fondest memory was when we were playing that chess game in Plymouth, that one time when you managed to beat me."

"Oh yes, I remember this, the one game that I managed to checkmate you. I actually thought that you had let me win on purpose."

"No, not at all. I had every intention of beating you, but I had become complacent, and I wasn't paying attention to you knight and queen, which checkmated me."

"I can't even remember how I won, all I remember is moving my queen and you told me that it was checkmate, you could have lied to me, and I wouldn't know the difference."

"Yeah, I was thinking that I should have lied so that I could win every game. I knew that your knight was being a pain in the ass, I should have defended better."

"Yes, you should have defended better, then we wouldn't be having this conversation."

"Yes, all right, Mum."

"What about Anna, what was her favourite memory?"

"I'm pretty sure you can guess it, it's always about animals when it comes to Anna Sommervale."

"Was it the time when I bought her Peter the pet rabbit?"

"Not really but close. It was the time when she had that fever, I think she was nine years old, you carried her off the sofa and tucked her into bed."

"Oh, I remember that she had been moaning and groaning for hours. I carried her to her bed and checked her blood pressure then gave her antibiotics; I used my experience as a nurse to help her."

"She told us that you changed her bedding to Hello Kitty to help her rest, and you also dressed her in Hello Kitty pyjamas to make her feel comfortable, because you knew that she liked animals," Alexander said.

"I remember that she usually stops moaning and groaning when you give her something that has a connection to an animal," Rose said.

"I remember that animal family that she made you and Dad get. Grampa tortoise, grandma barn owl, aunt parrot, uncle hare, cousin hedgehog, papa rabbit, mummy goose, sister hamster and brother ferret," Alexander recalled.

"I remember getting most of those from the animal rescue shelter, but did we have them all at once?"

"I think we actually did, that's why she called them a family. She wants to become a vet," Alexander said.

"I'm not surprised, I know that she will make a great vet," Rose replied. "I heard she had that accident and ended up in hospital."

"Yes, she was trying to rescue a cat that was stuck up a tree, but she ended up falling after a branch snapped," Alexander replied.

"Why would she attempt to climb a tree herself, she is no Tarzan," Rose said.

"I think that her passion for animals and her kind nature may have got the better of her," Alexander said. "It was a very difficult time for all of us, I struggled to enter the hospital, the terrifying thought that I might lose her kept me awake the whole night."

"But you found the courage to face up to reality."

"It did take a lot out of me to sit next to her unconscious body, but I managed to hold onto hope."

"So, what about William, what was his greatest memory?"

"You know William, he likes objects, a very objective thinker, his best memory was of him opening a birthday present and discovering that it was *Call of Duty*."

"Really, that was his best memory of me?"

"Unfortunately, yes."

"I fondly remember grounding him until he tidied his messy room, it took him two hours to do a ten-minute job."

"I was there, he was so stubborn and defiant, he would never apologise for anything. He does remember that trip to Cheddar Gorge, he does enjoy day trips," Alexander said.

"I remember that William would always dress up and wear different types of outdoor clothing, like that cowboy hat he used to wear and those army boots," Rose said. "What does William want to do as a career?"

"He wants to be a lawyer?"

Rose started laughing and Alexander joined in. "Why does he want to be a lawyer?"

"He wants to be a lawyer because it is a flashy job, and it pays well and he likes watching horror films so he can have the full experience."

"I hope that he is prepared for all the long hours and paperwork that is needed," Rose replied.

"I think that the paperwork will be easy for him because he is an academic, he wants to call himself Sherlock Holmes," Alexander said. They both laughed again.

"What about your father's favourite memory?"

"That was your chaotic wedding day," Alexander replied.

"I remember his mother kept interrupting the pastor and he and his cousin arrived late, and the pastor was late too."

"He told us that he and Cousin Derick drove to the wrong wedding."

"Oh yeah, I remember Cousin Derick has no sense of direction at all."

"Derick allowed him to drive his car as if it was a rocket because dad threatened to sue him if the wedding got cancelled," Alexander replied. "Is it really true that Grandma Margeret interrupted the pastor three times over photos and a charity donation?"

"Yes, it is definitely true, Margaret was incredibly impulsive, and she had a last-second memory."

"I hope that if I have a wedding it does not end up like that."

"No need to worry, Alexander, you will have better luck than us."

Rose held Alexander's hands then told him to stand up. She pointed out of the window (the time of day frequently changed in the mid-reality). The sunset was awe-inspiring. "Are you familiar with the theme tune from *Chariots of Fire*?" she asked him.

"Yes, we watched that film, I am familiar with the instrumental," Alexander replied.

"You see the sunset."

"Yes, I see it."

"The sun is your goal, your goal is a vision, a sight, something that you aim to reach, you just have to start the race and keep on running until you reach your target. Don't worry, I will be running with you every step of the way."

Alexander and the spirit of his mother began to jog on the spot, they started slowly but then gradually increased speed until they were running as fast as they could. This was a race that would change Alexander's life, a race that he needed to start. This was a race that only Alexander could finish, months, years, decades, a lifetime, who knew how long this race would last, but all anyone knew was that you had to start a journey in order to finish it.

"Now it is time to set your own pace, run with the wind until you create a storm."

Alexander was now determined to finish this race. "That was exhausting, I haven't done any exercise in weeks," Alexander said panting.

"Why don't you take a rest," Rose advised him.

Outside, the sunset was fading, the night was falling. "I like staying up late, I'm not ready to go to bed," Alexander said.

"Remember, Alexander, it's a school night, you need to sleep early."

"OK, I suppose one early night won't hurt."

"Why don't you get your ass up the wooden ladder then?" Alexander reluctantly climbed up Pvormlu's wooden ladder and pulled the duvet over his body.

"I know you are 25, not five, but I have a nursery rhyme for you. I haven't written it myself, it was created by the shadow figure, but I will read it to you.

"OK, I look forward to hearing it," Alexander replied.

One o'clock, the hopeful smile, when the dove arrives with the Amazon package.

Two o'clock, the rush of joyous emotion when the perfect swan drifts with elegance heading in your direction.

Three o'clock, the drill of fear, a woodpecker drilling into your soul.

Four o'clock, pelicans busy at work providing daily fish for their family.

Five o'clock, the shameful chicken lingers around, wishing that it was a human, waiting for its execution date.

Six o'clock, the depressed penguin shivering in fear, wishing that it was on a warm beach.

At seven o'clock, the lonely parrot echoes phrases from its owner in the belief that it might set him free.

Eight o'clock, the wise owl commends you for your meticulous decision-making.

Nine o'clock, the mighty ostrich glares at you with its laser eyes, daring you to make the first move.

Ten o'clock, the vibrant peacock flashes its feathers creating a scene of shocking beauty.

Eleven o'clock, the flamboyant flamingo invites you to a dance.

Twelve o'clock, the bald eagle soars above you, creating a divine display that could have only been orchestrated by God himself.

At some point during this long nursery rhyme, Alexander fell asleep. Whether this was due to his fatigue or the long nursery rhyme, we will never know.

"Oh, you are sleeping, that's the applause I get for reading this nursery rhyme." Rose then tucked Alexander into bed. "Goodnight, Alexander."

Alexander woke up. "Goodnight, Mum."

"Love you, Alexander."

"Love you, Mum."

Rose kissed Alexander's forehead as he went back to sleep. Thoughts of enrolling at Oxford University and when he might see Garcia again were elegantly drifting in his mind. He was looking forward to this next chapter in his life, but before he embarked on this next chapter, he must say farewell to the spirit of his mother, Anna Sommervale. She gradually faded away, but not without watching over Alexander like an angel. The lights from the light crown went out, followed by the candle flames. The clock hands were spinning counterclockwise, resetting all of Alexander's troubles so that he could move on with his life. The time was now 12:30am on the 9th of August. The speed increased until it looked like Pvormlu was going to explode.

Ten, nine, eight, seven, six, five, four, three, two, one; a bright white flash.

Narrated by Mr Green.

www.ingramcontent.com/pod-product-compliance
Ingram Content Group UK Ltd.
Pitfield, Milton Keynes, MK11 3LW, UK
UKHW032303100225
4532UKWH00001B/26

9 781836 151180